The Perfect Daughter

The Perfect Daughter

Gillian Linscott

St. Martin's Minotaur
New York

THE PERFECT DAUGHTER. Copyright © 2000 by Gillian Linscott. All rights
reserved. Printed in the United States of America. No part of this book
may be used or reproduced in any manner whatsoever without written
permission except in the case of brief quotations embodied in critical arti-
cles or reviews. For information, address St. Martin's Press, 175 Fifth
Avenue, New York, N.Y. 10010.

www.minotaurbooks.com

ISBN 0-312-27296-0

First published in Great Britain by Virago, a division of Little,
Brown and Company

First St. Martin's Minotaur Edition: April 2001

10 9 8 7 6 5 4 3 2 1

For Celia Haddon, with thanks.

Chapter One

THE TIDE HAD TURNED AN HOUR OR SO ago and was on its way up again, but not enough to make any difference yet. The river was still no more than a streak of silver between the mud banks of the estuary and everything was becalmed in the early afternoon sun. The reeds in the inlet were motionless, long collars of dried grey mud round their stems, not a shiver of breeze to move them. In the middle of them the streak of brighter grey and white that was a heron dozed, stiff and upright as the reeds. It hadn't moved in the half hour I'd been sitting there. Neither had the rowing boat in mid-channel between the gleaming slides of mud. Probably a salmon fisherman and also, quite likely, asleep.

'You'll hear the motorcar when he goes.'

That's what Verona's mother had said. Since then I'd been sitting on a rock outcrop in a wood of stunted oaks overlooking the estuary. I'd heard seagulls yelling and curlews gurgling. I'd heard little ploppings of mud falling as the salt water started pushing its way up again. But no motor.

'He won't stay. Just long enough to pick up his golf clubs, then off again.' Alexandra's eyes were anxious, begging me to understand. A Siamese cat, draped over her shoulder like a long spillage of Devonshire cream, looked a command at me from its squinting blue eyes: Go!

1

'Ten minutes at most,' she begged. 'You could wait in the summerhouse.'

I'd been tempted to stand my ground. I hadn't come all the way down from London to scurry away from a commodore, especially not one who was my least favourite cousin. But Alexandra was desperate.

'Ben doesn't even know I've written to you. Please, Nell.'

In the face of her panic I'd given in, let myself be hustled out of the garden door and pointed to a wooden summerhouse that perched on the far edge of the lawn with the sweep of the Teign estuary behind it. As she closed the door after me I heard Ben's voice from the front of the house announcing to wife and world that he was home, dear.

Commodore Benjamin North. There's a respectable strain in my family that I usually prefer not to think about, and he was its pride and joy. One of my mother's sisters married a diplomat and gave birth to an infant who'd probably insisted on three rings of gold braid round the sleeves of his christening robe. Ben was ten years my senior. In twenty years we'd met at precisely three family gatherings and quarrelled at two of them. Ben made a highly suitable match with Alexandra, a general's daughter who whiled away his long absences at sea painting watercolours and breeding Siamese cats. The cats were superb examples of their kind, which was more than you could say for the watercolours. Still, I preferred Alexandra to my cousin. There was just a hint of the unconventional about her that being married to Ben hadn't entirely smothered. They'd produced two children, a boy who was currently a cadet at the Britannia Royal Naval College just down the coast at Dartmouth and his elder sister, Verona.

Verona North, nineteen years old, was the reason I was sitting on a rock watching the tide go out. Her young

2

perfections had figured in the interrupted conversation with her mother.

'Always totally fearless. When she was seven she galloped her pony at a wall that must have been all of three feet high. I froze. I thought she'd break her neck. She went over it laughing.'

When I stood up on my rock I could see that very pony, pensioned off now, knee-deep in grass and buttercups in a field below the house. A solid little bay, sensible enough to save a spoilt seven-year-old from her folly. The house itself was solid too, built of granite blocks, door and window frames outlined in fresh white paint that caught the sun – all very shipshape. The granite, like the pony, came from Dartmoor. If you looked inland you could see the blue outline of the moors and Hay Tor perched on top like a jagged molar. The sea and the moors – a good place to grow up.

'And she handled the dinghy better than her brother did. Out in all weathers. Archie Pritty used to call her his little midshipman.'

I didn't ask who Archie Pritty was, for fear of setting off even more Verona worship. Alexandra's little sitting-room was crammed with photographs, including one of two curly-haired moppets in sailor suits with a black labrador lolling at their feet. Senior moppet had a protective hand on junior moppet's shoulder and beamed at the camera, sure of the world's approval. That was Verona. If you looked round at the surface of the baby grand piano, the windowsills, the little tables, there were more of them. Verona standing beside the pony festooned with rosettes, Verona in a rowing boat with her father as passenger, Verona and brother in sailing dinghy – and the same confident smile in all of them. I tried not to be irritated that for this girl's sake Alexandra had begged me to come down here to Devon, two hundred miles from London, and thirty-four shillings return by Great Western. Alexandra should have known, even in this backwater, that the world was falling in pieces around me and my friends.

'Ben's taken the motorcar to Shaldon to see him. When he gets back you'll have to keep out of the way for a while, Nell. You won't mind, will you? Only all this with Verona has hurt him so much and although I don't think you're to blame in any way – no, of course I don't – the fact is he . . .'

Stated more baldly than Alexandra would ever bring herself to do, the fact was that in my cousin's opinion his darling horse-riding, dinghy-sailing daughter had gone totally off the rails and it was entirely my fault. Eight months ago, a few weeks after her nineteenth birthday, she'd shocked the family by announcing her intention to go off to London to study art. Up to that point she'd shown no signs of talent or enthusiasm, but after all there were Alexandra's watercolours to prove art ran in the family, plus the rooted belief that Verona could do anything if she set her mind to it. When she announced she'd been accepted at the Slade, they found her lodgings in a respectable house and probably hoped she'd be back home by Christmas. One more thing. Alexandra wrote to me, presumably as the supposed expert on London and the Bohemian life, and asked me please to keep an eye on Verona. Cousin Ben didn't know about that. He'd have rather put her in the care of the bears at London Zoo.

I hadn't been pleased. I didn't know Verona. I'd only seen her once in my life when she'd been a bridesmaid at a family wedding, all silk roses and sugar-pink satin. Admittedly it was unfair to hold that against the girl as she would only have been eight or nine at the time, but there was nothing in her life to make her a soul mate of mine.

Still, with a lot of other things on my mind, I'd done what Alexandra had asked. Back in December, a few weeks after her arrival in London I called at Verona's lodgings with a pot of hyacinths and a fruit cake substantial enough to keep a student fed for days. I found a slim, polite girl with wary brown eyes and hair the colour of beech leaves in autumn. She'd struck me as subdued and I guessed that she might be finding student life in a London winter grimmer and colder than she'd imagined. To my surprise, she wanted to talk. She asked me about the suffragette movement and socialism and pacifism, and sat there taking in the answers with an intent, hungry look. Then she wanted to know how you joined – as if all the whole quarrelsome lot could be rounded up in one nice tidy party, entrance tickets two shillings and sixpence with tea at the interval. I explained that things were more complicated than that and added that if she were really interested in the fight for the Vote she could join the Women's Social and Political Union, address Lincoln's Inn House, Kingsway. Whether she wanted to get involved or not was her decision alone. That was all. That was the extent of my sin against Family and Duty and Pure English Girlhood and goodness knows what else. A few weeks later, in the early days of 1914, I received a letter from Cousin Ben written like fifty strokes from a cat-o'-nine-tails. Verona had joined the suffragettes, got in with a bad crowd, ruined her young life, worried her mother into a decline, blighted her brother's naval career – and it was all my fault. I didn't answer it. I had a lot more on my mind at the time than other people's rebellious daughters.

Then, in March, another pleading letter had arrived from Alexandra. She'd heard from Verona, who'd left her respectable lodgings and moved in to a house in Chelsea with some other students. Would I please, please, go to the address

5

given and see that she was still all right? Cursing, I'd done as ordered. It was a chaotic place, that student house, but Verona had struck me as a lot happier there than when I'd seen her three months before in her respectable lodgings. When I went in she was sitting on a broken-down chaise-longue, feet bare and hair down, smoking a cigarette. She was watching a short man with a ginger beard trying to juggle three oranges and pretending not to notice a tall dark-haired man who was perched on the windowsill, sketching her, not saying a word. She said 'Hello, Nell', very assured and woman-to-woman, and talked about a march she'd taken part in, as if she'd been deep in suffragette activity for years. I suspected it was as much to impress the men as for my information, and tried not to be annoyed. After all, she was young, thrilled with her independence and probably convinced that she and her fellow students were the first rebels in the history of the world. I remembered how it felt. We'd chatted for a while.

'I'm learning ju-jitsu too.'

She'd said it off-handedly but gave me a challenging side-ways look.

'Ah, Mrs Garrud's Suffragettes' Self-Defence Club, I suppose. Do give her my regards.'

If Verona thought that was something new, she was wrong. Edith Garrud's classes had been going for years and most of us had learned to swing an Indian club or twist out of an armlock under her tutelage. She was under five feet tall but I once watched her throw a thirteen stone policeman – by way of demonstration, not in anger. When I'd had occasion to try the technique in earnest on a policeman of my own it wasn't so successful. I didn't notice his nine stone colleague creeping up behind with a truncheon. Still, I was glad Verona was getting out and taking exercise. I didn't mention the suffragette march or the ju-jitsu lessons when I dropped

Alexandra a note to let her know that Verona was safe and well.

After that, I'd forgotten about Verona again. My friends and I had more serious things on our minds, including fighting the government's iniquitous 'Cat and Mouse Act'. It worked like this. If we were sent to prison for suffragette activities, we went on hunger strike. When the authorities decided we were likely to die on them, we'd be released on licence until we were well enough to be re-arrested, then the cycle would start all over again. Our response was to do our damnedest to see that once a woman was let out, the police didn't get their hands on her again. It was wild work, involving disguises, deceptions and sometimes downright confrontation, and it was taking most of our time and energy. Even today, when I'd been listening to Alexandra talking about Verona, half my mind was on something that should be happening back at home in Hampstead.

'The thing is, Nell, she was always good about letters. When she was at boarding school and we were away in Gibraltar she wrote twice a week without fail. Wonderful letters. We used to say she could be a successful writer if she wanted . . .'

I'd left the key where my friends could find it, then the plan demanded that I should ostentatiously leave at first light as if for a long journey, carrying a bag. I'd improved on the plan by taking the train to Devon. If it hadn't suited me for that reason, I doubt if I'd have responded to Alexandra's increasingly urgent appeals.

'Just to disappear. I can't believe she'd do that. She'd know how much it would worry me.'

I wondered if a man from Scotland Yard's Special Branch had followed me to Paddington. Probably not. They only had a hundred officers and we knew most of them by sight.

Just five days ago our headquarters in Kingsway had been raided and taken over by the police. I dragged my attention back to what Alexandra was saying.

'Something must have happened to her. Ben gets angry if I talk about it. I tried asking Archie for help – he has to go to London a lot – but he's so grieved, so puzzled. I'd go up there myself, only Ben would know and . . .'

Verona hadn't written home for three weeks. There'd been no reply to the increasingly urgent telegrams Alexandra sent to her at the student house.

'When was the last you heard from her?'

'I had a note on Sunday the third of May, saying she was well and working hard.'

'I think I might have seen her since then.'

'Where? When?'

Alexandra rocked forward, almost dislodging the cat. It mipped a protest and dug its claws in, but she took no notice.

'Outside Buckingham Palace last Thursday.'

Alexandra said 'Oh' and closed her eyes. Then, faintly, 'That terrible riot, the deputation.'

Since we were getting no sense from parliament, we'd decided to send a deputation to the King. The police had other ideas. They put a cordon of 1,500 men round Buckingham Palace and manhandled any of us who tried to get through it. They backed into us with horses, hit us with truncheons, picked us up and deliberately let us fall. Or, as *The Times* preferred to report next day, 'In the scuffle, two or three women slipped to the ground'. Altogether, it had turned into one of our most violent confrontations. It wasn't surprising that Alexandra was first shocked, then angry. Not with the police, of course; with me.

'You let her go to a thing like that?'

'I'd no idea that she intended to go.' (Not that I'd have

8

tried to stop her.) 'And I'm not quite sure it was her, even now.'

There had been a girl in a group of other people, her hair the colour of autumn beech leaves streaming down her back. She had the right colouring and build for Verona, but it had been no more than the briefest glance.

'Didn't you make sure? Didn't you go to her?'

Just after the point when I thought I'd glimpsed Verona, a lot of other things happened. A hefty constable grabbed one of my friends by the breasts – admittedly she'd been laying about him with a dog whip at the time – and a police horse was deliberately backed into me when I went to help her. I was tempted to tell Alexandra that, but it would only have worried her more.

'I did have other things to think about at the time.'

'What was she doing? Who was she with?'

'She was in a group, I think. Probably students. They were near the Victoria Memorial, not right in the thick of things.'

'Anything could have happened to her. She could be in prison, in hospital.'

'She's not. I can promise you that.'

One of my jobs in the days following the fight had been to keep lists of who'd been hurt or arrested. It wasn't easy, because most of the sixty-six women who appeared in Bow Street police court the next day refused on principle to give their names to the magistrates. But I was satisfied we'd got everybody accounted for, and Verona's name hadn't figured anywhere.

'She might have dragged herself off to her lodgings and be lying there hurt, too ill to write. I think I'll come up to town with you, whatever Ben—'

'Don't bother. She isn't there. I checked two days ago.'

I wasn't quite dead to family duty. When Alexandra began

9

her bombardment of letters to me, I'd found time to go back to the student house. There'd been no sign of the dark-haired man or the ginger-bearded orange juggler. When I described them the other residents thought they were away somewhere, but had no idea where or for how long. As for Verona, they were pretty sure she'd moved out some weeks ago.

'One of the girls there thought she might have gone home.'

'Home? Here?'

It was spring, so they were all feeling migratory. Gone home, gone to roam, gone to Paris, gone to Rome. People strolled out of the door with sketch pads in their rucksacks and a few pounds in their pockets, and came back when it suited them. I'd liked their attitude, it brought back memories, but I knew it wouldn't appeal to Alexandra.

'But it's not like her, Nell. She wouldn't behave like that.'

I was saved from having to say anything to that by the sound of the motorcar drawing up on the gravel outside and her urgent need to hide me away from Ben. The one advantage of the situation was that it gave me time to work out whether to tell Alexandra about my guess.

I'd been fidgety, couldn't settle on the knobbly rustic bench in the summerhouse, so had come down to this rock outcrop nearer the water. The heron still hadn't moved. When you looked closely it was standing beside a stream that showed as no more than a dark crack in the field of reeds. Where the stream joined the river there was a neat boathouse of brick and timber, probably commissioned by Ben to keep the family rowing boats and dinghies. With the tide so low, it was separated from the water by an expanse of shining mud and brown bladderwrack. I thought I might have to tell Alex, or hint at least, about what I'd guessed on that second visit to Verona, when she'd been so much happier. That woman-to-woman air had more to it than shared politics. She'd given me a smile that . . . well. It was the quality of that smile that I was wondering how to explain to her mother. 'Alex, do you remember when you and Ben first . . . ?' Not good enough. I couldn't imagine any woman ever smiling that way over anything cousin Ben might do. 'Alexandra, when you stroke one of your cats on a wall in the sun and you can feel it practically melting with smugness . . .' Safer perhaps, but would it tell her what I was sure was the case, that sometime between December and March her daughter had begun her first love affair? Now I asked myself – as Alex would ask more forcefully if she knew – whether I should have done something about it. I was a relative after all, however distant, nearly twice Verona's age. She was away from the protection of her home and parents and – I could almost hear her father spluttering – 'in moral danger'. But, looking at it another way, she was an independent and healthy young woman in the second decade of the twentieth century, in love for the first time and starting to live. She and her man – orange man, dark man or perhaps somebody else altogether – had probably run off to a warmer more southern sea than this one. They'd be back when love or money ran out. There was no point in moral cluckings even if, with my disorderly life, I'd been in any position to cluck. When I was only a little older than Verona I'd done much the same myself, in a more censorious generation. Normally, as far as I was concerned, Verona could have kept her secret and I shouldn't have dreamed of hinting at it to her mother. But wasn't my guess better than any of the horrors Alexandra was imagining? Then I looked up at the solid house and the pony in the buttercups, down at the boathouse and the estuary, thought of the ideal I'd be shattering and knew I couldn't do it. I couldn't even hint at it.

The heron made a sudden dive into the reeds then heaved itself into the air, beak empty. I heard the creaking of its wings as it flew over. Still no sound of a motor. Now the decision was taken there was nothing I could do for Alexandra. I wanted to be back in Hampstead, where our plan would be near its critical stage by now. If Ben wasn't gone in half an hour I'd walk the four or five miles back to the ferry across the estuary then to the railway station without bothering to say goodbye. Bored with sitting on the rock, I decided to pass the half-hour having a look at the boathouse. I'm not sure why. Perhaps I was half envying Verona her uncomplicated childhood and her present hypothetical happiness with her lover. I had the childish idea of spending the time sitting in one of the boats, seeing if the tide would come back soon enough to set it afloat. I slid down the bank under swags of wild roses and honeysuckle to the start of a wooden walkway over the reed bed. It had been newly creosoted and the smell fought with honeysuckle and seaweed. The landward end of the walkway joined a narrow path that led up through pasture and orchard to the house. The seaward end went to a small door at the back of the boathouse. I followed it across the reed bed and opened the boathouse door.

The light hit me. The narrow silver channel of water between the mud flats was blindingly bright against the darkness inside the boathouse. I was standing on a wooden platform with the masts of two dinghies in silhouette. Seagulls were swooping outside, flies buzzing inside. As my eyes adapted to the contrast of light I saw that the platform turned a right angle and went on down the long side of the boathouse

12

to the left. There were a couple of rowing boats moored there, one long and slim, the other a little tub. I started walking towards them and turned the right angle. Concentrating on where I was stepping, I was only half aware that something was hanging over the space on my right above the mud. If I thought about it at all I probably assumed it was a fishing net or a clutch of oilskins hung up to dry. But I'm not sure I even thought about it until flies came up in my face, and the smell wasn't creosote or seaweed. I think I probably put up an arm to wave the flies away and that disturbed the air just enough to set it moving, revolving.

There was something white in the net or oilskins, as if somebody had hung a mask there. A grotesque mask with a swollen face and protruding tongue. I heard my own voice saying something. I don't know what. Then I'd got a boathook from somewhere and was hooking at the hanging thing. It was some way out from the platform. I could only just reach it with the boathook. It was the jacket belt I hooked. The thing came reluctantly to me, bottom half first, swollen mask tilted away. It was heavy, soaked. A skirt, smelling of wet wool. Then the belt came unbuckled from the weight of it and the thing was swinging out over the mud, then in again towards me, half turning as it came. I dropped the boathook, fell on my knees and grabbed a handful of the skirt. Something rattled against the platform. A plank of wood. The bottom of the thing was lashed to a long soaked plank. The feet, still in their stockings and shoes, green weed trailing over the insteps, were tied with ropes to a piece of wood. I must have let go because she swung out again, over the empty space where the tide had gone away. I called as if she'd come back.

'Verona!'

Chapter Two

❧

'HER SKIRT WAS SOAKED,' I said. 'THE TIDE must have been up at least once.' The constable didn't write that down. He'd already got most of the things they'd need for the coroner's officer. I'd been on a visit to my cousin's wife. I'd happened to wander into the boathouse. When I'd found Verona I'd gone straight up to the house and Commodore North had reported to the police by telephone. They were very considerate, these policemen. The sergeant spoke with a gentle Devonshire burr and the constable managed to write and look sad and respectful at the same time. Commodore North and his family were well known locally. I counted as family and I think they were genuinely shocked and sorry for me. It wasn't an attitude I was used to from the police. I'd answered their questions as well as I could, but with most of my mind going in and out with the tides as it had been for the twenty hours or so since I'd found her. I'd looked up the tables. I had nothing much else to do, waiting in the boarding house where I had stayed overnight behind the East Promenade. Yesterday, the day I found her, the tide had been high around eight in the morning. Its slow drag out might have been strangling her even while I was travelling down from Paddington on the train. High again at about quarter to eight the evening before, half past seven the morning before that, broad summer daylight every time.

'When did you last see Miss North?'

I explained about the Buckingham Palace deputation. I sensed a little change in their attitude. They were surprised, even hurt, that the commodore's daughter should have been mixed up in anything like that. It made the sergeant's next question sharper than it might have been otherwise.

'Did Miss North ever give you any indication that she was thinking of taking her own life?'

'None whatsoever.'

'Can you think of any reason why she might have?'

'No.'

Silence. There was sunshine coming in at the window, a smell of fresh paint and the sea. The sergeant sighed.

'I'm afraid we shall have to ask you to come back for the inquest, Miss Bray. We'll let you know the date.'

'Does that mean you don't need me any more at present?'

They didn't. They asked if I'd be going back to my cousin's house and whether I needed a cab. I said no, thanked them and walked out into the sunshine.

I walked to the railway station, checked that the next train for London would leave in an hour and went back along the seafront towards the boarding house to pick up my bag. It was the Friday before the bank holiday weekend and Teignmouth, the resort at the mouth of the estuary, was getting ready for visitors. An ice-cream seller on a tricycle was attracting a few early customers. White cumulus was building up out to sea, and a stiff breeze was fluttering the canvas of the Punch and Judy booth. On the beach of red-brown sand, old-fashioned bathing machines were lined up on both sides of the pier on their big iron wheels, advertisements for Pears

15

soap and Fry's chocolate painted on their sides. Some children and their parents were down at the tide line. The children's skirts and trousers were hitched up and they were playing games with the tide, advancing a few steps into shallow water as a wave bubbled away, retreating squealing when it thudded back.

I turned inland to the lawns and flowerbeds behind the promenade and watched two gardeners planting out pink begonias round the edges of a big floral clock, with the hours picked out in house leeks. More house leeks against a white background spelt out two words on either side of the clock face: HIGH TIDE. Someone would move the hands round, twice a day every day. No getting away from it anywhere. Verona would have known the tides. She grew up with them. She'd have known exactly how far each day the water rose and fell inside the boathouse. Known how long she'd stand there, feet bobbing on the plank, rope round her neck, until the tide went away and there was nothing under her but air and mud. The rope would have tightened before then, though. Tide drawing out of the boathouse, body following, feet first, until the pressure of the rope round her throat . . . Surely she'd have struggled? It couldn't be in human nature not to struggle. But the commodore's daughter was a girl of strong will, we all knew that.

I was furious with Verona. If she'd appeared in front of me, I'd have slapped her. Of all the vain, selfish, hurtful, self-dramatising things to do. Killing herself was bad enough. Creeping home to do it, so that she'd almost certainly be discovered by her father or mother, was worse. Doing it in that horrible, self-tormenting way meant she'd put something into all our minds that would never go away. A girl, on a summer morning or evening, walking past her house, down through the paddock with the old pony nuzzling her for titbits, the walk out over the reed bed with the tide coming in and only the tops of the reeds showing. The tide draining out of the boathouse and the woman self-pinioned, waiting for it to strangle her. She'd wanted to make an impression on the world – I'd sensed that about her. But the world, in her first few months of trying, turned out to be less easily impressed than she expected. Perhaps the love affair went sour. So she'd turned back to the place that had been kind to her, and destroyed it and the people there more surely than if she'd planted a bomb.

Half an hour to train time. I left the beach, emptied sand out of my shoes and picked up my bag. The police had assumed that I'd stayed overnight with my cousin and his wife. It was a natural assumption, but then they hadn't been there the day before when Verona's body had been carried up to the house on an old door grabbed from the woodpile, covered with a tarpaulin from one of the boats. A gardener and her father did the carrying. They put it down on the gravel outside the front door, so that Ben could make sure that Alexandra was upstairs before they carried it into the house. It was at that point, just before he went inside, that Ben spoke to me for the first time since I'd told him. He turned on the step and gave me a look as blank as slate.

'She was the perfect daughter before you got to her. The perfect daughter.'

Chapter Three

◈

IT WAS A LONG JOURNEY BACK TO LONDON. All I had to read was the newspaper from the day before. Durbar II had won the Derby at twenty to one. The Queen had attended the Derby Ball at Devonshire House. Parliament had shut down for the Whitsun recess – in spite of the fact that everybody expected civil war to break out in Ireland within days – and most of the party leaders had gone away somewhere to play golf. Paddington in late afternoon was full of families with hampers and buckets and spades getting away for the weekend to the coast or the river. I took the tram out to Haverstock Hill, then walked up to Hampstead, telling myself that I had to put Verona out of my mind for a while and concentrate on the job in hand, otherwise a lot of other people would be in trouble. It was reassuring to see a familiar figure lounging on the corner as I turned out of Heath Street.

'Good afternoon, Mr Gradey.'

When I say he was lounging, I mean he was trying very conscientiously to lounge. I dare say they run classes on lounging and loitering for police officers of the Special Branch at Scotland Yard, but Gradey would never have won any prizes. The clothes were wrong too, a navy-blue suit and waistcoat, a bowler hat nicely brushed. He might as well have kept his uniform on and have done with it. I didn't wait to see if he touched his hat to me – sometimes he did, sometimes he didn't – but I was aware of his eyes on my back as I walked along the street. That was what we wanted. It was all part of the plan.

I kept to the pavement opposite my house, stopped and had a good look at it. Things weren't as I'd left them the day before. The blind on the first-floor window was drawn almost all the way down. There was a narrow gap between the blind and the windowsill, just enough to show the top of a table inside and a row of medicine bottles standing on it. Although it was a warm day, a trail of smoke came up from the chimney. On the ground floor, the curtains of the living-room were drawn all the way across. Then, as I watched, one of them was twitched aside and a face looked out warily. It was a young woman's face, round and pale, with the sort of red hair that looks as if it's had an electric shock. Her name was Gwen Hoddy. She saw me, nodded and let the curtain drop back. I crossed to my own front door and knocked. She opened it.

'Hello, Gwen. Everything all right?'

'Where have you been, Nell?'

'Something happened. Did things go alright here?'

She nodded uncertainly and opened the door to let me in. I hesitated on the doorstep, giving Detective Constable Gradey time to get a good look at us.

'She's upstairs?'

'Since yesterday night.'

'Any callers?'

'No.'

'I passed Special Branch on the corner.'

'The plump one in the bowler? He's been prowling up and down all afternoon.'

19

'Did anybody see the stretcher come in?'

'Half the neighbourhood probably.'

I took my hat and coat off and sprawled in the armchair. It was hot in the room with the fire going and there was already an invalid fug to the place.

'You look tired. Want some tea?'

I said yes please, though it was obvious from the violet rings round her eyes that Gwen was tired as well. She got the teapot and warmed it from the kettle on the hob, moving easily around my book- and paper-cluttered living-room in spite of the iron brace on her wasted leg.

'Shouldn't Amy be here?'

'She's on duty upstairs.'

We were speaking in low voices, the way you do in a house where somebody's seriously ill. We said nothing while the tea was brewing. Gwen and the others were owed an apology because I should have been back the night before, but I didn't want to explain about Verona.

'So June had a bad time?'

She nodded, not looking at me. June Price and Gwen shared lodgings and were inseparable most of the time, except when June was in Holloway. Gwen couldn't take part in the kind of things that got people sent to prison because of her leg, so she probably suffered worse than June did.

'She's worn to nothing, transparent nearly. Heart palpitations. And she's got abscesses from when they broke her teeth trying to get the tube down. It'll kill her if they get her in there again.'

The boards creaked upstairs. Somebody was moving around in the bedroom. Gwen sighed, poured two more cups of tea, one strong, one weak and milky. I opened the door for her to take them upstairs. When she came down a few minutes later, she was looking worried.

'How is she?'

'Restless.'

'Given her temperament, that was predictable.'

'She says she hates being passive – hates just waiting.'

'No choice at the moment.'

'She expected the police to come yesterday.'

'Yesterday midday was when the licence ran out?'

Gwen nodded, staring out of the gap between the curtains. I'd have liked to pull the curtains aside, open the window, let some air in, but Gradey might be watching.

'Why haven't they raided us already, I wonder.'

'We've been discussing that. We think they may have been waiting for you to come back, Nell.'

'And charge me with harbouring an escaped prisoner?'

'Or obstructing the police in the course of. They can always think of something.'

It wasn't a comfortable thought. If that was what they were waiting for, Gradey could have telephoned a message to Scotland Yard by now. A car-full of police might be rumbling up the hill towards us.

'Gwen, you're not to attack them. Understand? Let them come in, let them search, let them take her away if it comes to it. Just don't lay a finger on them whatever they do.'

She turned away.

'Do you understand, Gwen? It's an order.'

Still she wouldn't look at me.

'When I think what they did to her. You too, come to that. Let alone lay a finger on them, I could bloody kill them.'

I put a hand on her shoulder. Her muscles were knotted like . . . like hemp ropes knotted around feet, swollen from seawater. Gwen flinched, so I suppose my fingers must have tightened. I said I was sorry, moved my hand.

21

'You see, Nell. You feel just the same as I do.'

'Perhaps. Only don't do it. It wouldn't be worth it.'

We sat there, drinking more tea, watching the sky change from bright to dark blue through the gap in the curtains. They usually came in daylight, but they were getting more desperate these days so you couldn't be sure. We let the fire go out. At around ten o'clock Gwen said: 'Doesn't look as if they're coming today.'

'Dawn then, probably.'

'Miss their bloody breakfasts.'

We lit the gas, warmed some soup for the four of us and decided that Gwen would take the night shift upstairs.

'Do you want to come up and see her, Nell?'

'Better not. She'll only start arguing again if she sees me.'

Gwen said goodnight and went upstairs with the soup. Amy came down, looking exhausted. She's a dance teacher in ordinary life and weighs about as much as a litter of kittens, with twice the energy, but the waiting was wearing her down. We sorted out our sleeping arrangements. Amy was persuaded to have the chaise-longue. I made a nest of blankets on the rag rug in front of the fireplace. We took our shoes off, but didn't undress. I made sure I'd put my shoes under a chair where I could find them easily when the knock on the door came. You're at a disadvantage meeting police boots in stockinged feet.

None of us slept much. Now and then I heard boards creaking upstairs. Amy lay on her back, arms at her sides, too disciplined. I dozed now and then but the slightest noise brought me immediately wide awake. The only point when I came near deep sleep I imagined I was back in the dark of the boathouse and must have made some noise.

'What's up, Nell? Are they here?'

I was right. Amy hadn't been sleeping.

'No. Sorry. Go back to sleep.'

We both pretended. It got light around four. Just after five, horse hooves and wheels outside brought Amy and me to our feet but it was only the milkman. At six Gwen came down, rubbing her eyes.

'She's asleep, thank God.'

By seven there was so much traffic noise from Heath Street that we wouldn't have heard platoons of police arriving. It was the holiday, of course. There were charabancs of people on outings grinding uphill to Hampstead Heath, motor buses hooting, and children shouting. It looked a dull weather day, but it didn't sound as if that was bothering anybody.

'Perhaps they won't come when it's a holiday,' Amy said.

Gwen and I didn't answer. Then, just as Amy was talking about having a wash and I was looking for the coffee grinder, it happened. There was a knock on the door. We hadn't heard wheels or tramping feet. It was quite a soft, apologetic knock, not the thundering we'd expected. Still, it froze us. Amy stood, blouse half unbuttoned and slipping off at the shoulder. I noticed the coffee grinder propping up a pile of dictionaries but left it where it was. Gwen's eyes closed and her fists bunched. The only movement came from upstairs. It was bare feet hitting the floor.

I hissed at Gwen, 'Go up there. Stay with her.'

Gwen went, reluctantly. Whoever it was, standing on the other side of the door, might have heard her going upstairs. I'd expected another knock by now, more demanding, but he was as patient as a cat at a mouse-hole. Amy buttoned her blouse, fingers trembling. This was her first experience of this sort of thing. The second knock at last, a little louder. I prepared my expression of respectable and puzzled householder (not that it would deceive them in the least, but there

23

are conventions about these occasions) and went to open the door.

It threw me. I was totally and completely at a loss. I'd expected a policeman in uniform on the doorstep, several more behind him, a vehicle waiting at the kerb. I'd even expected to be shoulder-charged against the door frame, dispensing with the 'puzzled householder' formalities. Nothing would have come as a surprise except what I saw. A man in plain clothes. Not the Special Branch's version, but country tweeds that looked as if they should have bits of heather and dog hairs clinging to them. He was tall and thin, with dark eyes set deep into their sockets and a quiff of dark hair falling over his forehead. He held a brown trilby hat in his left hand. His right hand held a plump bunch of lily-of-the-valley. He'd been smiling, but the smile faded when he saw my face. For a few seconds we stared at each other then he handed the lily-of-the-valley to me.

'Good morning, Nell. I hope I'm not too early.' My hand closed round the cool stems of the flowers. Their scent came to me like something from another world. I could see he was disappointed.

'You said if I got here early we could go somewhere like Box Hill and walk. But we'll have to be back in time for the opera.'

'Opera?'

'Boris Godunov. I managed to get tickets for this evening. Chaliapin's singing.'

From inside, Gwen's voice, sharp and anxious. 'Nell, what's happening?'

He'd already registered there was something wrong. Now he was annoyed as well. He'd come all the way from Manchester and goodness knows what the opera tickets had cost.

24

'You've got visitors? I'm sorry. I didn't realise.'

He'd gone stiff and formal.

'Bill, I . . .'

'Only, when I suggested coming down at Whitsun you said . . .'

'Oh God, so I did.'

'Nell, who is it? If I'd realised there were people staying with you, I'd have . . .'

'You'd better come in.'

Gwen was standing with her back against the table, glaring. Amy's eyes were wide and scared. The two of them took in Bill then looked beyond him for the rest of the squad.

'It's all right,' I told them. 'It's only a friend.'

The room was in more of a mess than usual. There were bedclothes folded on the chaise-longue, blankets piled on the armchair, ashes in the grate. Bill's air of having just walked in from the country made the sickroom fug from upstairs seem worse than ever. I introduced him to Gwen and Amy as a friend of mine, a barrister, Bill Musgrave. They shook hands guardedly, obviously wondering why I'd gone and invited him during this crisis. There were men who supported us, but somehow Bill at first sight didn't fit the picture. I said, 'I'd like to offer you a coffee, but you'd better go.'

Even Gwen looked shocked at this lack of hospitality.

'I could make the coffee, if you like, Nell. Shall I put these in water?'

I was still clutching the lily-of-the-valley. She took them from me and went out to the kitchen.

I said to Bill, 'You can have a coffee, if you like, then you really must go. We're expecting the police at any moment.'

He raised his eyebrows. 'Have you been burgled?'

It took me a while to realise he was joking.

25

'They're looking for a woman who was out on licence. The Special Branch have been watching this place for days.'

'I think I passed one of them on the way here.'

'How would you know?'

'Plump, pink face, bowler with curly brim.'

'Gradey.'

'Polite bloke. I asked him for directions.'

'But you knew where I live.'

'Yes. Just wanted to see his expression.'

He grinned at me. This was all new to him, but Bill was a quick learner.

'Bill, I'm sorry I forgot I invited you, but so many things have . . .'

'Evidently. Mind if I sit down?' He moved the bedding aside and settled on the chaise-longue.

'I shouldn't sit down for long. It won't do your career any good to be arrested.'

The floorboards creaked overhead. Amy looked at me then went upstairs in a hurry.

'What for?'

'Aiding and abetting.'

'I suppose I shouldn't ask who's upstairs.'

'No.'

'So I'm supposed to drink my coffee, get the train back to Manchester and leave you to it?'

'I'm sorry about the tickets. I'd have liked to hear Chaliapin. They say he sings the—'

Which was when it happened of course, just when I'd started for a few seconds to think like a normal human being. There must have been the sound of a car turning into the street, but I didn't register it until it stopped outside and simultaneously Amy's voice came high and sharp from upstairs.

26

'Nell, I think it's them.'

This time the knock on the door was thunderous. Gwen came through from the kitchen and took up position beside me. She glanced at Bill who was still sitting on the chaise-longue, looking no more than politely interested.

'We can't put him out the back door. They'll have a man there.'

'Yes. Remember, Bill, it's nothing to do with you. You just happened to be visiting.'

Another thunderous knock. 'Open up! Police!'

I was annoyed my heart was thumping so much. I smoothed my hair and went to the front door. A sergeant in uniform was on the step with two constables behind him.

'Are you Miss Eleanor Bray?'

He'd cut himself shaving. There was a nick on his cheek-bone with a bit of cotton waste stuck to it surrounded by a tuft of blond bristles. He was already angry, probably at having to work on a holiday. I said nothing – usual policy.

'We have reason to think you are harbouring a licence-expired prisoner. I have a warrant to search these premises.'

'May I see it?'

He put it into my hand, standing aside as he did it so that the constables could get through. I let them barge in, pray-ing that Gwen would do as she was told. She managed not to raise a hand to them, but only by gripping the edge of the table so hard I thought her fingers would make dents in the wood.

'Who's she?' said the sergeant, following them in, looking at Gwen.

'Seen her before, sir,' one of the constables told him. 'She's June Price's friend.'

'And I suppose your little friend is upstairs, is she?'

The sergeant moved towards the stairs. Gwen let go of

the table and lurched at him. I tried to grab her and missed. Then suddenly Bill was on his feet, blocking her path. The police were so intent on Gwen and me that they hadn't noticed him sitting there quietly.

'Good morning, sergeant. May I see your identification, please?'

Bill was taller than the policeman and managed, in spite of the country tweeds, to radiate an air of authority. I suppose it came from cross-examining police witnesses in court. The sergeant stopped with his foot on the first stair. Gwen's rush was checked just enough for me to grab her hand and squeeze it warningly.

'So who might you be, sir?'

'My name is William Musgrave. I'm a barrister.'

The sergeant gave me a hurt look. Having lawyers ready on the scene wasn't part of the game.

'Are you resident at these premises, sir?'

Bill ignored the question. 'Your identification, sergeant.'

Reluctantly, the man unbuttoned his tunic pocket. Bill took his time checking the document and handed it back.

'Have you a search warrant?'

I was still clutching it. I handed it to Bill who read it through slowly as if trying to memorise it, moving his lips as he read. I knew he was a fast reader who could take in documents at a glance, so it was a good act. It gave time for my heartbeats to slow down and Gwen to unclench her fists and move back to the table, even if she couldn't stop herself glancing upstairs. It was all quiet up there.

'It all seems to be in order.'

Bill handed the warrant back to me. Gwen looked betrayed. I think she hoped he might have found some flaw in it.

'So if you've no objection, sir, we'll be getting on with our duty.'

Bill stood back. The sergeant went upstairs, followed by the two constables. Their studded boots sounded like riveters in a shipyard.

Bill said to me: 'I'm sorry I couldn't do more, Nell.'

'You tried.'

I was grateful, but all my attention was on what was happening upstairs. I heard the sergeant's steps stop on the landing, heard the bedroom door creak. Then Amy's voice, trembling with fear and anger.

'Have some respect. There's a sick woman in here.'

Then a little gasp of pain. I found out later one of them had trodden on her toes – accidentally of course. The door creaked wider. Heavy steps approached the bed.

'Miss Price, your licence expired . . .'

Then, silence. Not a word or a slither of a boot stud. A silence buzzing with amazement. Gwen looked at me then bent her head and crossed her arms on her chest, rocking backwards and forwards. The silence was broken by the sergeant's voice.

'Where's she gone?'

Then a constable: 'The window's open, sir. She's gone out of the window.'

It was our turn to be surprised. Gwen looked at me – alarmed, questioning.

Three pairs of boots came thudding down the stairs. The sergeant and constables rushed out of the front door in a blur of navy blue. I heard the sergeant yelling to somebody else, presumably the man they'd posted at the back door.

'Interesting,' said Bill. 'Do you think we might go out and see what's happening?'

Bill, Gwen and I followed them out on to the street. People were leaning out of windows, collecting in groups on the pavement, asking each other what was going on. All of them were looking up to the rooftops, although there was nothing to see but disturbed pigeons fluttering about. A gang of urchins who'd decided this was more interesting than the fairground were whooping and cheering. Our three policemen plus the one from round the back were standing in the middle of the road, also looking up. If the urchins' cheers were for them they were doing nothing to deserve them. They stood at a loss, not noticing us. Then there was a louder whoop from the boys, and a shout of 'There she is.' I looked up where somebody was pointing. There was a chimney stack between my house and the next, with six chimneypots on it. A figure in a dark dress was standing on the stack, arm hooked round one of the pots. Gwen gasped and grabbed me by the shoulder.

'Surely she's not . . .'

The figure raised its free arm, acknowledging applause. The urchins had changed sides and were now cheering her. For a moment I shared Gwen's fear that she was going to jump, a last gesture of defiance to the police and the whole corrupt business, but I should have known her better than that. She picked her way carefully round the chimneypots, sat astride the roof ridge, then disappeared down the other side of the roof.

'A skylight,' I said. 'There'll be a skylight.'

The sergeant must have come to the same conclusion and realised that when she did come down to earth, it would be in the next street. Two constables were sent running back towards Heath Street to cut her off that way, the sergeant and the other constable rushed along the street and round the corner in the other direction. The constable was shrilling on his whistle, goodness knows why. Some of the boys and a couple of dogs were sprinting after them. I joined the chase with some vague but not very hopeful idea of trying to create a diversion and heard Gwen's limping run coming after me. The police rounded the corner and came to a halt, looking up. Then a new noise added itself to the uproar. Behind us, in the street we'd just left, a motorcar horn was parping like a giant bullfrog. From the same direction there were cries of 'There she is!' The sergeant and constable looked at each other then started running back the way they'd come, almost cannoning into Gwen who'd just turned the corner. Gwen looked at me, pale-faced, panting.

'They'll get her. Why didn't she . . .'

'She'll think of something.'

The two of us were alone now, in the street at the back of my house. Gwen, shaking with the effort of running, wanted to get back to where things were happening, but I made her wait. Then, halfway down the street, a door opened. A figure in a dark dress slipped out of it and came dashing down the street towards us. As she passed, she gave us the thumbs-up sign. Then she was gone, scudding away towards Hampstead Heath, where she'd be lost within minutes among thousands of holidaying Londoners. Gwen clung to me, half laughing, half crying.

'Nell, I can't believe it.'

'Shall we go back?'

We walked shakily back round the corner. The pandemonium in our street was worse than ever. When we got back Amy and Bill were there in the crowd. Amy was worried, looking for us. Bill was actually chatting to the sergeant, who looked red-faced and depressed.

'Ah, here you are, Nell. I was just explaining to Sergeant Hedger that no offence has been committed.'

The door and ground-floor windows of my house were wide open. A constable put his head out of the living-room window.

31

'Nobody here, sergeant.'

'Have you looked in the attic?'

'Evans is doing it now.'

An upper window opened and another constable put his head out. His face was covered with dust and there were cobwebs on his tunic.

'Not there either, sir.'

Disgustedly, he told them to come out.

Bill said. 'So you're confirming that there's nobody wanted by the police in Miss Bray's house?'

'There was, sir.'

'How do you know?'

'They'd got the Price woman up there in the bedroom. She skipped out over the roof. You saw her yourself.'

'No, sergeant. I saw a person on the roof who appeared to be a woman. I've no idea of her identity. Have you?'

'It stands to reason.'

'How? Are you able to identify her as Miss Price?'

'No, but they'd had her up there since Thursday so it must have been her.'

'How do you know?'

The sergeant said nothing. The activities of Special Branch were supposed to be secret.

'When your officer went into the bedroom there was nobody in the bed. Is that correct?'

'Because she'd just gone out of the window.'

'But there was nobody in the bed?'

'Well, no, but . . .'

'So where's your proof that it was the woman you were looking for? Had she been kind enough to leave her card on the pillow?'

By then the sergeant was looking like a man defeated. Bill pressed his advantage.

'So the facts are as follows. In pursuance of your duty, and properly equipped with a warrant, you carry out a search of Miss Bray's house. The person you're looking for is not present and you have no proof that she ever was present. I'd suggest that your proper course now is to apologise to Miss Bray for the inconvenience you have caused her and to carry on your search elsewhere.'

'What about the woman who went out over the roof?'

'If one of Miss Bray's guests chooses an unconventional way of leaving, that's hardly a matter for the Metropolitan Police.'

The sergeant wouldn't apologise to me, of course. He'd have sooner been rolled down the Heath in a spiked barrel. He glared at me, organised a search of yards and dustbins up and down the street just to make a nuisance, then they all piled into their car and went. The crowd dispersed reluctantly and the four of us went back inside. Amy, Gwen and I clung together, half laughing, half crying.

'Oh God, when I saw her coming out of that house . . .'

'So she got away? She got right away?'

'I told Gwen she'd find a skylight.'

'I wonder what the people in the house thought?'

'Oh God, I can't believe we've done it.'

Bill sat on the chaise-longue and watched us, but I could see there was something bothering him.

'Your friend, June Price – I gather they released her from Holloway on licence because she was seriously ill from her hunger strike?'

Gwen bit her lip and left it to me.

'Yes, that's right.'

'Then they withdrew the licence later because they decided her health had improved enough to serve the rest of her sentence?'

'Only it hadn't, that's the point. They withdraw the licences before people are anywhere near recovered, then the whole process starts all over again.'

'But it seems Miss Price was well enough recovered to perform acrobatics on rooftops.'

Gwen turned away. Amy took a sudden interest in tidying up papers on the table. My decision. I'd known Bill for only a matter of months, been with him only a few days in those months. I decided.

'June Price is still very ill. The last I heard, just a few days ago, she couldn't walk let alone climb roofs.'

Bill looked at me, an unreadable look.

'That wasn't June Price up there. It was a friend of ours called Bobbie Fieldfare. The whole thing was a diversion to keep Special Branch busy while we got the real June Price somewhere they won't find her.'

Gwen said, happier now I'd made the decision: 'Only Bobbie didn't keep to the plan. She never does.'

'That's right. The idea was simply that the police should go upstairs, pull the covers off the bed and – surprise – it's not the woman they're looking for. Since Bobbie isn't actually wanted for anything at the moment, they'd have had to let her go.'

'But being Bobbie, she naturally decides to improve on that and take to the rooftops.'

We started laughing again, but when I got my hands on the coffee grinder at last, they were shaking so much I could hardly pour in the beans. At least the police hadn't been destructive in their search. The place wasn't much more of a mess than it had been. When I went into the kitchen to fill the kettle the unexpected scent of lily-of-the-valley was flooding the place and I felt a surge of regret for Bill. He'd done well, very well, but I shouldn't have let him in for this.

*　*　*

As we sipped our coffee he said, 'I'm afraid it's a bit late for Box Hill now, but what about a look at the fair on the Heath?'

Amy and Gwen said, far too quickly and politely, that they must go, they had things to do. Gwen, I knew, would be going back to a lonely flat in Paddington that she usually shared with June. She knew where we'd taken June for safety, but it was a long way from London and she was a marked woman so she couldn't visit or even write to her. They went, leaving me and Bill alone, too alone. There was a lot I didn't know about him, far more he didn't know about me. He knew I was a suffragette, of course, but this was his first look at what that meant.

'Thank you,' I said. 'You helped a lot.'

That was less than he deserved. Without his authoritative manner, we'd have still had police crawling all over the house. Still, it had been convention that worked for him and he knew now what an outlaw I was.

'Glad to be of use.'

Which told me nothing.

'Sorry I didn't get a chance to introduce you to Bobbie. She's a wild woman.'

'So the rest of you are tame?'

'You know, they might have caught her if it hadn't been for that horn making such a row. Was it the police panicking?'

He shook his head.

'Anywhere there's a motorcar, there's an urchin just itching to get his hands on the hooter.'

'So it was one of the boys?'

'With a little encouragement, yes.'

'Encouragement?'

'I gave him a shilling and suggested he should see how loud it was.'

'Bill!' I stared at him. 'When you did that, you thought you were assisting the escape of a prisoner!'

'Just don't tell them that at the Inner Temple, that's all.' He smiled. I realised I was staring at him and stood up.

'So what about that walk on the Heath?'

'Yes, you look as if you need to relax. Not surprising, I suppose, with all this on your mind.'

I hadn't forgotten about Verona, but the raid had been a diversion from the nagging questions. Now they were starting again.

'I'm afraid it's not only all this. Come on, let's walk.'

Chapter Four

❧

THE CROWDS WERE THICKEST ROUND THE FAIR IN the Vale of Health. A steam organ on the roundabout was pumping out *Soldiers of the Queen*. Smells of hot sugar and fat from food stalls hung in the air under a cloudy sky. I noticed a cart selling a Bavarian type of sausage. A big grey-haired woman spiked them out of a boiling vat. A small dark man who might have been her son swaddled them in twists of paper, dabbed on mustard and put them in waiting hands, threepence each.

'Hungry?' Bill said.

'No. Just looking at the name.'

The name on the side of the cart was Harry Black, amateurishly painted. Underneath you could just make out another name – Hans Schwarz.

'Poor blighter,' Bill said: 'The *Daily Mail*'s got a lot to answer for.' Hunting for spies had become a national sport in the past few years, with Germany talking peace but building battleships, so it wasn't a good idea to do business under a German name, especially as far as London crowds were concerned. The most inoffensive barbers, café owners or shopkeepers were potential agents of the Kaiser.

We walked halfway across the Heath to get away from the the crowds and sat down on a grassy slope with London

37

stretched out below us in the haze. I told Bill about Verona and was grateful at least that he didn't fuss, say how awful for me or any of the conventional, useless things.

'So you weren't close to her?'

'Not in the least. I only looked her up out of duty.'

He gave me a long look.

'You think I'm callous?'

'I know you're not. But . . .'

'You think I should have taken better care of her?'

'It isn't a question of care. You weren't *in loco parentis.*'

'Her father thinks I as good as killed her. A good happy girl, apparently, until I got her involved in politics.'

'From what you tell me, that's nonsense.'

'Yes, of course it is.'

'So why are you feeling guilty?'

With anybody else I'd probably have exploded and said I wasn't feeling guilty at all, why should I be? But Bill had such a matter-of-fact way of looking at things that I didn't resent it.

'Doesn't everybody feel guilty when somebody they know commits suicide? You know – if I'd written that letter, or sent him ten pounds or gone to see him, then he wouldn't have done it.'

'Yes, but it's not rational. Anyway, you did go and see her.'

'Maybe I should have gone back. But that last time, with the two men there, I could see she didn't need me. She had her own life. If it had been after that first visit, in December when she hadn't been in London long, I might have understood.'

'You thought she was suicidal then?'

'No, of course not or I'd have done something. Only, she struck me . . .' I had to stop and think about it. Bill asked if I minded if he lit his pipe. I liked the smell of his tobacco.

It had a musty sweetness to it, like apples stored in a loft.

'. . . she struck me as somebody who'd taken a leap and was close to regretting it. It can't have been easy for her to leave a close family and the house where she'd grown up.'

'Why did she, then?'

'The usual things. Independence. Ambition.'

'Ambition as an artist?'

'My guess is that studying art was just an excuse to get out into the big wide world. Then she got there and didn't know quite what to do. She was asking me about all sorts of things – socialism, pacifism, even anarchism. She struck me as somebody looking for a cause.'

'Then she found one,' Bill said.

'Joining us, you mean? It's one thing to go on a march or two but that's not the same as being committed.'

'If you saw her at that Buckingham Palace riot—'

'Deputation.'

'If you saw her there, that's pretty committed.'

'I'm not even sure it was her. But if it was, that bothers me.'

'Why?'

'Let's assume it was. Even if she's not in the thick of things, she cares enough to be there. Exactly a week after that, I find her dead. If she was that despairing about things, why bother to go to a political demonstration? Why does anything matter if you've decided to kill yourself?'

Bill lay back and closed his eyes. 'There's a story somebody told me once. A man with all sorts of troubles decides to end them by jumping off the pier. Police fish the body out, ask if anybody saw him before he jumped. Oh yes, says the man in the ticket booth. We had an argument. He reckoned I'd given him a dud halfpenny in his change.'

Music drifted over from the fairground, now *Down at the*

39

Old Bull and Bush. Two children came rolling down the slope, laughing, nearly cannoning into us. I followed Bill's example and lay back on the grass, looking up at the grey sky. After all that had happened it was good just to lie there thinking of nothing in particular. Or it would have been, if it had lasted for more than half a minute.

I said, 'I could talk to people I know. Find out if it really was her outside Buckingham Palace.'

'Will that help?'

'I'd like to know. And I could go back to the student house again. I suppose there'll be things of hers there. Her mother will want them.'

I remembered that her lodgings, on that first visit, had been decorated with little souvenirs from home – a framed photograph of her parents and brother, a painting of the estuary, a pennant that looked as if it came from a sailing dinghy.

'Do you have to do that?'

'I can't leave it to Alexandra. I could take them when I have to go down for the inquest.'

'Do you want me to come to the inquest with you?'

'All the way to Devon from Manchester? Why?'

'You might want a friend there.'

'It's all right, I've been to inquests before.'

I don't know if he was hurt, but he went quiet for a while. I hadn't meant to snap at him, but I was surprised he was so concerned. All I had to do was describe how I found her. It would be the coroner's job and the jurors' to draw conclusions, not mine. In spite of that, I couldn't help worrying away at it, trying to visualise it. Walk into the boathouse, into the shadows. Salt water lapping against the walls, dinghies and rowing boats floating. It would be brighter than I remembered it, with the tide up and light reflecting from the water. There'd be plenty of rope in a boathouse, she'd know where to find it, and the girl who sailed a dinghy better than her brother would tie seaman-like knots. Stand on the wooden walkway, throw one end of a rope over a roof beam. It might take two or three tries, but she'd be efficient at that as well. Tie the rope, leaving a long end hanging down. Knot a noose, then sit down on the walkway and tie your feet to a plank of wood, firmly round the ankles so that they won't get loose. They'd been good knots. I'd struggled to undo them before I realised it wasn't any use. Then what? Noose round neck and push off into the water. You'd keep upright, couldn't prevent your-self doing it. Her hands hadn't been tied. They'd close round the rope that went up to the beam above her head, while her feet floated on the water. So she'd stay there, conscious, waiting for the tide to go out, feeling the tug of it on the plank, first a twitch then a drag that pulled her legs and body out towards the silver expanse of water that was getting narrower all the time. She'd surely fight it. Even if you wanted to die, you'd fight it. But sooner or later, the strength would drain out of your arms like the tide draining out of the creeks, and the noose would tighten.

Bill said, 'Do you think she hoped somebody might come and save her?'

So he'd been thinking too.

'Who? Nobody knew she was there. Her parents thought she was still in London. Her brother was away.'

'There's an element of gambling in some suicides, don't you think? If anybody in the world loves me, I'll be saved.'

'But to stack the odds so much against herself? If there's anything that's certain, it's tides. She grew up with that.'

'You sound angry with her.'

'I am, if—'

41

'If what?'

I didn't answer. After a while we got up and started to stroll back across the Heath.

'Boris Godunov this evening?'

'Why not?'

After all, we did have a victory over the police to celebrate, only I wasn't as happy about that as I should have been. A suicide insults everybody left alive. All the things you think matter, from a great cause to the next cup of tea, hadn't counted for anything in the suicide's eyes. Devalued currency.

'What's going on there?' Bill said.

We were back near the funfair. At first I thought Harry Black and his mother at the sausage cart were just having a rush of good business, then I heard the raised angry voices, saw the cart rocking and realised it was nothing as innocent as that. There was a chant going up.

'Ger-man spies. Dir-ty Ger-man spies.'

Above the heads of the crowd, trapped inside the cart, I saw the scared faces of the old woman and the dark-haired man. He was trying to reason with them, getting nowhere.

'Nell, wait! Leave it to the police.'

But Bill didn't take his own advice. We both ran over. The air round the crowd was heavy with beer fumes. They were mostly young men and a few girls, having some holiday fun as they saw it, but once they'd started it was taking them over, growing vicious. As they chanted and pushed against the cart it rocked almost off its wheels. Another few heaves and it would be over with the the two people and a cauldron of boiling water inside. I shouted to the crowd to stop it but it did no good. Bill grabbed a couple of men by the collar and dragged them aside, so of course they turned on him. For once in my life I was glad to hear a police whistle shrilling and see navy-blue uniforms. Bill's attackers melted away. He took my arm and dragged me to one side.

'Just let them get on with it.'

The police didn't even need to use their truncheons and nobody hung around to be arrested. In a few minutes all that was left to show there'd been trouble was an area of scuffed grass with burst sausages trampled into it. The Blacks were still inside the cart, the woman sobbing and trembling, the man apparently arguing with the police who didn't seem sympathetic. We watched as a policeman escorted the man to fetch his donkey from where it was tethered under a tree and stood over him while he harnessed it to the cart. The woman emptied the cauldron on to the grass, stowed away the mustard jar and they rolled off towards the road. Some of the drunks cheered from a distance as they went.

Bill and I followed the cart out to the road and watched it going slowly down the hill. We'd both had enough of the Heath and the holiday, although it was still only midday.

I said, 'I suppose I could go to the student house this afternoon, get it over with.'

I hadn't intended Bill to come with me, but he seemed to take it for granted that he would and I was feeling too down to argue. We decided to take the underground into the centre of town. While we waited on the platform Bill asked: 'You're hoping her friends might give you some idea why she killed herself?'

A train was coming, which saved me from having to answer. Bill had been through enough already today. I couldn't bring myself to tell him something that had been growing in my mind since I found her. Supposing the question wasn't 'why' but 'if'?

43

Chapter Five

⊗

THE STUDENT HOUSE WHERE I'D LAST SEEN VERONA alive was in one of the small streets behind Cheyne Walk in the stretch between Battersea Bridge and Albert Bridge, close enough to the river to hear seagulls and smell the mud when the tide was out. It was mid afternoon when we got there after a walk along Chelsea Embankment, not saying much. I wished, to be honest, that Bill weren't there but after what he'd done for us, I could hardly tell him to go away. I hadn't paid much attention to the outside of the house on my other visits, beyond noting that it looked run-down, so before we went in I stood with Bill on the pavement opposite and had a good look at it. The general impression was of a house that hadn't woken up yet, even on a holiday afternoon. There were curtains drawn over the downstairs windows, yellowed linings turned to the street. The sash windows of the two upstairs storeys were closed, one of them pinning down a thin blue towel hung out to dry, flapping languidly in the breeze coming from the river. The sill next to it, with cream paint flaking off the stonework, supported a milk bottle and a dead geranium in a pot that looked as if it would slide down into the street at any moment.

'Probably all out,' Bill said, sounding unconcerned.

We crossed the street. The front door, probably blue once,

44

had faded to grey blistered with paint bubbles from sunnier days than this one. The knocker was broken, hanging from one side. I knocked, waited, and knocked again.

'Who's there?' It was a man's voice, with a foreign accent.

'Verona's cousin.'

Father's cousin, but too complicated to explain that through a closed door. A long silence then, 'She's not here.'

The voice was lazy, a little hostile, as if he'd just been woken up. Bill looked at me and raised his eyebrows.

'May we come in, please?'

Another silence, then much fiddling with bolts or catches, and a curse in a language I didn't recognise at first. I'm usually good at foreign curses. By the time the door opened I'd had a chance to think about it. Standing there, eyes half closed, looking far from pleased to see us, was the silent man who'd been sketching Verona with such intense interest. He was older than I'd realised, probably nearer thirty than twenty, and had a world-weary air as if he'd just woken up from a sleep centuries long and found nothing changed. He wore white flannel trousers stained with paint, held up with an even more stained piece of rag knotted round the waistband, a parody of the way university rowing types use their college ties to hold up their trousers. His feet were bare, his toes unusually long and slender and bent like bird's talons as if he needed to keep a good grip on the floor. The dark hair flopping over his forehead looked as if it hadn't been washed in a long time. I thought, with a little stab of loss, that when I was silly and romantic and Verona's age I'd have found him attractive, then with a stab of something else that I refused to recognise I realised that I still did. He pushed his hair back with fingers yellowed with nicotine – elegant fingers though – and stared at us from half-shut eyes as if wondering whether we were worth the trouble of getting in focus. He managed at the same time to be half asleep and so arrogant that I could sense Bill going tense with dislike.

I said 'Good afternoon' to him politely – in Hungarian. His dark eyes opened wide and focused. He said, 'Who are you?' also in Hungarian. I said in English, 'As I told you, Verona's relative. May we come in?' I only knew five phrases of Hungarian and we'd already got through two of them. Still, it had been enough to wake him up. He turned his back and took a few steps into the passage, leaving the door open. I followed. Bill came behind me and closed the door. The dark man went up the stairs without looking back, into a room on the right. It was where I'd last talked to Verona and seemed to be a common room for everybody in the house. At the time, it had struck me as a cheerful creative sort of place, but today it felt like the inside of dustbin. A thick green blind was drawn over the window. There was a smell of linseed oil, stale beer and wine, and cigarette smoke. Something else too, a smell of human bodies and stale sweat.

'Must have been quite a party,' Bill said, sounding unconcerned. I realised that he was talking to me because the dark man had gone. We could hear his bare feet padding back downstairs.

'We'll just get Verona's things and go.'

The Hungarian had said, 'She's not here.' Did he know why? It seemed an age since I'd found Verona, but it was only two days ago.

Bill walked to the window and took hold of the blind. It went up with a rattle like a goods train and something in the room gave a screech of protest. Bill spun round and in other circumstances I'd have laughed at the expression on his face. There was a beautiful half-naked woman lying on the chaise-longue. It was the same broken down chaise-longue where I'd seen Verona posing. The woman had long dark hair, legs bare to the upper thigh and just covered there with a rucked-up net petticoat, white breasts spilling out of a flesh-coloured chemise. You could have toasted bread on Bill's blush. He backed towards the door, started apologising. The woman, entirely unworried, sat up, pulled down her petticoat and stretched like a lazy lioness.

'Ah, I see you've met Maria.'

The Hungarian was back, bringing with him the young man with the ginger beard, the orange juggler. He too looked as if he'd had a long night and while the dark man carried himself with a kind of jaded glamour, Ginger-beard simply looked ill. His round amiable face was pale, his eyes blood-shot, his hair wet as if he'd just dunked his head in a basin of water. Still, he had the manners of a polite schoolboy and came towards me with his hand out.

'Miss Bray, isn't it? Verona's aunt.'

I didn't argue. It was horribly clear now that I'd have to break the news to them.

'I don't think she introduced me last time. Toby's my name. Toby Menteith. That's Maria, as you've heard, and this is Count something-or-other I can't pronounce, known to his friends, police and creditors as Rizzo, as in Bloated Arist-o-crat.'

The Hungarian didn't respond. He was rangeing around the room looking for something.

'Cur, did we drink all the wine?'

'We did, Rizzo. We drank all the wine in the whole wide world.' He explained to us, 'I'm Cur, as in Dog Toby.'

Bill was looking at a mural on the wall behind Toby. It was done in black, white and greys, a man walking along the street with his shadow stretching across the pavement and

47

up a wall behind him. Only the man and his shadow had changed places so that the shadow was walking upright, the man angled and stretched out behind it.

He asked Toby, 'Is that yours?'

'God no. That's Rizzo's. He's a genius whereas my only talent, he assures me, is for being completely devoid of talent.'

The count called Rizzo went on searching, ignoring us. Toby stood looking at us, willing to please but not bringing himself to ask what we wanted. In the end he picked up a Spanish guitar that had been lying on a table and sat himself down cautiously beside Maria. The guitar seemed to comfort him. He plucked a chord or two, inexpertly, and risked a question.

'Well, how's Verona?'

I wished I were anywhere but there. I thought it quite likely that one of these men had been Verona's lover. He didn't deserve to hear she was dead like this, in the ruins of a party with people around him. The question was, which one? Gentle, reassuring Toby seemed the more likely bet, but there was no telling for certain.

I asked Toby, 'You haven't seen her, then?'

'No. Is she all right?'

Toby, through his hangover, was starting to sense something was wrong. From across the room, Rizzo yelled, 'Throw them out, Cur! Throw them out!'

'Rizzo, that's hardly hospitable.'

'Beware the family. Beware the family.'

Rizzo was glaring at us but there was something stagey about his anger. He was too self-absorbed to pick up the atmosphere as Toby had.

Toby explained, like a man who'd had to do it before, 'Rizzo's an anarchist. We all are.'

I'd met angora rabbits that struck me as being more

anarchistic than Toby. It was no more than typical student posing, but it wasn't helping. I asked Rizzo, ignoring the glare, 'Why should you beware of Verona's family?'

He looked at me in silence, then turned away. Again, Toby explained for him.

'He thinks her family will make her go back home and get married.'

I asked Rizzo's back, 'You're against that?'

'We're against marriage, possessing people and so forth.'

That was Toby again, clearly unhappy. He plucked a few more tentative sounds out of the guitar, single notes this time. Beside him, Maria stretched and yawned. Bill caught my eye, questioning. I still couldn't make up my mind, so there was no choice but to tell the whole roomful of them.

'I'm sorry, but I've got some very bad news for you. Verona was found dead on Thursday.'

For a few seconds, the guitar notes went on, Toby's fingers working while his mind tried to catch up. In those seconds Rizzo turned slowly, eyes wide. His face had been pale before, now it was grey. He looked like the shadow-man in his picture. Maria asked in Spanish what was up. Nobody answered her. Toby asked: 'How?' He was shaking so much he could hardly get the word out.

I said, 'She was hanging in a boathouse.'

'H . . . hanging? You mean she k . . . k . . . ?'

'There'll have to be an inquest, of course, but it does look as if she might have committed suicide.'

Toby screamed, a high little scream like a child's. He stood up, unsteady on his feet. His right hand still clutched the guitar. He looked as if he was going to be sick and I expected him to rush for the door. Instead he hurled himself across the room at Rizzo.

'It's your fault. You made her go away. It's your fault.'

49

I don't know if Rizzo's failure to defend himself was due to arrogance or surprise. Before we could do anything Toby lifted the guitar in the air like a man doing a serve at tennis and brought it down with a splintering crash on Rizzo's head. Then they were both on the floor, Rizzo with the remains of the guitar round his head, Toby apparently trying to strangle him, not very effectively. Between us, Bill and I got them apart. Rizzo simply stood up, picked bits of wood off himself and walked out of the room without a word. Toby leaned against Bill, crying unashamedly, tears running down his beard. 'I loved her. I loved her.'

With the help of Maria, who seemed to have woken up at last, we got Toby upstairs to bed. It was a sparsely furnished cubicle on the top floor, like a boarding school bedroom. The only thing by way of decoration was a charcoal sketch of a girl on a bed, barefoot, smoking a cigarette. I saw Bill looking at it and mouthed, 'Verona.'

It was the sketch Rizzo had been doing when I was there. The paper had been crumpled and carefully smoothed out – probably rejected by the artist and retrieved by Toby. When we'd got him quiet, Bill and I left him in the care of Maria and went out onto the landing.

'So what now? Do we still want to collect her things?'

I was about to say no, we'd leave it, when a door across the landing opened and a girl stuck her head out, looking annoyed.

'What's going on now? Are they fighting again?'

I said Toby had had some bad news.

'Oh God, there's always something in this house.'

'Have you been here long?'

'Three weeks, and it's a lifetime too long already. I'm moving out tomorrow.'

'Did you know Verona North?'

'No. I've got her room, but I never met her. Are you looking for her?'

I explained. She was apologetic, introduced herself as Janie, asked us in. It was just like Toby's bleak little room opposite, except it had a skylight in the roof that gave good light. Janie had a table exactly under the skylight with a box of watercolours, a jar of fine brushes and a spray of marsh marigold in a vase. There was a half-finished picture of it on an easel, done with beautiful precision.

'There's nowhere to sit but the bed, I'm afraid.' The accent was Home Counties. She seemed a world away from the chaos downstairs. 'You won't mind if I go on with this? I'm supposed to have it done by tomorrow.'

The bed was a pallet against the wall, narrower than in a prison cell. She must have trained herself to sleep without turning over. I sat on it and after a moment's doubt, Bill joined me. I asked if she was at the Slade too.

'Yes. Was Verona? We don't tend to socialise much with the first-year people and I've been busy. First commission.'

'You say this was her room?'

'That's right. I was sharing with somebody, but when I got this commission I needed somewhere to work on my own. I heard on the grapevine that this was vacant so in I came. Serious mistake. It's like trying to work in the middle of Trafalgar Square.'

'On the grapevine? Can you remember how exactly?'

'Not sure. I think I heard about it from a woman who went to life class with somebody who knew the man they call Rizzo . . .'

'The aristocratic Hungarian anarchist?'

She snorted. 'Egoist, you mean.'

Bill said unexpectedly, 'I thought his painting was good.'

'Oh he *paints* well enough. He'd be even better if he stopped posturing and did some work.'

I asked, 'And Toby?'

Another snort. 'No talent whatsover. He should go home and be a vicar, which is what his father is, wouldn't you have guessed.'

'Did you get the impression that Toby was in love with Verona?'

Janie looked at me as if I'd asked about the habits of warthogs.

'Not interested. Even if I were, there wouldn't be any point in this house.'

Bill asked why.

'Like trying to draw a map of a desert in a sandstorm. Always people coming and going, shouting at each other, drunk or worse half the time.'

'Worse?'

Janie picked up another brush and drew an outline of a leaf.

'Smoking. Going to China, Rizzo calls it. First time I heard it, I said would he bring me back some calligraphy brushes.'

I said, 'Opium, you mean?'

She nodded.

Bill said, 'It seems a funny sort of place for a vicar's son.'

Or for a commodore's daughter, come to that.

'Oh, I'm sure Toby thinks he's seeing life. He'll grow out of it.'

Grow out of life, did she mean? Which brought us back to Verona. I was going to ask another question, but Bill got in first.

'The man they call Rizzo had done a drawing of her. Do you think he was attracted to her?'

'What's the connection? He spent days at a hospital once painting a gangrenous foot.'

52

Bill persisted. He was good at that. 'Do you think he's the kind of man women find attractive?' (Had he picked up that rogue thought in me? I hoped not.)

'Perhaps, if they've got no sense. Rizzo thinks love is a bourgeois affectation. I expect he offered to deflower her.'

Bill blinked, but rallied. 'Why do you think so?'

'He did it to me the first time we met – offered, that is. He says any virgin over fifteen years old is an offence against nature.'

'What did you do?'

'Poured a bottle of turps over him. I shouldn't have reacted like that. Waste of good turps.'

She went on calmly painting the flower. Bill seemed to have run out of questions, so I came in with mine.

'You say you moved in here three weeks ago. That would be near the start of May?'

'Monday May the fourth.'

Janie was as precise about dates as in her painting. As far as I could remember, Verona had last written to her mother the day before, May the third, saying she was well and working hard. There'd been nothing said about moving.

'And you got the impression that Verona had moved out for good, not just gone away for a while?'

'Nobody's that definite about anything here, but I certainly got the impression it was vacant for the foreseeable future or I shouldn't have taken it. I must say I was annoyed, though, to find she'd left some of her things here.' Bill glanced at me. I asked, 'What sort of things?'

'An old jacket, some books, a not particularly good landscape.'

'Of an estuary?'

'Yes.'

'Anything else?'

'A flag of some kind, a few seashells, a pair of shoes.'

'What did you do with them?'

'Put them in a box and shoved it in the corner, out of the way.'

I looked round the room. No sign of a box. I said, 'If you can find them, we'll take them away with us and return them to her family.'

'No need. They've come for them already.'

'When?'

'Yesterday. I didn't know she was dead then, or of course I'd have said something. I thought they were just collecting them for her.'

'They?'

'Two men.'

'What sort of men?'

'Pretty standard bi-pedal hominids, I'd say. One thin with a bowler, one fat with a cap and red muffler.'

'Working men?'

'Oh yes.'

'What did they say?'

'I can't remember too clearly because I was working and they were a nuisance. I think the thin man said something like was this Miss North's room? I suppose I said it had been and he said they'd come to take away her things.'

'Did they say who they were?'

'No, and I didn't care. I just pointed to the box and said there they were and they took it away.'

'Nothing else said?'

'The thin one said was there anything else of hers in the house? I said I didn't suppose so, but if she'd left anything lying around downstairs it wouldn't have lasted long.'

* * *

54

She didn't raise her eyes from the painting as Bill and I let ourselves out. There was no sound coming from Toby's room across the landing, no sign of anybody on the other two floors. When we got outside we turned without saying anything to the embankment and stood looking down at the river. There was a steam tug pulling a long line of empty barges against the current.

I said, 'We didn't find her body until Thursday. On Friday, two men arrive to collect her things?'

'Some people react like that. Get it over with.'

'Ben and Alexandra were in a state of shock. Besides, those two sound more like removal men than family.'

'The coroner's officer will have to find out if there were letters.'

'In a room she hadn't lived in for three weeks? Besides, it would be a job for the police.'

We started walking towards Albert Bridge. There was a man in a striped blazer and yellowish straw boater on the other side of the street, looking as if he'd got separated from his friends. After a while Bill said, 'She does seem to have got in with a rum crowd.'

'They're students!' For some reason, I needed to defend Verona.

'Opium smoking and seducing virgins?'

'More talk than anything, I expect. I went to an opium den in Limehouse when I was about their age.'

Bill gave me one of his looks that I hadn't learned to interpret yet. I suppose at that stage I was still trying to find out where his limits were.

'On your own?'

'A little group of us – thought we were terribly modern and daring. To be honest, it was a bit of a disappointment. It was this big room with white walls and a lot of cubicles

55

like coffins with people sleeping in them. And two very neat and polite Chinamen preparing the pipes.'

'Did you smoke?'

'A few puffs. So as not to lose face.'

The man in the yellowish boater still hadn't found his friends. He was walking slowly, taking a great interest in front gardens. A horticulturalist perhaps.

Bill said, 'She does seem to have plunged into student life quite quickly.'

'That's the only way to do it. Weren't you like that?'

I really wanted to know. Bill and I had spent an intense few weeks working on a case together back in the autumn, but I still hardly knew him.

'I think maybe it was different in Manchester.'

He sounded not resentful exactly but I did have the feeling that my youthful frivolities – mostly modest enough on the whole – were being put firmly in their place.

'You think it happened because she plunged in too rapidly?'

'Look, Nell, by your account, up to about six or seven months ago she was the model daughter, with nothing in her head except ponies and dinghies.'

'That's what her mother thought. There must be more to any nineteen-year-old girl than that.'

'Still, she was an ordinary girl with a conventional upbringing.'

'Certainly conventional. Ordinary? Is anybody?'

'Let's say, nothing remarkable about her that we know of.'

'No.' Nothing remarkable. Except that she'd put a noose round her neck, lashed her feet to a plank and waited for the tide to go out. Perhaps.

'Yet within those six or seven months she's stopped writing to her parents, taken an interest in radical politics and moved in with a household of drug-takers and anarchists.'

'Are you implying I should have looked after her better?'

'You *know* I'm not. Still . . .'

He left it. We came to Albert Bridge, strolled to the middle of it, watched a steamer full of trippers going underneath, strolled back again. The man in the yellowish boater strolled too, on the opposite side of the bridge. I didn't draw Bill's attention to him. After all, I might have been wrong.

Chapter Six

⊗

W E WENT TO BORIS GODUNOV AFTER ALL, BUT if you want
a detailed critique of Chaliapin's performance you'll
have to find somebody who stayed awake. From the clam-
our of cheers and bravos that jerked my head up from Bill's
shoulder, I assume it was up to standard. Going home afterwards in a cab, I couldn't stop apologising.

'Honestly, I've never done that before.'

'Then I'm sorry my company is so uniquely unstimulating.'

'Oh God, I didn't mean that, you know I didn't. Only . . .'

'It has been quite a day. Or is that normal with you?'

At least he didn't seem offended. We were close together
on the hansom seat and I'd have liked to rest my head on
his shoulder again, but didn't have the excuse of going to
sleep. In the traffic, we were stopping and swerving too much
to make it plausible.

'I assume it didn't end happily.'

'Correct. *Macbeth* without the jokes.'

He saw me to my front door, I said thank you for everything, he said to let him know if he could help. Then he
took the cab on to the friends he was staying with in Camden.
He had to get the train back to Manchester in the morning.
That was it.

* * *

For the next ten days or so I tried to put it all out of my mind and just get on with work, both the kind that got me into trouble and the other kind that paid the rent. The first category was getting grimmer all the time. It wasn't just a case of demonstrating and window-smashing. These went on but they were almost echoes from an age of innocence compared to what was happening now. This summer, the conflict between ourselves and the authorities was so bitter and violent that neither side could see a way out of it short of a catastrophe worse than anything that had happened before. We weren't just a nuisance to be shrugged off: we were enemies of the state. The police searched homes, arrested some of our people on suspicion of bomb-making, stayed in occupation of our headquarters and seized our incoming mail. We moved to our Westminster offices in Tothill Street, almost within the shadow of the Houses of Parliament, then they raided us there as well.

One of the immediate consequences for me was that plain clothes observation of my movements became almost constant. I thought Special Branch must have been doing some hasty recruiting because though some of the old familiars like Gradey were still around, there were people I hadn't seen before hanging about on the corner of my street or loitering in libraries I happened to be using. Gradually, they too became a part of the landscape. Then, glimpsed two or three times on street corners or on the far side of cafés, was the man I always thought of as Yellow Boater. Not that he wore the boater after that first day. I assumed it must be the plain clothes' idea of how to be inconspicuous on a bank holiday weekend. Sometimes he was in a bowler, sometimes in a flat cap. Under the varying headgear was the face of a man in his thirties, clean-shaven apart from a neat dark moustache, with a dutiful, melancholy air.

The reports on my movements, from Yellow Boater and

the rest of them, must have been monotonous reading for somebody. Subject left home in the morning at eight o'clock. Spent morning either in libraries, usually the London Library in St James' Square, or in police courts observing cases involving suffragettes, or at homes of known associates, most of them with police records. Consumed lunch of tea and Chelsea bun in ABC café (the amount of Special Branch petty cash spent on tea and buns in the course of duty would soon need its own column in their accounts), spoke at meetings in evening at which various derogatory things were said about Prime Minister, tram to Haverstock Hill and walk home, arriving 11 p.m. approx. What they couldn't record, because it wasn't happening, was any more evidence that I was assisting the escape of prisoners on licence. The spiriting away of June had been a coup for us, but it meant we couldn't use my house again. I was surprised the watchers hadn't worked this out for themselves, then I decided I might be overestimating the average intelligence of Scotland Yard.

The reason why my watchers were getting so much time to improve their minds in libraries was that I'd managed to get a useful piece of freelance translation work. That's my job, nominally, though what with one thing and another it had got neglected – to the point where many people who'd sent me work in the past diverted it to translators who were less likely to be in prison or tied up with murder investigations. Just when my finances were at their lowest, a friend recommended me to a children's publisher who wanted translations of German fairy tales. It was the most interesting professional work I'd had in a long time, and a welcome distraction from everything else.

Now and then, between work and the demands of being an enemy of the state, I thought of Bill. To be honest, I thought of Bill quite a lot. I hadn't heard from him since he'd driven away in the cab and I wasn't surprised. There he was, turning up for a day out, with his bunch of flowers and his expensive tickets and what had I given him in return? A police raid, a minor riot and a fight. On top of that, when I should have been taking pity on him, I'd gone in for some pointless boasting about my own student days that probably convinced him I was no fit company for a man with a career to think about. Not that Bill was a conventional ambitious barrister. We'd met because he'd been desperately trying to save a client from the gallows. We managed it, but he'd had to take some risks along the way. He'd known from the start that I was often on the wrong side of the law. What he couldn't have known, until he turned up on my doorstep at the wrong time, was what that meant in practice. He'd done well, magnificently well, but I couldn't blame him if he decided that was more than enough. Still, I cared about not hearing from him more than seemed reasonable and wished the day could have turned out as he'd wanted. I craved ordinariness. I wanted to do what other people did – what I'd done myself in days that seemed now a lifetime away. I wanted to go for walks in the country, eat meals with time to enjoy them, go to concerts and walk down streets without wondering if anybody was following. Bill wasn't ordinary in himself, but for a while he'd seemed to open a door back to that kind of life. Well, the door had closed again, just as I should have closed my door on him and kept him out of trouble. Stop fretting about it. Get on with work.

So I got on with work, until something else happened. It was two days after the police turned us out of Tothill Street. We'd had to set up another emergency headquarters all the way out in Notting Hill, knowing it would only be a matter of time before they pounced on us there. Somebody, I remember, sang two lines of a music-hall song to the stony-faced constables, 'I've been thrown out of better joints than this before, so you won't hurt my feelings if you chuck me out again.' I'd had to put aside my translation work yet again. It was a long day and nearly midnight when I got home, only wanting to make a cup of tea and collapse for an hour or two. I turned my key in the lock and, even before I lit the gas, realised that some-body had been in while I was out. I'm not sure what it was that gave me the first warning, maybe no more than a smell or some sort of animal instinct. I lit the gas mantle, curious but not too worried. My neighbour and a dozen or so friends knew I kept a spare key under the back doormat. It was useful for making sure the cats were fed if I had to go away in a hurry or if a friend in trouble needed a refuge.

I said: 'Anybody at home?'

I wouldn't have been surprised – though not pleased, as I wanted to sleep – if Bobbie or somebody had called from upstairs. Nothing. The gas flame steadied and light spread round the room. No sign as far as I could see that anybody had been in, but since the living-room hadn't been tidied for months, it wouldn't be easy to tell. Bill's lily-of-the-valley, faded now, were still in their vase on the piano. The place really was a mess – dust thick as a mouse's fur on the piano top – except for a few inches. There was a narrow fan shape with no dust at all, just clear varnished wood. It was along-side some sheet music, Schubert, that had been lying on the piano since goodness knows when. Very recently, too recently for dust to settle, somebody had picked up the sheet music and put it down again. Who? I hadn't played the piano since my New Year's Eve party more than five months ago, or given even a passing thought to Schubert. There was a chair that might have been moved back from the table. A line of dictionaries on the bookcase that I thought had been level with each other now had one sticking out. The piles of letters waiting for answers beside my typewriter were tidy, which was a bad sign. They usually weren't. Even so, I wasn't totally sure that something was wrong until I sat down at the table and looked at my work in progress. Because everything else round me is usually in chaos, I'm ridiculously orderly about my translation work. I like to have my pad and pencils, my dictionaries and the book I'm working on placed so that I can sit down and pick up work exactly where I left it. This was all wrong. The pencils were on the left side of the pad, the dictionaries at right angles to it, not parallel. The postcard of Venice I was using to keep my place in the book was address-side uppermost, when I knew I'd left it photo-side up. I sat there, still in my coat, and shivered.

Why? After all, almost everybody I knew had been raided. The police had been through the house only eleven days ago. We were all suspected criminals under observation. The simple fact that somebody had been in and searched my house quite thoroughly while I was away shouldn't have rated as much more than the normal course of events. The trouble was, I knew it was anything but that. The normal course of events was police coming in loudly and mob-handed, opening doors and cupboards, carrying crates of papers away. It was a rough but quite open business, a world away from this expert and surreptitious search that might easily have gone unnoticed. What made me shiver, what I couldn't understand, was why anybody had gone to all the trouble. There was very little in my life that was secret – sometimes I'd felt I was living all of it on a public platform – but somebody believed there was and that it mattered.

I slept. I was too tired to do anything else. In the morning I asked the neighbour who fed my cats if she'd noticed anybody going into my house the day before.

'I try not to be nosey, dear.'

Which was true. She was on my side personally, if not politically, and was good at ignoring the goings-on next door.

'Police?'

'Oh no, nothing like that.'

With some prompting, she thought she might have seen two men in the street outside in mid afternoon, ordinary working men in caps and rough jackets. Thinking of the men who'd collected Verona's possessions from the student house, I asked if one of them had been wearing a red muffler. She hadn't noticed. It was going to be another day with no progress on the fairy tales.

I did what I'd done before when sorely perplexed and made my way to a little low building a few hundred yards from Liverpool Street Station. It has a cross over its corrugated iron porch and a faded mural of Jesus teaching the children on the wall inside. It was built as a Sunday school but now the sign outside, in neat white letters on a blue board, reads Archimedes J. Stuggs Chess Forum. It's the haunt of some of the best chess players in London and – coincidentally or not – some of the most left-wing political desperadoes in Europe. Since my old friend the journalist Max Blume is passionate about both chess and politics, it's usually a safe bet that I'll find him there and I was lucky. He was standing by the tea urn, looking out over a room dotted with small tables. Three of them were already in use for chess games and he was probably following all three. Max looked even thinner and more worried than usual. He's capable of being depressed about the political situation in places most of us could hardly find in an atlas.

'What's wrong, Nell?' He didn't waste any time in conventional chat. He guessed it wasn't a social visit.

'I'm being followed. My home's been searched.'

His eyebrows went up. He wasn't shocked at what I'd said, only that I was making a fuss about something as obvious as rain being wet.

'I don't mean in the usual way, Max. Followed most of the time and a secret search I wasn't supposed to know about.'

I told him about the escape coup and what had happened since. He listened, still apparently absorbed in the three chess games.

'Have you been consorting with revolutionaries?'

'No more than usual.'

'Suspicious foreigners?'

'Not particularly . . . oh God, yes. But surely . . .'

I hadn't told him about the Verona business at first, partly because I didn't want to, partly because I couldn't see that it was relevant. Now I remembered the student house and the man they called Rizzo. If Germany was the big bogey of the spy scares then Austria-Hungary came a close second. I explained what had happened, from finding Verona's body to the disorderly household in Chelsea.

'But they were just artists and students, Max, trying to be important. I can't imagine that even Special Branch would waste time watching a crowd like that.'

But now I came to think of it the first time I'd noticed Yellow Boater was when Bill and I left the student house.

Max said: 'It might not be Special Branch.'

'Who else would be that stupid?'

'Have you heard of something called MO5?'

'No.'

'It hasn't been going long. War Office department, supposed to be spying on the spies. Then there's the SSB.'

'Must we talk in initials?'

'Secret Service Bureau. Probably War Office as well, but

65

they work with Scotland Yard's Special Branch sometimes.'

I was going to ask how Max knew about them, but decided not to.

'What are they for?'

'Tracking German spies, anarchists, saboteurs, Sinn Feiners. Also other dangerous elements like trade unionists and Labour MPs.'

'Seriously?'

'Ask Keir Hardie next time you see him.'

'And you think they're being used against us now?'

He took his eyes off the chess games and looked at me.

'No, I don't. You people should come under Special Branch. If MO5 or the SSB are really taking an interest in you personally, that's for something else.'

'For heaven's sake, what else could there be?'

'Contacts with Germany?'

'I'm a *translator*, Max. It's what I do. Do they think witches and wood sprites are some kind of code, for goodness sake?'

I must have raised my voice because one of the chess players looked round. He had dark greasy hair down to his collar, a drooping moustache, face yellowish from cigarettes.

Max smiled. 'It might not be a bad one.'

'You can't seriously think . . .'

'No, of course I don't. But it's a question of what *they* think.'

'They can't be investigating all the people in London who know German on the off-chance they might be spies.'

'No, so if it is MO5, they think they have some other reason to suspect you. You genuinely can't remember anything except those art students?'

'No. Surely they're not under observation?'

'From what you say, I shouldn't have thought so. I agree

with you, they don't sound worth the trouble. And yet . . .'
His eyes were back on the chess players, but most of his
mind wasn't. Max was worried. 'This cousin of yours . . .'

'Cousin's daughter.'

'You say her father's a commodore. Would she have talked
about that?'

I started saying I didn't know Verona well enough to have
any idea what she'd talk about, then I saw where he was
heading.

'You mean, somebody might have taken up with her
because . . . ?'

'I'm trying to make sense of this. There's this naïve young
woman, by your account, on her own in London, probably
thrilled to be among more exotic people than she'd meet
down in Devon. Supposing somebody noticed her and
thought she might be a useful source of information.'

'Rizzo?'

'Or somebody else using him. His friend told you he's a
count. Suppose he has powerful friends back in Budapest?'

'Max, this is worse than the *Daily Mail*. It's pure spy
fantasy.'

'Yes. But just because there are spy fantasies, it doesn't
mean there aren't such people as spies.'

'You're trying to tell me that Verona was taken up by a
spy ring?'

'No, I'm not. I'm trying to see why the secret service
people are taking an interest in you – if they are. It's like
trying to get into your opponent's mind when you're playing chess. Look at it from the opposition's point of view.' I
tried and didn't like it.

Max said, looking across the room, 'It's a pity we can't
ask him what he thinks.' He was staring at the long greasy
hair of the chess player who'd turned to look at us.

'Why?'

'He's one of them. An MO5 man, we think. One of the initials anyway.'

'How do you know?'

'Sticks out a mile. Calls himself Weaver.'

Weaver seemed to be intent on the game now, under the unimpressed eye of his opponent, a cadaverous man with a grey beard.

'The man he's playing comes from Prague. He has a reputation worldwide as a lepidoptericide.'

I was so keyed up that it took me longer than it should have to work it out.

'Kills butterflies?'

'One of Europe's foremost collectors. Naturally he corresponds with people all over the place in several languages. Weaver's convinced he's a master spy.'

'Why don't you throw Weaver out?'

'Why? He's doing no harm here and he might elsewhere. Anyway, we're getting a lot of enjoyment out of him. Everybody wants to challenge him to a game.'

'You mean he's a good player?'

'No, the game is to make as many deliberate mistakes as you can and still beat him. Thirteen's the record at present.'

We watched as Weaver hesitated, moved a piece, sat back to watch the grey-bearded man.

Max shuddered. 'If that's the best the War Office can do, we'd better pray even harder for peace.'

Back at home that evening, I found an official letter with a Devon postmark among the mail. My presence as a witness was required at the opening of the inquest on Verona North at 11 a.m. on Wednesday 17 June.

Chapter Seven

ॐ

W HEN DID YOU LAST SEE VERONA? THEY MIGHT reasonably ask me that at the inquest and I'd have to reply
that I wasn't sure. There could have been any number of
young women with reddish-brown hair outside Buckingham
Palace on 21 May, and even if I could have identified her
for certain, that still left a larger question unanswered. Where
had she been during the rest of the twenty-five days from
the time she left her room at the house in Chelsea to when
I found her in the boathouse? Unless somebody could answer
that, nobody could even make a guess at her state of mind.
There was no reason why I should be the one to provide the
answer, but I felt belatedly – and uselessly – responsible. Over
the next few days I worked on the Buckingham Palace angle
and found it as difficult as I'd expected. There'd been around
twenty thousand people there in a constant eddying battle
between our side trying to get to the palace and the police
hellbent on stopping us. Everybody I spoke to had her own
story of the day, but none of them included a girl answering Verona's description until the Sunday before the inquest
when myself and a few others were having a quarrel with a
flat-bed printing press in an old coach house in Clerkenwell.
Two days before, the inevitable had happened in the shape
of yet another police raid on our makeshift headquarters in

Notting Hill. This time they'd taken away boxes of posters and pamphlets. We needed more in a hurry and a nervous supporter had volunteered the use of his press, provided he wasn't present. The coach house was paved with flagstones and plastered with cobwebs, and the press looked and behaved as if it dated from Caxton's time and had been put together in a bad mood by one of his less promising apprentices. Add to that spiders the size of coffee saucers scuttling out of dark corners and a cataclysmic thunderstorm outside with rain pouring in gallons through holes in the roof, and you have one of the low points of our campaigning experience. Still, we got some posters printed at the cost of a lot of wasted ink and paper and several crushed thumbnails. One of the team was a woman called Cecily who'd been in the crowd around the Victoria Memorial. She remembered seeing a girl with long reddish-brown hair down her back.

'I noticed the hair, because it struck me she must be new to all this. For goodness sake, wearing your hair down like that's a positive invitation to the police to grab you by it. They were pushing us back and some of us were getting crushed against the railings. You either had to break out somehow or get over the railings on to the grass.'

Cecily had taken the more aggressive option and broken out through a gap in the police cordon, but before that she'd noticed a little group of about half a dozen people helping each other climb the low railings to the comparative safety of the grass island round the monument. The girl who looked like Verona had been one of them.

'Around nineteen?'

'Could have been anything from sixteen to mid twenties. Do you want these in that box?'

'Leave them, they're not dry yet. Did she look as if she was with friends?'

70

'I don't know. You just help if you can, don't you, whether you know somebody or not? There was one person I recognised though.'

'Who?'

'Vincent Hergest. That was the other thing that made me remember her, that and the hair.'

Distinguished company. Vincent Hergest was one of the best-known novelists in the country. He was in his early forties but still had a reputation as an interpreter of modern youth, particularly of independent-minded young women. People who worried about modern youth read Vincent Hergest to have their worst fears confirmed. Young people who hoped they were modern read him to find out what the qualifications were. He was a socialist in politics and, naturally, a firm supporter of the suffragettes. His great line was campaigning for peace by bringing the youth of the world together. He used some of the profits from his books to finance weekends and summer camps where students and workers from all over Europe held high-minded debates, and went swimming and hiking together. It was no surprise that Vincent Hergest had been at the deputation. No surprise either – to me at any rate – that he'd managed to keep out of the worst of the trouble. To be honest, I liked him less than a lot of my friends did. I had to acknowledge his financial generosity to us and I enjoyed his angry, witty letters to papers, but to me there was the whiff of opportunism about him. He managed to support risky causes in a way that ensured his reputation and sales figures didn't suffer and he could go safely home to his mansion out Guildford way, to his wife, his collection of paintings and his little fleet of motorcars.

'You didn't see what happened to any of them after they climbed over the railings?'

'Of course not. Did you know you've got purple ink on your nose?'

That night I wrote a note to Vincent Hergest, care of his publishers, explaining about Verona and asking if he remembered meeting a girl like her on the day of the deputation. I wasn't hopeful. Events like that throw complete strangers together for a few minutes, then they get separated again. Even if he did happen to remember a girl like Verona, his description would probably be no more conclusive than Cecily's. I delivered the note to his publishers on Monday morning. The clerk in the post-room promised to forward it but warned me that it wouldn't get to Mr Hergest for some days. He'd just left for Paris to do research on his latest book and wasn't expected back before next week. Then I walked to Oxford Circus, jumping gutters still flooded from yesterday's storm. Thinking back to my last conversation with Verona in March, I had another idea for trying to fill in those blank twenty-five days. She'd informed me, rather smugly, that she was studying ju-jitsu and confirmed that it was at one of Edith Garrud's classes. Just beside Oxford Circus, in Argyll Place, the sign over the door, painted in vaguely oriental lettering, read 'Garrud's Academy of Ju-jitsu'. From upstairs, regular thudding sounds and a female voice – 'One, two, three and *swing*' – indicated that class was already in progress. I opened the door and walked up the stairs. There were photographs on both sides of the stairway showing men and women in martial poses, mostly Edith Garrud and her husband. When I opened the door at the top of the stairs the familiar smell of sweat, wintergreen oil and coconut matting came out at me.

'And three and swing, and four and swing. Miriam, you're letting your shoulder drop. Concentrate. One and swing . . .'

Indian club exercise. Edith believed in a thorough warm-up routine before letting anybody practise ju-jitsu. She was wearing a white sleeveless tunic that ended at mid-calf and had a club in each hand. There were ten women swinging clubs in the bare mirrored room dressed in various versions of sportswear. Nine faces were red and sweating already. Edith turned as the door opened without breaking rhythm.

'You're late, Nell. Get changed quickly and remember what I told you about keeping your shoulders relaxed. Supple joints, supple mind.'

I hadn't been to one of her classes for six months at least. Edith never forgot. She'd stopped swinging the clubs but flexed her knees and shoulders as she talked.

'I'm afraid I'm not here for the class.'

'Police after you again? Strip off quickly, then.' Some time ago, Edith had saved several of us from arrest when the police were chasing us after some window-smashing in Oxford Street. We'd dashed into her studio, stripped off our outer clothes and when the officers came in she assured them that we were just there for the ju-jitsu.

'No. Not directly at any rate. I want to know if you remember somebody. Verona North.'

She nodded. 'What's wrong with her?'

'I'm afraid she's dead.'

Her face changed, but her knees and shoulders went on moving. She called, without turning round. 'Look up, Erica, look up. Eyes down, heart down.' Then to me, 'Accident?'

'Of a kind.'

'Take over, Kitty. Put the clubs away and get them down on the floor.'

As we went through to the office the tenth woman – the only one who wasn't red in the face – moved to face the class. She was not much taller than Edith herself, and looked as lean and fit as a ferret. Her hair was dark and cut almost as short as a man's. Even in the office, grieved at the news I'd brought, Edith couldn't stop exercising. She signalled to me to take the only chair, kept standing and swung one foot in its white tennis shoe up to the corner of the desk.

'What happened?'

'They think she might have killed herself. I found her. I've got to give evidence at the inquest.'

I couldn't see her face because it was turned away from me, resting against her knee but the shudder she gave was enough. Violence against your own body went against all that Edith believed.

'I'm trying to find out what happened to her in the last few weeks. When I saw her in March she said she was coming to your classes.'

'In March, yes, not in the last few weeks.'

The fingers of both hands were laced behind her instep. Kitty's voice came through the closed door, commanding the class to stretch, really stretch. It was an Irish accent, harsh north of Ireland, not soft south.

'When did you last see her?'

'April. She stopped coming here in April. I can give you the date if you want.'

She returned her leg to the floor, opened the desk drawer and took out a big diary. Every page in it had lists of names in columns.

'Here we are. She came to my Tuesday classes. The first one was back here in February, through to 14 April, then she just stopped coming.'

'No letter? No explanation?'

'No, but then it's like that with some of them. All enthusiasm at first, then when they find they're not going to learn how to throw twenty-stone ruffians over their shoulders in the first few weeks they get impatient and give up.'

'You thought that was what had happened?'

'Yes. To be honest, she had struck me as an impatient type, only . . .' She closed the book and put it away, '. . . I liked her. I thought she had something about her.'

'For ju-jitsu?'

'Not necessarily for that. It was too early to tell. I liked her because she was serious about it and she worked hard, as if she needed it.'

'Needed to defend herself?'

'Needed to be strong.'

'Strong for what?'

'I don't know. I'd assumed it was for the cause but . . .'

I waited. It wasn't usual for Edith to hesitate about anything.

'. . . Thinking back, I don't know. I said she was impatient, but it wasn't quite like the others. It was . . . well, it was as if she was expecting something to happen and thought she might not have enough time to get ready for it.' Her head was up against her knee again, her voice muffled.

'But she didn't say anything to you about what it was she expected to happen?'

'No. What I've just said to you – I'm not sure I realised it at the time. Just, as I said . . . thinking back.'

'And then, in April, she just stopped coming without any explanation?'

'Yes.'

'And you never saw her after that?'

'No.'

When we went back to the studio, Kitty was kneeling on the mat, knee to knee and palm to palm with one of the pupils.

The girl looked heavier and more muscular than Kitty and was pressing with all her strength but getting forced back on her heels, panting.

'Stop that, Kitty. You're not on stage now.' Edith explained as we went downstairs: 'I'm training Kitty as my assistant, but she does a strong woman act in the halls and I'm afraid she's got into some bad habits.'

Outside the sun had come out and the pavements in Oxford Street were steaming. I'd done nothing to fill in the blank of Verona's last twenty-five days, only added another reason to be worried. 'As if she was expecting something to happen . . .'

Chapter Eight

☙

THE NEXT DAY I WENT BACK TO TEIGNMOUTH and stayed overnight at a guesthouse, ready for the inquest. It was held in a meeting-room next to the town hall, behind the big hotels that lined the street nearest the sea. I got there too early and found the door locked so had to kill time looking in shop windows and watching the traffic. It consisted mostly of carts loaded with barrels of fish on their way to the railway station, tradesmen's carts and a few smarter gigs. There weren't as many motorcars as in London, so it wasn't surprising that the big black one nosing its way among the fish carts had people turning to look at it. But the murmuring from the people near me, low and respectful, wasn't from admiration for the car. It was the shivery mixture of curiosity, sympathy and the thank-God-it's-them-not-me you get at accidents.

A woman said, 'Poor things.'

The man driving the car, wearing a black peaked cap, was the gardener who'd helped carry Verona's body up to the house. In the back seat, straight-backed and looking directly ahead, was my cousin Commodore Benjamin North, in civilian clothes with bowler hat and black armband. The bowed figure beside him, face hidden under a heavy black motoring veil, must be Alexandra. I turned away quickly, glad they hadn't seen me. It was bad enough for them to have to be in the same room as me at the inquest. I knew logically that Ben was unjust in blaming me, but at a time like this he was entitled to be unjust, and since I'd arrived the night before, guilt had been getting a tight hold on my mind. It was to do with being in Verona's home territory. She'd have come in to town as a child, bought bull's-eyes at the sweet shop and ice cream from Antonucci's near the harbour. Her family was known and respected here. (Some old men were actually touching their hats as the motorcar drove past.) And in the end, she'd come back here to die.

I waited until the car was out of sight and strolled slowly back to the yard behind the meeting-room. The black car was parked there with the gardener at the wheel, and no sign of Ben and Alexandra. They must have gone inside. It was twenty to eleven and the doors were open now, with a constable standing outside. I decided to wait until the last possible minute and watched as more people arrived, first in ones and twos and then in a steady stream, mostly men. One man, in his sixties with a neat grey beard and very upright bearing, brought the police constable snapping to attention. He was dressed like Ben in dark suit, armband and bowler, and walked quickly, eyes straight ahead, like a man who was used to people getting out of his way. There was a shiny pink scar down the left side of his face from hat to beard, just missing his eye but dragging the corner of it down. He nodded an acknowledgement to the policeman and went inside without looking round.

A few minutes later a governess cart came skidding into the yard, scattering gravel. It was drawn by a useful-looking bay and driven by a girl about Verona's age. She had a round open-looking face, flushed with anxiety and hurry, dark curls under a schoolgirlish black felt hat. Almost before the cart

78

came to a halt the door at the back opened and a middle-aged man jumped out.

'That's the doctor,' somebody said.

The man hurried into the building. The girl blew out her cheeks with relief at having got him there in time, slackened the reins and stayed sitting in the cart. Five minutes to eleven. I moved towards the door then took a jump backwards. Somebody was coming out – a woman, hurrying, stumbling. She was dressed in black, head down, with a black motoring veil hiding her face. Alexandra. Beside her, holding her by the arm, practically holding her up, was the man with the scar and grey beard. He was angry now, jostling people aside. A sharp command to the policemen, and the people trying to get in were held back to let them through. The gardener was already holding the door of the motorcar open and together he and the bearded man got Alexandra on to the back seat. She was slumping sideways. They had to prop her up like a doll. The girl in the governess cart was watching horrified, mouth open. She started knotting the reins round the rail of the governess cart, as if with the idea of going to help, then just stood there uncertainly. There was no uncertainty about the bearded man. He grabbed an onlooker by the shoulder and made him help the driver start the car then got in beside Alexandra. She slumped again, letting her weight fall against him. Her black-gloved hand was clamped against her eyes, over the veil.

'Too much for her,' a woman said. 'They shouldn't have let her come.'

After what seemed like a long time the car started and they drove off, a policeman clearing the way for them.

Eleven o'clock. I went to the door, asked a constable where the witnesses were supposed to wait and was directed to a

79

room off the corridor. I'd expected to have to face Ben there, assuming that he'd be a witness too, but there was no sign of him. There were just two people apart from myself, the doctor who'd arrived in such a hurry and a sharp-faced man in a grey suit who had a professional air about him. He and the doctor were sitting next to each other, talking in low voices, very much two medical men together. The doctor still looked hot and anxious. They glanced at me, stood up and said good morning, sat down and went on with their conversation. From the room next door we heard chairs scraping, the low boom of a man's voice, probably the coroner's. I knew enough about the procedure to guess what was going on – first the formal opening, name of the deceased and date of her death. The coroner would already have been to view the body, probably days earlier. Then the swearing-in of the jury, followed by evidence of formal identification. Ben would do that and normally it wouldn't take long, but the coroner might decide to question him about Verona's state of mind. After that, it would be the discovery of the body. My turn. The two medical men had finished their talk now and were staring straight ahead, trying not to catch my eye. It was a warm day, with sunshine and the sounds of a town going about its business coming through the open window. I wondered if there was anybody back at the house to look after Alexandra, wished I could do something for her but knew I was the last person in the world she'd want to see.

'Miss Bray.'

The coroner's officer. I followed him along a corridor, through a door, was sworn in. The coroner was an ordinary conscientious-looking man with a bald patch. The jury were ten respectable tradesmen in their Sunday best, middle-aged mostly, showing no hostility in the way they stared at me. Not yet. Ben was sitting to one side of the front row. He stared too, beyond me, as if at something far out to sea. The room was full, five rows of people. The coroner asked questions about how I came to find Verona, making it easy. I was family after all. Naturally I'd be visiting Alexandra, taking a stroll to the boathouse. We came to finding her hanging, pulling in the body with a boathook. The coroner took a long time writing it down.

To make sure my eyes wouldn't come into contact with Ben's, I looked towards the back of the room – and found myself staring at Bill Musgrave. The last man I'd have expected to see. He should have been in court or in his chambers in Manchester, not travelling hundreds of miles to inquests that had nothing to do with him in Devon. He gave a kind of twisted smile that might have been encouragement, sympathy or even an apology for surprising me. I looked away, trying to give my mind a chance to catch up. There was a woman sitting next to him, small, in her thirties, with glossy dark hair and big beautiful eyes. She was staring at me, lips apart, very intently. I'd never seen her in my life before. It was almost a relief when the coroner stopped writing and started asking questions again, but the relief didn't last long. He wanted to know when I'd last seen Verona alive. I told him about probably seeing her outside Buckingham Palace a week before I found her body, on 21 May. In what circumstances? So, of course, it all came out about the deputation. The coroner managed to keep the disapproval off his face although not out of his voice. A few of the jurors looked downright hostile. In the next pause for writing I couldn't help looking at Bill. He was worried. Had he come all this way to try to protect me, for goodness sake? I wished I could tell him that I was a lot more used to this than he was.

The coroner wanted to know whether I'd seen much of Verona in London. Just twice, I said. Had I formed any judgement about her state of mind? I'd expected this and had my reply ready.

'As far as I could tell, she was starting to settle down in London, making friends.'

Scratch, scratch, his pen went. Bill was still looking worried. The dark-haired woman next to him was looking even more intent, as if this part of the story mattered a lot to her. But why should it? If she'd been friends or family, she'd have been sitting up at the front near Ben. Press? Just possibly. Her jacket and turban-style hat were more fashionable than you'd expect at a seaside town inquest.

'Would you have expected her to confide in you if she'd had problems of any kind?'

When the coroner asked that, I felt an electric charge in the air. At the time I had no idea why. It was an obvious enough question after all. We were talking about a suicide. But there was something happening I didn't understand. It had to do with Alexandra's sudden flight, with the bearded man's anger.

'No,' I said. 'I shouldn't have expected her to confide in me.'

That was it. I was allowed to step down and listen to the rest of the proceedings. There was a spare seat on the end of the second row, at the far side from Ben.

The next witness was the man I'd seen getting out of the governess cart, the family practitioner, Dr Maidment. He was there because he'd been the one to certify Verona dead. After getting that on record, the coroner asked if he'd known the deceased for some time.

'Yes, indeed. I took up practice here soon after she was born. I have the pleasure to be doctor to Commodore North and his family.'

'Had you seen Miss North recently?'

'Not very recently. The last occasion was back in the autumn. She came to say goodbye to my daughter before going to London.' (Presumably the girl who'd been driving the governess cart.)

'And you hadn't seen her since then?'

'No, sir.'

It was all simple enough, and yet the family doctor was clearly unhappy, even more unhappy than you'd expect in the circumstances. The feeling that there was something worse to come was growing. We all felt it. Dr Maidment was allowed to step down and paced heavily to a seat near the back of the court.

Next witness, Dr Stephen White, pathologist. The other man from the waiting-room was sworn in. It seemed to take the coroner for ever to note down his string of professional qualifications. Yes, at the coroner's request, he had carried out a postmortem examination on the body of Miss Verona North on 28 May 1914. Had he formed any opinion as to the cause of death? The pathologist hunched over his notes, reading in a monotone. Chair legs squeaked on the linoleum floor as everybody strained forward to hear him, all except Ben.

'. . . congestion of face and cyanosis typical of asphyxia, engorged tongue, burst capillaries in eyes, considerable bruising and abrasions on neck and throat, consistent with pressure from a tight ligature . . .'

I closed my eyes but still saw the silver light of the water in the estuary, smelt mud and creosote.

'. . . some abrasions and bruising on the ankles and over the insteps, also consistent with pressure from ligatures . . .'

Feet still in their stockings and shoes, green weed trailing.

'. . . compression of the jugular vein and trachea, no rupture

83

of spinal cord and no significant displacement of neck vertebrae . . .'

The hangman's fracture, they called it, that deplacement
of the neck vertebrae. But if the hangman got it wrong, the
victim died from strangling not a broken neck. That was what
had happened to Verona. The coroner wanted to get it quite
clear, for the jury.

'In layman's terms, Dr White, in your opinion death
resulted from strangulation.'

'Yes, sir.'

Feet being pulled out and out by the tide, noose slowly
tightening. Her arms weren't tied. Surely she couldn't have
helped doing something to relieve the pressure? I was sitting
on the edge of my seat. I wanted to stand up and ask Dr
White, 'Were her nails broken? Were there scratch marks on
her neck?' The coroner asked Dr White if he had made any
more observations the court should know about.

'Yes, sir.' He turned over another page of his notes, seemed
to hesitate, then went on in the same monotone. 'I observed
a deep puncture wound in her upper left arm, some three
and a half inches above the elbow joint, surrounded by superficial bruising.'

Whispering and rustling in court. The coroner frowned.

'Did you form any opinion as to what might have caused
the puncture?'

'In my view, it was consistent with an injection from a
hypodermic syringe.'

'An injection?'

'Yes, sir.'

'Administered by the deceased herself or by some other
person?'

'Either. The position of the puncture would be consistent
with self-administration.'

The coroner looked at him steadily for a long time.

'Is there any evidence of what might have been administered?'

'Yes. On examination of the internal organs I found distinct traces of morphine.'

Gasps around the court. Ben was staring straight ahead. The coroner had been making a note of what the pathologist was saying but stopped, pen in hand.

'You've given your opinion that death resulted from strangulation?'

'Yes, sir, and that remains my opinion. I had further analysis done of the internal organs which confirmed that though morphine was present, it was not in sufficient quantities to have caused death.'

The coroner sighed, then wrote for a long time.

'Any other observations?'

'One.' Dr White was on the last page of his notes now. He seemed reluctant to get to the end of them. The court was as quiet as the inside of an ice cave. 'The deceased was well advanced into the first trimester of pregnancy.'

More gasps. I happened to be looking towards Bill at the time and the dark-haired woman in the turban hat sitting next to him. She wasn't the one who'd gasped, but the expression on her face was more than concern. It was pain.

The coroner said, 'By first trimester, you mean . . . ?'

'The deceased was somewhere between two and three months pregnant, in my opinion somewhere between eight and ten weeks.'

Like everyone I couldn't help glancing at Ben. He gave no sign that he'd heard, none at all. They'd warned him, which was why he'd got Alexandra away. The court had been struck silent at first, but now a rustle of whispering started.

The coroner put down his pen.

'Thank you, Dr Smith. Please call the next witness.'

The next, and last, witness was a young police constable who'd arrived about an hour after Verona's body was discovered. I remembered him asking me a few questions and how he'd seemed awed both by Ben's position and the event itself. Now he gave his evidence stolidly, not looking at Ben. He'd arrived at the house where Dr Maidment was already present and had certified death. He'd spoken to Commodore North and arranged for the removal of the body to the mortuary. Later he'd made a search of the boathouse and taken possession of the following objects.

A hemp rope, one end knotted in a noose, the other cut.

(I'd gone running up to the house for help when I knew I couldn't get Verona down on my own and Ben had run back with me. We'd got her into one of the rowing boats. I'd held her while Ben cut the rope with a sharp seaman's knife. When we'd got her back on the wooden platform Ben had somehow got the noose off and flung it down.)

A large plank of wood with hemp ropes knotted round it, some cut.

(I remembered Ben kneeling on the planks in the boathouse, hacking at the ropes round Verona's feet. No use, of course, but the useless things seem important when there's nothing you can do.)

A woman's overcoat, with the label of a London store. The constable had found it in one of the dinghies moored to the platform, as if flung there. It was blue-grey tweed, not nautical wear. (I couldn't remember an overcoat.) In the pocket of the coat he'd found an object. I almost missed what he was saying. I'd been thinking about Ben's fingers trying to loosen the knots, wondering if he still hoped then that she might be alive. A collective gasp brought me back

86

to what was happening, with the coroner asking the constable to repeat that to make sure the jury heard it.

'Yes, sir. A hypodermic syringe, in the pocket.'

'Did you take possession of the syringe?'

'Yes, sir.'

'Was there anything in the syringe?'

'It was nearly empty, sir. Just a bit of stuff at the bottom.'

'Stuff?'

'Liquid, sir.'

'Did you have that liquid analysed?'

'Yes, sir.'

'And what was the result?'

'Morphine, sir. Solution of morphine.'

Chapter Nine

THE JURY TOOK UNDER AN HOUR TO DECIDE that Verona
North killed herself while the balance of her mind was
disturbed. When it was over Ben walked out first in complete
silence. When he'd gone the murmuring started again and
the rest of us filed outside. I hung back to give Ben plenty
of time to get clear and found Bill beside me.

'Are you all right, Nell?'

'What are you doing here?'

'Would you rather I weren't?'

I was so angry – not so much with him as with everything – that I almost said yes, but didn't know if I'd mean
it, didn't know anything. Besides, there were people all
round us in the corridor, hungry for more drama. We went
with the crowd, out to the yard where the cars and carts
were parked. I hadn't given Ben enough time after all. He
was sitting in the big black car with the engine running and
the driver at the wheel. The man with the grey beard and
scar was standing beside the car with one foot on the
running board, leaning in and talking to Ben. I tried to
make myself inconspicuous in the crowd but the bearded
man turned and looked straight at me. He turned back to
the car, said something to Ben and nodded. It looked as if
he'd asked a question and got an answer. He took his foot

off the running board, stepped back and the car drove away. The man watched it out of sight and started walking towards me.

'Somebody you know?' Bill asked.

'No, but he must be a friend of the family. I'll have to talk to him.'

The last thing I wanted to do was stay and collect more blame, but I needed to know about Alex. Bill took a tactful few paces back. The man stopped, raised his hat.

'Excuse me for troubling you, but am I speaking to Miss Bray?'

Yes, I said.

'My name's Archie Pritty. Ben asked me to make apologies on his behalf.' His voice surprised me. It was soft and likeable with a touch of West Country accent in it. From his manner, I'd expected something more peremptory. Seen close to, he was younger than you'd have guessed from the beard, late fifties or early sixties probably. The beard was a bright silvery-grey, his face had a light tan that made the scar stand out and the eyes that were looking into mine were the colour of the sea on a cloudy day. The pupils were small and that gave his look an intensity, as if you were being recorded by a pin-hole camera. Perhaps he was aware of that, because he had a way of looking then glancing away.

'Apologies?'

'For not speaking to you. I'm sure a time will come when he and Alexandra want to talk about what happened, but at present . . .'

He waited.

I said, 'I'm not sure that Ben will ever want to speak to me again. Please tell Alex, if she ever does, I'll come and see her at any time.'

'Yes.'

I took that more as a promise to deliver the message than a sign that Alex might want to see me.

'And if you think she needs to hear this, please tell her that I had no idea, no idea at all.'

It was odd, saying this to a man I'd only met a minute before, but it was in my mind that Alex might think I'd known about the morphine and the pregnancy and hadn't told her.

'Verona hadn't confided in you at all?'

I guessed then that Ben had offered no apologies and that Archie Pritty was there entirely as Alex's messenger.

'No. I wish with all my heart that she had.'

'I'm sure we all wish that. I'm very sorry indeed to have troubled you, Miss Bray. Are you staying here or going back to town?' Back to town, I said. To my annoyance he glanced at Bill, standing just out of earshot, acknowledged his presence with a nod and got one back.

'And may I offer you my most sincere sympathies. She was a remarkable girl, Miss Bray. A quite remarkable girl. Good morning. I'll give her mother your message.'

The voice was quivering on the last few words. As he put his hat on and turned away I saw that tears were gathering in the corner of the down-turned left eye, trickling down the line of the scar. I watched him walk away and Bill came and stood beside me.

'Distinguished-looking chap. What did he want?'

'Alex can't face seeing me, but I think she's trying to keep the lines of communication open.'

'Poor woman.'

'I can't do anything. I must be like losing Verona twice over, first her dying and then all this.'

'Let's get away from here, shall we. I thought you might like . . .'

I didn't find out what I might like, because we'd got to the gateway of the yard and had to stand back to let out Dr Maidment in his governess cart. He was red-faced and jerking at the reins like a man in a bad temper. He was alone in the cart. I looked round for the anxious girl with the dark curls whom I took to be his daughter and saw her leaning against the wall, hat askew, with her back to everybody and a hand up to her face. Verona had liked her enough to say goodbye before going off to London.

'Bill, I'd better go and see if . . .'

'Will you stop worrying about other people for once. She'll be all right.' I didn't argue. We started walking, but the street was quite crowded and I recognised some of the people who'd been at the inquest stopping and talking to friends who hadn't. Little groups were gathering. The air was buzzing with a combination of shock and self-satisfaction. The commodore's daughter. Her poor parents. Who'd have thought it. Just shows. I was jostling against people, getting angrier. Bill kept pace with me, saying nothing, and we eventually found ourselves sitting on a bench by a flowerbed.

'I simply don't believe it.'

'It will take some time. It's come as a shock to you.'

'I don't mean I can't believe it because it's a shock. I mean, I simply don't believe it happened like that.'

'What bit of it don't you believe?'

'What they were implying. That she's pregnant, addicted to morphine, sunk so low that the only thing to do is come home and slowly strangle herself.'

'Are you disputing the medical evidence?'

Bill was being desperately patient, the way he'd be with any difficult client.

'No. If the patholgist says she was pregnant, she was pregnant.'

91

We were having to speak in low voices. There were people walking by and the whole town would know by now.

'Or that there were traces of morphine in the syringe?'

'I assume the police can analyse morphine. There was bruising round the puncture wound.'

'Superficial bruising. I imagine you could do that injecting your own arm. You'd brace your elbow against something and press down.' Bill mimed it against the back of the bench. He might think I was deluded, but at least he gave me credit for not being squeamish.

'Miss Bray . . .'

I was just about aware of the little voice from behind but I was seeing Verona in the boathouse, sleeve rolled up, elbow pressed against the wall.

'But you'd have the syringe in your hand, so how could you be bruising yourself at the same time?'

'Miss Bray, could I talk to you please?'

Bill groaned. I looked round and saw the doctor's daughter. She was more flushed than ever, hair all over the place. Her face must have got dusty in the drive to get her father to the inquest in time and her tears had made tracks down it. You could see that she'd been properly brought up, so that accosting strangers in public places wasn't her normal behaviour, but there was a desperate determination about her.

'What about?'

'You're her relation, aren't you? Verona's. I want to know . . . I mean, what people are saying, only nobody will tell me.'

I said, as gently as I could, 'Don't you think you'd better go home and wait for your father? I'm sure he'll tell you when he gets back.'

'He won't. He won't discuss it. He wouldn't after she'd

killed herself and now . . . what they're saying . . .' She stared at me for a while, then burst out, '. . . that she was enceinte?'

Then she seemed to register Bill's presence for the first time and her round face went as red as a geranium. I looked at him. He sighed again and stood up.

'Ten minutes, Nell?'

The girl watched as he walked away round a corner.

I said, 'You'd better sit down and tell me your name.'

'Prudence Maidment.'

She sat.

'How old are you, Prudence?'

'Eighteen.'

'And you and Verona were friends?'

'Always. We went to the same school until we were fifteen. She'd stay with me sometimes and she'd take me out in her boat and . . . we'd always tell each other our secrets. Always.'

There was still so much of the schoolgirl about Prudence that it reminded me of how far and fast Verona had travelled in such a short time. This girl was a world away from the young woman lounging in a cloud of cigarette smoke. Scrumped apples would probably be Prudence's idea of wicked indulgence.

'Is it true?'

It had taken a lot of nerve for Prudence to speak to me. She didn't deserve evasions.

'Yes. I'm afraid it is.'

'Oh.' Her head went down. 'How . . . how did it happen. Did . . . did somebody force her?'

'Why do you think that?'

'Because . . . we'd talked about it.'

'Having babies?'

She shook her head so violently that her hat fell off. When I picked it up and gave it to her she didn't put it back on

93

but turned it round and round in her fingers, mauling the brim.

'No. About not getting married or getting . . . getting silly over men or anything like that until we'd done something in the world.'

'Done what?'

'Done anything. I . . . I wanted to be a nurse. Daddy doesn't want me to, but Verona was going to help me persuade him. He liked Verona, everybody did. He'd have listened to her. Now . . .'

'And what did Verona want to do in the world?'

She hesitated a moment and smiled, probably at some memory of schoolgirl confidences, drifting in a boat or lazing under the apple trees.

'She wanted to join the Navy.' Prudence mistook my surprise for disapproval.

'It's all right, we knew she couldn't, not really. But she wished she could be a cadet like her brother and then serve on her father's ship, so that when another war starts she could go with him.'

'She thought there was going to be a war?'

Prudence stared at me. 'Of course there will be! Why are we building all those battleships if there's not going to be?'

'So Verona took an interest in naval affairs?'

'Oh yes. She was so good at identifying ships and things. When we visited her godfather in Shaldon we'd always take his old telescope up to the Ness and watch the ships going past. She knew the names of all of them and where they were coming back from. I saw him talking to you. He must be so upset too, poor man.'

'Saw who?'

'Verona's godfather, Admiral Pritty.'

'The one with the beard and the scar?'

94

'Yes, isn't it awful? It happened on an exercise. A shell exploded. Daddy says he must be in pain from it all the time, but you'd never guess and he's always such fun with us. He's got a house at Shaldon, that's on the other side of the estuary, right down by the water. We'd have races across the river in his rowing boats. Verona would nearly always win. He called her—'

I finished it for her, '—his little midshipman.'

It was falling into place now, that conversation with Alex, a few minutes before her world fell apart.

'Even when he had to be away in London he'd tell the bosun to let us in . . .'

'Bosun?'

'His butler, sort of, but we call him the bosun. He used to be on one of the admiral's ships. There'd be the telescope and a basket with ginger biscuits and lemonade for us to take up the Ness with us, and when the admiral got back we had to tell him all the ships we'd seen while he was away. Verona even knew the tonnages. She never got one wrong. Well, hardly ever.'

Remembering it, Prudence was talking herself back into cheerfulness. She wasn't to know she was sinking me deeper and deeper in gloom. We sat there in silence for a while, Prudence staring at me as if there were still questions she wanted to ask. I had no answers for her, only more questions of my own.

'Were you surprised when Verona told you she was going to London?'

'Yes.'

'When did she tell you?'

'Back in the autumn sometime, late September or early October. We'd been away, so I hadn't seen her for nearly three weeks. I thought we'd have a lot to talk about but she seemed quieter than usual. I wondered if she'd been ill, but she said no. Anyway, there was one afternoon when Daddy went off to play golf with the admiral and Verona and I went out in her dinghy. There wasn't much wind, so we just sat there and talked and it was then she told me.'

'What?'

'That she was probably going away to London. She said it wouldn't be for a few weeks and I wasn't to talk about it because her mother would be upset.'

'Did she say why she was going?'

'She thought probably art school.'

'Was she interested in art?'

'She did a very nice painting of our puppies once, except she couldn't get the paws quite right.'

I'd heard that the Slade's entry standards had been slipping, but they couldn't be that low.

'Did you have the impression there might be other reasons?'

'Other reasons?'

'Was art school just an excuse for getting away from home?'

'I don't know.'

'What did you say when she told you?'

'We . . . we quarrelled.' She tugged at the hat brim, close to tears again.

'You didn't want her to go?'

'I wanted her to wait for me. We were going together, you see. I'd start training at a hospital and Verona would do whatever she was going to do and we'd stay friends. So I said why not wait until we'd both persuaded Daddy.'

'And she wouldn't wait?'

'No.'

I gave her my handkerchief and waited until she'd dried her eyes.

'But you made up your quarrel before she went?'

She stared at me.

'Your father told the inquest that she called on you before she went to London.'

'She called, yes.' Her voice was doubtful.

'But she didn't make up?'

'No. I don't know. I mean she . . . she was different.'

'How different?'

'More . . . grown-up. I mean, she talked to me as if she were a grown-up and I wasn't.'

'What about?'

'Normal things, like how were my family and her family and so on.'

'Did she talk about London?'

'She said she'd finished her packing and was going in two or three days. Her mother had found lodgings for her.'

'Was she excited about going?'

'I'm not sure. She was just, well . . . odd. There was something she wasn't telling me.'

'Did you ask her?'

'No. The way she was, I couldn't ask her the things I wanted to.'

'Perhaps she was nervous. It was a big step, after all.'

Prudence thought about it. 'I think she might have been. She was keyed up. You know, like at school, when it's your turn to sing the solo.'

'When she got to London, did she write to you at all?'

'Yes. Once before Christmas and once after.'

'What did she say?'

'The first letter said she didn't like London and she was missing the sea, but she was working hard and it would be worth it one day.'

'The second one?'

97

'That was just a few weeks ago. She said she was making a lot of friends and having an interesting time.'

'I wonder if you'd let me see the letters.' I gave her my card. 'I'd take great care of them and post them back to you.'

She considered. 'Would it be alright if I copied them and sent you the copies?'

'Of course. Thank you.'

A man wheeling two bicycles came along the path between the flowerbeds.

Prudence stood up. 'I'll have to go and see about Daddy's dinner.'

'Prudence, one thing. If you really want to be a nurse you should do it. I'm sure that's what Verona would have wanted.'

I was sure of no such thing. There was hardly a person on the planet I understood less than Verona at that moment. Still, it seemed to be what Prudence wanted to hear. She gave me a tear-stained smile, jammed her hat on her curls and went. The man propped the bikes against a seat opposite and came striding across.

'Bill, what in the world are you doing with those machines?'

'Getting us out of here. Come on.'

It's a long uphill ride from the sea to the edge of Dartmoor. We arrived late afternoon, hot and so thirsty that before anything else we had to find water. We propped the bikes against a boulder and followed a sheep track uphill until we came to a stream pouring itself into a little pool. There was bright green sphagnum moss round the pool and white quartz sand at the bottom. We knelt on either side of it and gulped moss-tasting water from our cupped hands, splashed it over our sweating faces.

'How did you know this is what I needed?'

'You can have too much of the grieving friends.'

'Poor Prudence.'

'You don't have to talk about any of it. We could just walk for a bit.' My hair had come down. I must have been shedding hairpins all along the road. I put it up again with the few I had left and decided to carry my hat. Bill had left his trilby with the bicycles, but we were both wearing city clothes, suitable for inquests but not hiking. Heather shoots and bits of pink bilberry leaf clung to my skirt as we went on uphill. It was a beautiful day, the sky clear blue, shrilling with skylarks. After a while we came to a cluster of granite boulders where the heather gave way to thin sheep-cropped turf and, without saying anything, decided to stop. Bill sat on a boulder and lit his pipe.

'It may not be the Pennines, but it will do.'

We sat for a while looking out over the sea in the distance. The ships on it were as small as toys. I told Bill about Prudence.

'She said Verona could recite all the ships of the line and their tonnage.'

'So could I, when I was about nine and wanted to be Lord Nelson.'

'Could she have known anything that a spy would want to know?'

Bill looked at me through a cloud of pipe smoke, sceptical.

'Why in the world should you think that?'

'Just something a friend said.'

'Nell, these things are published in the papers and discussed in Parliament. If Germany doesn't already know how many dreadnoughts we've got, all they need to do is enquire politely and enclose a stamped-addressed envelope.'

'The point is, it shows Verona was seriously interested in naval affairs and until a few months ago she lived in a household where her father and godfather would be talking about them all the time.'

'Just because your cousin's a commodore and her godfather's a retired admiral, that doesn't mean the Admiralty would be consulting them about their secret plans.'

'Prudence says the admiral's sometimes away in London.'

'Anyway, if either of them did know naval secrets, they'd surely have more sense than to chatter about them in front of the children.'

'Isn't that just what they might do? They'd assume the children wouldn't understand.'

'But you've just been proving to me that Verona would have understood down to the last marlinspike or whatever they use now. You can't have it both ways.'

'You think I'm getting spy mania?'

'I think that complicated brain of yours is doing anything rather than think about what really happened. That's understandable.'

'Oh? So what really happened?'

'A young woman went out into the world and got destroyed by it. Not the first time and I'm afraid it won't be the last.'

'Yes, I thought that too. Until the morphine.'

'That's part of it.'

'No. I'll believe almost anything about what happened to Verona in those few months in London, but I won't believe she'd started injecting morphine.'

'Evidence, Nell.'

'A puncture wound in her arm and an empty syringe. It doesn't prove she did it herself.'

'She was living in a house in London where people talked quite openly about smoking opium.'

'That's simply the kind of thing art students talk about. It's a very long way from that to being a serious addict.

Certainly a lot further than you'd go in the few months she had been there.'

'But you wouldn't claim to be an expert on morphine addiction?'

'No, but I do know something about it.' This time I wasn't seeing if I could shock him. I just wanted him to understand. 'There's an actress I know. I'm not going to tell you her name, but you've probably seen her on stage. She played Nora in *A Doll's House* better than anybody's ever played her before or since. I got to know her because she supported us. Anyway, she took to injecting morphine and it destroyed her. If there'd been any sign of that in Verona or the people she was with, I'm sure I'd have picked it up.'

'You only saw her at that house once.'

I didn't answer, stubbornly sure that I was right.

Bill said, 'Even if she wasn't addicted to the stuff, she could still have injected it before she killed herself.'

'Why?'

'Do you know what it feels like?' I thought he meant being as desperate as Verona. 'Morphine, I mean.'

'No.'

'I do. A while ago, I fell down a rock face and broke my shinbone in a couple of places. It took a long time to get me to a hospital, so they filled me up with the stuff to ease the pain. Quite a nice effect. You're conscious but you feel as if you're watching yourself from a distance, calm and easy as if it had nothing to do with you.'

I watched a skylark take off and spiral up to the point where it would start singing. Bill went on talking.

'Perhaps one of her friends had told Verona that. So, if she'd decided to do what she did, she might have known morphine would make it . . . easier.'

'If she wanted it easy, why did she do it that terrible way?'

101

'I don't suppose she was thinking very clearly. She had a problem and could only see one way out of it.'

'The pregnancy? But there wasn't only one way out of it. If she'd only come to me, I could have helped her. She could have stayed with me.'

That had been the worst thing about the day – the hard fact that I could have helped Verona, if only I'd seen more of her, got her to trust me. Bill moved closer. I felt his arm round my shoulders.

'You're not responsible for the whole world.'

But for once, I could see myself through Cousin Ben's eyes and I didn't like it. Nell marching for this and campaigning for that, not caring about anyone's feelings.

I said, 'That's assuming she knew she was pregnant.'

'Uh?'

'Only two months. She might not even have known. I don't suppose you want me to go into details but . . .'

'I don't mind. My father was a doctor.'

'So was mine.'

'You mean she might not have noticed that she hadn't menstruated?'

It was a relief to find him so unembarrassed and I thought how few men, even among my friends, I could have talked to like this.

'It's just possible if her periods were irregular, and not all women feel sick.'

'Alright, granted that's possible, but if she didn't know she was pregnant, why did she kill herself?'

'*If* she killed herself. Don't you see how neat that pregnancy made it? She's supposed to have committed suicide but there isn't any motive. Then, after the postmortem, she's pregnant and a morphine addict so naturally she killed herself and it can be all wrapped up and put away and we needn't worry.'

Bill said, 'I'll admit one thing still puzzles me, and that's the speed of it. She leaves home in November, very much the conventional girl from a good family. And by your account, things haven't changed a lot when you see her in December.'

'No, except she was wanting to get involved with things her father wouldn't have approved of.'

'And she managed it with impressive speed. Next time you see her, three months later, she's living in a household of anarchists and free lovers and, in your view, has already started on her first affair.'

'Things do move fast when you're nineteen.'

'That fast? Then another two months later she's pregnant, injecting morphine – and dead. That's less than six months from beginning to end. I'd guess that whatever happened to her started longer than six months ago.'

'Prudence said she was keyed up before she went to London "like at school, when it's your turn to sing the solo".'

'Poor kid.'

Prudence or Verona? We sat there for a while, looking out to sea – at least I thought he was looking out to sea, but when I turned to say something, he was looking at me instead. To be honest, I'm not sure whether I kissed him or he kissed me, or perhaps it was like one of those decisions in anarchist communities, emerging by popular will without any need to take a vote. I'd told him that things move fast when you're nineteen. Thank the gods, that's true sometimes when you're nearly twice that age.

Chapter Ten

⊕

WE RACED EACH OTHER DOWNHILL ON THE WAY back to Teignmouth, disturbed the bicycle hirer at his supper to return our machines and managed to get the train back to London that night. It was too late for the friends in Camden, so Bill spent the night with me in Hampstead, not without some fussing about my 'reputation'. I told him it would give the initials – the way I thought of the watchers after that talk with Max Blume – something to write home about at last.

He had to get up at first light to catch an early train back to Manchester and I went to see him off. There were the usual awkward few minutes before the train left, with me standing on the platform, Bill hanging out of the window and smoke from the engine drifting back into our faces. More to cover the awkwardness than any real curiosity, I asked him about the fashionable woman who'd been sitting next to him at the inquest.

'The one in the odd hat? No, I don't know who she was. She came in just after things started, a bit breathless and nervous. There was an empty seat beside me and she took it. I assumed she was a friend or relative.'

'Not a relative that I've met. Did she seem to know anybody else there?'

'No. One thing I did notice about her was how quickly she got away afterwards, while you were talking to the admiral. She had a sporty little green car in the yard. She drove off so fast a couple of people had to jump for their lives.'

The whistle blew and the train started moving. Bill waved through the smoke, shouting something about seeing me soon. When the train was out of sight I walked back up the platform, working out dates in my head.

If Verona had been two months pregnant, it dated from somewhere near the time back in March when I'd last spoken to her at the student house. It was no consolation now that I'd been right about that woman-of-the-world look. If only I'd been less tolerant or, as her parents would see it, more careful of her morals, I'd have got her to talk to me. We'd have quarrelled, probably, but at least she'd have known that I cared about her. Only I hadn't, or not enough. I was angry with myself, angrier still with somebody else. If I'd been free I'd have gone straight from the station to the student house in Chelsea, only I wasn't. There'd been a message in my mail that the old press in Clerkenwell was giving trouble again and I was needed urgently to knock some good manners into it. It was well into the evening by the time we got it working, more or less, and printed a batch of leaflets. When I caught a motorbus for Chelsea I was covered in printer's ink, had added a couple of injured fingers to the bashed thumbnail from my last battle with it and was in a mood for taking things out on somebody. It was dusk when I got to the student house. There were lights on in the windows, raised voices inside. The front door was ajar. I pushed it open without knocking, went straight upstairs and flung back the door of the common room. Two pairs of eyes turned towards me through the cigarette smoke, Rizzo's and Toby's. Toby was sitting on a chair by the window, Rizzo lying on the chaise-longue with a glass of wine in his hand. A fair-haired woman I hadn't seen before was kneeling beside him holding a red-blotched handkerchief to his nose.

'I want to speak to you two,' I told Toby and Rizzo.

Toby said: 'She hit him with a bottle.'

'Good.'

The woman glanced at me and went, slamming the door behind her. She took the handkerchief with her. A slow trickle of blood oozed from Rizzo's nose. He was looking dazed, whether from alcohol, opium or violence I didn't care.

'Where did Verona go when she left here?'

Rizzo pretended not to take any notice.

Toby said, 'We don't know.'

'You let her go just like that – not even asking?'

'We . . . we tried to stop her. We begged her not to go.'

'I didn't,' Rizzo said. 'You did the begging.' His eyes were closed.

Toby said, 'But she'd made up her mind. She wouldn't listen.'

'She must have made up her mind quickly. She wrote to her mother on May the third, saying nothing about moving. The day after that her room's free and Janie's moving in. What made her decide to go?'

Rizzo groaned to the ceiling, 'Oh the inquisitions of families.' A bubble of blood appeared in his nostril.

'I'll tell you why. She went because she'd told you she thought she might be pregnant and you didn't care.'

Rizzo opened his eyes and turned his head towards me. The bubble broke and trickled down his face. I could have sworn he looked surprised, but it was no more than a flicker before the bored pose was back.

'Supposing she had been, why should I care about it?'

106

I had to press my fists together to keep from hitting him. '"Why should I care about it?" Was that what you said to her?'

He closed his eyes again. I stood up and went over to the chaise-longue. The rickety leg had been propped on a brick. I kicked it hard and the end of the chaise-longue collapsed. He slid off it as slickly as herring guts into a bucket.

'Answer me, or you'll have a lot worse than a nosebleed to worry about.'

He looked first at the toe of my shoe a few inches away from his ribs, then up at my face.

'I didn't say that because she didn't tell me she was pregnant. I didn't know until you just said so.'

'It's true. She didn't tell us.'

Toby sounded scared and miserable. He'd lost weight and his red beard was untrimmed and straggly. I turned to him but kept my toe within reach of Rizzo's ribs.

'When I told you she was dead, you blamed him.'

'Not for that. It wasn't for that.'

'So what was it for?'

Toby looked uncertainly at Rizzo. Even supine, the man controlled him.

'For quarrelling with her. It was his fault.'

'So there was a quarrel?'

'There wouldn't have been if Cur hadn't been trailing her like a mongrel after a bitch on heat.'

The yelp that Toby let out when he heard that did have something dog-like about it. He stood up and Rizzo scrambled to his knees, alarmed. I gave him a shove and he settled back, sitting on the floor against the broken chaise-longue.

'Sit down,' I said to Toby. He sat. 'For all I care, you can knock each other senseless when I've gone, but I want some

answers first or I'm telling the police that you know something.'

An empty threat. As far as the police were concerned the
case was closed when the jury foreman said it was suicide.
These two didn't know that. Rizzo, a self-proclaimed anarchist and an alien in a country that didn't like Hungarians
much more than Germans, couldn't take too many chances.
Toby had been brought up to be law-abiding. I was taking
unfair advantage, but I hadn't come there to be fair to
them.

I said to Toby, 'Were you trailing her?'

'No. Well, only because I was worried about her. I wanted
to help her, and . . .'

'Yes, in other words?'

He nodded, looking at the floor.

'Why?'

Rizzo said, 'Because he was besotted with her.'

Toby looked at me. 'Because I loved her.'

There was a desperate dignity about the way he said it, in
spite of a derisive noise from Rizzo. Once Toby had started
he went on talking, pouring it out. He wanted me to understand because I was the nearest he could get to Verona.

'She'd stopped going to art classes and meetings. We used
to go to a lot of meetings and things together.'

'What sort of things?'

'Political. Wild things, mostly. Pacificism, socialism, syndi-
calism – all the isms.'

I remembered her quizzing me about left-wing politics
soon after she'd arrived in London.

'Are you involved?'

'No. There are some rum people at those meetings. I went
along to protect her.'

'Did she seem particularly attracted to any of the isms?'

108

'No. She took a lot of notes. She said she was trying to make up her mind.'

It seemed oddly methodical to me. Most people just plunged in headlong.

'Then you say she stopped going? When?'

He thought about it. 'Around March or April. I didn't mind, at first, because the meetings were unbelievably dull. I hoped we could do other things like going to galleries and concerts together, but she never had time. She'd go out early in the morning and come home late at night and sometimes she wouldn't come home at all.'

Rizzo said, 'And after a few weeks of this, it began to dawn on Cur that she might perhaps have a lover.'

Toby yelled at him, 'It was you who said that. I'd never have thought of it if you hadn't suggested it.'

'Never mind who suggested it. So you followed her?'

'Only because I was worried. I thought if she was in some sort of trouble, I could help her.'

'Little Sir Galahad.'

He ignored Rizzo, looked at me, imploring me to believe him. I did, up to a point.

'Yes, I followed her. She went out one evening. I saw she'd left her scarf in the hall, and I thought I could catch her up with it . . . but she was walking fast. She went down the King's Road. It was dusk and there were some drunks around. I thought I'd keep an eye on her, in case anybody tried—'

Rizzo opened his mouth. I glared at him and he closed it.

'. . . in case anybody tried to accost her. She kept on going, all the way down to World's End. You know it?'

I nodded. It was a big public house at the place where the trams turned round. We sometimes went there distributing leaflets but it was quite a rough area. A basically conventional young man like Toby might well be worried about a girl going there on her own as dusk fell.

'Then?'

'She went into a shop. It was down one of those little streets near the pub.'

'What sort of shop?'

'Scrubby little place, mostly maps in the window and a few books.'

'Open at that time of the evening?'

He shook his head. 'No. It wasn't open. There wasn't even a light on. She had a key. She let herself in. I waited a long time, more than an hour, but she didn't come out. I wondered if she might have gone out the back entrance, but there wasn't one. So I came home, but she wasn't here. She didn't come in until nearly midnight.'

'Did you ask her where she'd been?'

'Yes. She was angry. She said it was nothing to do with me.'

'But you went on following her?'

'No. I didn't want to make her angry with me again. But I went back to the shop, several times. It was always closed. The maps and things in the window were all dusty. Then, one day, I saw a man going in.'

'Did he have a key?'

'He must have.'

'What was he like?'

'Ordinary. Just ordinary.' He said it in the puzzled way of any man wondering how a woman might prefer somebody else.

'I mean, what did he look like?'

He struggled. 'Older. Bowler hat, little moustache. Nothing special about him at all. I thought he might be the shop owner. I waited for him to open up so that I could go

110

in and buy something, only he didn't. I went over and rattled the door. I saw his face looking out of the window upstairs. He ducked down when he saw me looking at him. He didn't come down.'

'At which point,' Rizzo said, 'it occurred even to young Cur that the shop might be a *maison d'assignation*.'

'No, it didn't. You said that.'

'I suggested to Toby that we should take a stroll together one night, so we did. We followed Verona all the way to World's End, saw her unlock the door of the shop and go inside, just as he's told you. Half an hour later, along comes our bourgeois with the little moustache, all impatience, looks round to make sure nobody's watching, lets himself in. A light goes on in the room on the first floor. We settle down to wait . . .'

'I wanted to go. You made us wait.'

'. . . but we're not waiting as long as we expect because no more than five minutes later the door opens and out comes the man, looking angry. Just after that the light goes off and out comes Verona, grim and determined, and goes back up the King's Road so fast that she gets back here some time before us. That's when we quarrelled.'

'You shouldn't have said anything to her.'

'My dear Cur, I had your interests at heart. I merely suggested to her that if one lover had proved unsatisfactory, she could find another one nearer home.'

'By which he meant himself, of course,' Toby said.

'It would have been up to her to choose.'

I said, 'In any case, I take it she refused your generous offer.'

'He told her what we'd seen,' Toby said. 'She was furious with both of us. She said she was leaving. She said she'd been intending to leave anyway, but this was the last straw.'

111

'When was this?'

'May the first. She packed her suitcase and went next morning. That was the last I ever saw of her.'

So the letter to her mother, dated 3 May, had stretched the truth a little. If Toby and Rizzo were not lying, Verona was already at a new address by then.

'Will you show me this shop?'

'Now?'

'Now.'

It was a warm, soft night. Smells of horse dung and petrol vapour hung in the air, along with whiffs of river mud and coal dust from barges going up to the power station at Lots Road. In this part of London, even when you couldn't see the river you were aware of it as if its tides were dragging at the earth under the pavement and the foundations of the houses. We turned away from the river, Rizzo on my left, Toby on my right. King's Road was still busy, with lamps lit, men drinking pints at the doorways of public houses, a few women strolling arm in arm, cabs going up and down. As we walked further down the road in the direction of Fulham there were fewer people strolling and the public houses looked rougher. There was a fight going on outside one of them and men standing round, cheering on the fighters. I imagined Toby trailing Verona and had no trouble in believing that he was worried for her. We came to the tram stop and World's End pub. The windows were brightly lit and the subdued roar of men happy and drinking came from inside, along with wavering notes of *Nellie Dean*.

'It was down there,' Toby said.

We walked past the pub, turned left down a narrow street. There were terraced houses on either side, a few dark shop windows. It smelt of dog excrement and rotting fruit, and looked far from prosperous.

'It's still there.'

Toby sounded surprised. It was only six weeks or so since they'd watched Verona coming out. Did he think the shop would have gone out of existence because she had? The street was dim, lit only by a gas lamp at our end of it, no other lights showing. We walked slowly along the uneven pavement, stopped in front of a shop that looked as if it hadn't seen a customer in years. The name over the window said 'Townsend Bakers' but was so faded I doubted if it had sold a loaf since Queen Victoria's jubilee. A painted sign advertising Coleman's Mustard suggested it had been a grocer's in one incarnation but it had the air of a place where nothing survived for long. As Toby had said, its trade now seemed to be mostly maps, which in a place like this seemed to guarantee another failure. The door was firmly locked, the window in it covered with a net curtain, with a 'Closed' sign lodged at a slant between curtain and glass. Upstairs, another net curtain covered the dark window. Even allowing for the glow that being in love gives to places, it was altogether the least attractive assignation place imaginable.

'Nobody there,' Toby said, unnecessarily.

I looked in the window, which clearly hadn't been altered since its days as a bread shop. Two wooden shelves at waist level and eye level slanted back into the shop. There were a few books, some small framed pictures, folded maps. Somebody had tried to make the pathetic display more enticing by spreading out a couple of maps and tacking them between top and bottom shelf, where they'd faded so that you could hardly make out the detail on them. I tried out of habit, pressing my eyes against the cobwebbed glass.

'Oh, God!'

Toby jumped forward, all consideration. 'Are you all right? What is it?'

'They're not maps. They're charts. Sea charts.'

They both stared at me, puzzled, but then they hadn't seen Verona hanging, didn't have sea and the rise and fall of tides on their minds. The books, too. Some of them were tide tables. And what I'd taken for pictures were miniature seamen's knots, fancy splices and Turk's heads and so on, mounted on cards and framed.

Toby said, 'I hadn't noticed. We're quite near the wharves, after all.'

Which was true, except I couldn't imagine the most desperate mariner finding his way to this tatty collection.

Rizzo said, 'Why worry what they had in the window? It was what went on upstairs that mattered.'

True too, but of all the things to choose as window-dressing, why those? Toby had turned away, not rising to Rizzo's taunt. I believed him. I probably even believed Rizzo, but it didn't help much. We walked back together up the King's Road without saying anything. When we parted at a tram stop Rizzo walked on, but Toby lingered for a while.

'Please, when you find him, tell me. I want to know.'

I didn't promise.

I spent most of next day, Friday, looking for Bobbie Fieldfare. If you were sensible, Bobbie was the last person you'd think of asking for help. But what I was planning to do wasn't sensible.

Chapter Eleven

◈

MIDSUMMER'S A BAD TIME FOR BURGLARY. LONDONERS QUIT the streets as reluctantly as light leaves the sky. At eleven at night, with the horizon beyond the chimney stacks towards Fulham still smoky-pink from the last of the sunset, trams and motorbuses were more than half-full, couples walked the pavements hand in hand, conscientious constables on their beats returned slurred 'goodnights' from drinkers rolling peacefully homeward. Meanwhile the ones who, even stone-cold sober, had reason not to attract the attention of conscientious constables, skulked in side streets and passageways and killed time while they waited for the few hours of darkness to hide them. The ones like me. It wasn't my first burglary. A mental search of my curriculum vitae put the score so far at four, though I might have missed one. The difference was that in the other ones I hadn't been under observation already by a set of shadowy initials who had me tagged as an enemy of the state. Even the most outlandish things become part of the landscape in a surprisingly short time, and I was already taking it for granted that wherever I went a man would come trailing along behind. Admittedly, since I'd got back from Devon I hadn't spotted one of them, but that might mean they were getting better or I was getting careless. I'd taken a lot of trouble, that

Friday evening, to make sure that if there had been one, I'd lost him – leaving a meeting through the kitchens instead of the main entrance, stopping to stare into shop windows all the way along Oxford Street. I'd smashed a few of those plate-glass windows in the past, but tonight I was grateful for the way they mirrored the street behind me. I'd jumped on a motorbus at the last minute while it was moving away, jumped off a few stops later, also at the last minute, and seen nobody trying to follow. Now that my zigzag progress had brought me back to Chelsea and an alleyway just off the King's Road, I was sure I was on my own.

The next step was meeting up with Bobbie. We'd agreed on half past midnight, by the river wall at the western end of Cheyne Walk, upriver from Battersea Bridge. I was there by the time the clocks all over west London were striking midnight. The place was a few minutes' walk away from the chart shop at World's End, the less prosperous end of Cheyne Walk, a dip of comparative darkness between two stretches of light. Downriver, lines of lamp standards glowed along the Embankment between Battersea Bridge and Albert Bridge. Just upriver the four great towers of Lots Road power station hummed in a glow of their own electricity, and down at the water line bright electric lamps lit the wharves for barges bringing coal for the generators up from the Pool of London. A steamboat surged downstream along the middle of the river, sparks from the funnel and red port light glowing against the dark water. On one side of the street white house fronts and irregular roof lines stood out against the sky, with lights on in some upstairs windows. The side where I was standing had just an erratic line of small plane trees and a few street lamps, then solid London fell away to water. At night the smell from the sewer pipes that run under the Embankment seemed stronger than by day. There were big

116

posts sticking out of the water with sailing barges moored to them, survivors from an older and slower river life. Their copper-coloured sails, trussed in untidy bundles against the masts, looked black in the lamplight. The scent of fresh hay rose from the nearest one and mingled with the sewage smell. I watched and waited, not even daring to walk in case my footsteps disturbed people going to bed in the quiet houses opposite. A clock struck a single note. Half past midnight and no sign of Bobbie, but when had she ever been on time for anything?

'Nell.'

Her voice. I spun round and still couldn't see her. It seemed to be coming from the river.

'That you, Nell?' A dark shape was standing on the Embankment wall alongside the hay-scented barge. It flew through the air and landed beside me.

'Oh, that was so comfortable. I went right off to sleep.'

There was hay in her hair, clinging to her skirt and jacket. I started brushing it off to try to make her look halfway respectable, then remembered that we weren't and gave up.

'Where are we going, Nell?'

I'd told her only that I needed her help to break into somewhere. She'd agreed unhesitatingly. Now as we walked up a narrow street from the river I told her about Verona and the missing days.

'Nineteen days, from when she left the student house to when I think I saw her outside Buckingham Palace. I want to know where she was and what she was doing.'

Bobbie didn't argue about that, or make any pointless regretful noises about Verona. Her concentration was entirely on the job in hand.

'Have you thought about how we're getting in?'

'Depends if there's a back entrance. I don't think there is.'

Toby hadn't found one.

'You should have made sure when you were there.'

She was right, of course. No point in explaining to Bobbie the shivery feeling the knots and charts had given me. I concentrated on finding our way to the chart shop by the back streets. Before the clocks struck one we were standing in front of it. There was no sound except a late cab clip-clopping down the King's Road, only dim light from the one gas lamp on the corner. The drab window display was just as I remembered it from the night before.

'Back to back,' Bobbie said. 'We'll have to climb in.'

She sounded quite happy about it. I told her to hang on a minute and stooped down at the keyhole. I'd brought half a dozen assorted keys with me, some of my own from home and a few borrowed from friends. The place looked so decrepit that it seemed possible the lock would be no more than a formality, accessible with anything that fitted more or less. That was my first miscalculation. As far as I could tell in the dim light, the lock was the newest thing about the premises. You could even make out a wedge of new unpainted wood where it had been fitted into the door quite recently. While Bobbie waited impatiently I tried all my keys twice over, but none of them was any good. We stood back and looked at the front of the building and the single net-curtained window on the first floor. Just below it a course of brick stuck out from the rest, the builder's one conces-sion to decoration. Under the brick course was the wooden housing for the shop window blind. The blind itself projected by about six inches. It was part of the general dilapidation of the place that it wouldn't roll all the way back into its housing. Metal support struts angled down from the edge

118

of the blind into the window frame at about eye level. A drainpipe came down to the left of the shop window but it looked tinny and insubstantial. Slum builders have no consideration for burglars.

Bobbie said, 'If you make a back for me, I can stand on that strut and get up on top of the blind.'

'The whole thing's probably rotten. It could pull away.'

'What do you suggest then?'

We were talking in low voices and I'd been as quiet as I could with the keys, but we were already taking too long. Rotten or not, the blind looked like the best chance. Before Bobbie could get in there first I got a foot on the narrow sill at the front of the shop window, grabbed the strut and brought my other foot up to join it. By changing hands on the strut and leaning out, I could get a grip on the top of the window-blind housing with one hand. Getting the other hand up to join it meant taking a jump off the narrow sill. No point in standing thinking about it, especially with Bobbie panting to have her turn if I failed. I jumped and grabbed, scrabbled with my feet against the drainpipe. At the critical moment I felt Bobbie's hand against my buttocks, giving me a hearty shove upwards. I transferred my left hand cautiously to the drainpipe, tried to get my left foot on to the top of the blind, cursing skirts. Something ripped. I wasn't sure if it was my skirt or the old canvas of the blind. My chin was grazing the windowsill of the upstairs room. At least here the builder hadn't skimped. It was a good substantial slab and I threw myself at it, ending up with my right hand clasping it and my body sprawled on the top of the wooden blind housing, with six inches of unreliable canvas between me and a fifteen-foot drop to the pavement. From somewhere just below me Bobbie breathed, 'Well done.' I squirmed round so that I was kneeling on top of the blind, facing the window.

119

Everything depended on the window catch. If it was as new as the lock on the door, we were finished. When I saw the tail end of a metal lever on the inside of the dark glass I felt grateful after all to the slum builder. It was more what you'd expect in a place like this, a fastening of the simplest kind that swivelled into a notch on the window frame. And, even more blessedly, there was a gap between window and frame you could put a knife through. Which was what I did. I'd brought from home a blunt thick-bladed knife. I'd wrapped it in a duster, but that hadn't stopped it digging into my thigh on the way up. A little pressure from underneath lifted the catch. I swung the window open and went headfirst over the sill and into the room.

Carpet. A thin, dusty-smelling carpet that ruckled up under my hands and knees. I crouched, waiting for my heart to stop thumping, listening. If there'd been people in the house, they'd have been awake and yelling by now. After twenty or so heartbeats I rummaged a candle and matches out of my pocket, lit the candle but kept it at floor level so that it wouldn't be too obvious outside.

'Nell, are you there?' Bobbie's voice.

'I'll come down and let you in.'

The candle was throwing shadows on to the walls – cupboards, a chair, a table. I got up and walked over to the door. It opened on to a narrow landing with another door opposite and a flight of steep boxed-in stairs, uncarpeted. The lock on the inside of the front door was, as I'd guessed, new and from the look of it would have cost a month's rent for a place like this. There was no key. Bobbie, from the other side of the door, told me to hurry up.

I said, 'I can't open it. I'm afraid you'll have to wait outside. Cough if you hear anybody coming.'

That suited me, though I knew it wouldn't please her. There was just one inside door downstairs. When I opened it, it led into the shop. There was a counter, with tracks of rat feet in the dust and a few droppings, a ball of string, some old flour bins, three empty tea chests. One shelf held a dog-eared collection of maps and charts, but apart from that the shop's entire stock seemed to be on show in the window. Bobbie was pressing her face against the glass like a child locked out. I waved to her and went back upstairs.

The other door from the landing opened onto a room that was hardly more than a cupboard, windowless and entirely empty with distemper flaking off the walls. I went back into the main room, closed and latched the window and made sure the net curtain was pulled right across. It was a double layer of net, newer and of better quality than the rest of the place, like the lock on the door. Now my eyes were used to the candlelight I could make out more details. Two new filing cabinets stood on either side of the door that led to the staircase, a kitchen table and an office chair against the wall on the left. The wall opposite the window had no furniture against it and was entirely covered by what looked like a large map. I was taking the candle over for a closer look when there was a desperate tapping at the window. I drew the curtain back and there was Bobbie kneeling on the outside sill with one hand braced against the brickwork, mouthing curses at me. When I opened the window she came tumbling in, still cursing.

I said, 'I thought I told you to keep watch outside.'

'Have you found anything?'

'Only disproved something. Wherever Verona stayed for those missing nineteen days, it doesn't look as if it was here.'

There wasn't a sign about the place that it had been lived in recently, not a bed, a blanket, a washstand. It didn't have the feel of a room where anybody stayed. And yet according to Toby and Rizzo she'd come here, twice at least, and had her own key.

'Looks quite efficient anyway.'

Bobbie had produced her own candle and was looking at the cabinets.

'Efficient for what? You wouldn't need all this to keep a run-down little chart shop.'

'Perhaps it does most of its business by post. Probably what the map's for.' She took her candle over to it. 'Can't be much of a business, though. It's only London.'

I went to look. It was London and the surroundings, from Greenwich out to Hammersmith, down to Herne Hill and up to Highgate. The whole map was freckled with little blobs in red ink, dozens of them. Each blob had a number beside it, in black ink.

'There you are,' Bobbie said. 'Customers.'

'For nautical charts in Paddington?'

I looked at the Chelsea area, wondering if this place itself was marked with a blob. It wasn't, but there were a few red blobs not far away. The scale was so large that blocks of houses as well as streets were identifiable. One of them was familiar.

'What's up?'

'I think it's where Verona lived before she went missing.'

The student house, either that or very near it. Bobbie was looking at the top part of the map.

'There's one for you, Nell.'

'What!'

She pointed. The candle flame wavered over the familiar network of streets off Hampstead High Street. I saw my own street and about halfway along it, much where my house would be, a red blob and the number: 191. It scared me, and what scared me most was that I didn't know why it did.

'Nell, what's happening?'

Even Bobbie sounded concerned.

'I don't know. I promise you, I don't know any more than you do.'

I felt as if I had to convince her, as if the red blob was accusing me of something although I didn't know what.

'Why the number?'

'I don't know. It's not my house number. It's not anything.'

'It must be something.'

Bobbie walked over to the cabinet, pulled at a drawer.

'Locked.' She took a small screwdriver out of a pouch belted to her waist, signed to me to hold the candle close. 'Never travel without one.'

The wood round the lock splintered, the draw came open. Empty. She pulled open some other drawers, all released by the same lock.

'Ah.'

File cards, quite new, held upright by a spring arrangement in the drawer. It was the sort of system an efficient librarian might keep. Bobbie picked out a card at random and showed it to me. It had a number on the top right-hand corner in the same careful hand as on the map. This one was 52. A name, address, then a few lines in a different hand. 'Approx 5ft 7, swarthy complexion, dark hair, wears glasses. Schoolmaster. Holidays walking in Austria. Writes regularly to young woman in Vienna whose brother works in interior ministry.' I stared at it.

'I don't seem to be on the map.' Bobbie sounded regretful about it. 'I wonder what they've got on you, Nell. What was the number? 191.'

She rummaged in the file. I wanted to stop her, but couldn't think of a reason. She looked at a card and laughed.

'What does it say?'

She handed it over. I read: 'Eleanor Rebecca Bray (Nell). Dark hair, thin build, height 5ft 9 approx. WSPU. Communist. Travels frequently on Continent. Fluent in most European languages. Corresponds with associates Germany/Austria/Hungary. Three prison terms, most recent for attack on Rt Hon. David Lloyd George.'

'Attack, for heavens sake! All I did was throw stink bombs at him. And I'm not a communist.'

'Somebody seems to think you're dangerous anyway. Why you and not me?'

I ripped up the card, shaken and angry.

'Don't do that!' Bobbie said. 'They'll know who's been here.'

'They? Who? And I don't care.'

'In that case, we might as well take some of them with us – see who's on them and warn them.'

She picked handfuls of cards out of the drawer and stuffed them in her pouch.

I tried to get control of myself and concentrate on the work in hand.

'Can you find number 208?'

That was the number on the map near the student house. I was expecting, half-dreading, that Verona's name would come up. It didn't.

'Desperate character, 208. Hungarian anarchist.'

'Rizzo.'

She passed the card over. The address and description fitted and there was a short list of associates in London and Paris, but none of the names meant anything to me. 'Known anarchist' was all the card said about his political activities but since his friends shouted that from the rooftops it hardly suggested a high level of information, any more than my own card did. The ink on Rizzo's card was a slightly different colour from mine and there was a date on the bottom left-hand corner, '4 Feb. 1914.'

Bobbie was still truffling through cards.

'There's a whole lot of blobs on that chess place where your friend Max goes. Shall I see what they've got on him?'

'No.'

I hated the place, wanted to get out. Even that wasn't going to be easy with the door locked. I went over to the window to work out a way down, then froze.

'Bobbie!'

She looked up from the file cards, listened and heard what I'd heard. There was somebody coming down the street.

'Policeman?'

No, not the heavy official tread of a man on the beat. These footsteps were light, as if whoever it was didn't want to attract attention. Bobbie grabbed the candle and blew it out. I knelt by the window and looked down. It was a man in a dark coat and flat cap coming from the King's Road direction. At that angle, I couldn't see his face. Probably it was just a washer of glasses and pots from one of the pubs, walking back to his lodgings in the early hours. Except there was something about him that made my hairs bristle like a cat in a dog kennel. Quietly I checked the curtain and signed to Bobbie to close the cabinet. We couldn't see the man now, but by the sound of the steps he was just passing the shop window. Then they stopped. We looked at each other. I got off my knees and pointed silently to the door out to the landing. We went as lightly as we could, but boards creaked. I opened the door to the empty boxroom. She dived inside and I followed, pulling the door behind us. As we went, a noise came from below of a key turning in the front door lock.

'Who's there?'

A sharp voice, scared and trying to hide it. He'd heard something. The key turned in the lock again, this time from the inside. A match flared and the smell of paraffin drifted up the stairs. For a moment I thought he'd come to set fire to the place but he must have been lighting a lantern because a glow spread up the stairs and through a crack in the badly fitting door into the boxroom. His shadow came first. I saw it from where I was kneeling, slanting against the staircase wall. Then the man himself, just a glimpse of his face as he went past. A pale face in the light of the lamp he was carrying, nervous but determined, with a little dark moustache. He pushed open the door of the room opposite, took a step inside and stopped. I pulled the boxroom door open, got a foot on the landing then took the stairs in two jumps. Bobbie must have taken them in one because we landed hanging on to each other in the space at the bottom of the stairs. The man shouted, turned and came clattering down after us. He didn't bring the lamp with him so was no more than a dark mass. Bobbie hit out. He gave a gasp of pain so she must have connected with something. I grabbed the front door handle, turned and pushed but it didn't move. Locked. Then, scrabbling, I found he'd left the key in the lock. A turn, a push and I was hurtling on to the pavement, grabbing for anything I could reach of Bobbie. I got an arm and she followed. I slammed the door, turned the key in the lock from the outside. From the inside, the man was throwing himself at the door.

'Stop! You there! Stop!'

'Skirt! Confounded skirt's caught.'

126

We both pulled. There was a tearing sound, then we were both running down the street towards Cheyne Walk. The noise coming from inside the chart shop sounded loud enough to be heard on the other side of the river, but so far there was no sign of anyone taking any notice. We got to the Embankment, ran along Cheyne Walk towards Battersea Bridge, past caring now if we woke up anybody in the quiet houses. Between Battersea and Albert Bridges we slowed to a walk. I had a stitch and Bobbie was trailing bits of torn cloth like Cinderella after midnight. A long way after midnight. The city was so quiet that we could hear Westminster chimes and the strokes of two o'clock drifting upriver from Big Ben.

'He'll have got out by now.'

'Yes.'

Even if nobody heard him, which was unlikely, he could have climbed down from the window.

'What was he doing? Do you think he owns the shop?'

I told her to hold still. I'd found a couple of safety pins in my pocket and was trying to fix her skirt. Anybody seeing two women out at this hour would draw the obvious conclusion, but I didn't want to look as if we'd been brawling as well. It gave me a chance, too, to decide how much I wanted to tell Bobbie.

I suggested we should walk away from the river up Oakley Street. We knew a coffee stall near Sloane Square that stayed open all night for cab drivers and people going home from parties or, come to that, tired suffragettes who'd spent nights putting up posters. This part of London is never quite asleep. A man, hatless and in shirtsleeves, passed us without looking up, eyes on the ground. A hansom drove by, blinds down, a woman's giggle bubbling from inside it.

'Do we talk about it or don't we?'

127

If I'd said no, Bobbie would have accepted it.

'Yes.'

'If he was the shop owner, what was he doing there at that hour of the morning?'

'He wasn't.'

'Why so sure?'

'I've seen him before.'

It had only been a glimpse through the crack in the door, but enough to see that it was the man I'd dubbed Yellow Boater. I explained to Bobbie.

'So he must have followed you and waited until we were both inside.'

'Bobbie, I'm sure neither he nor anybody else followed me.'

'So how did he know you were there?'

'He didn't. Not when he came in. He knows now.'

He'd had one glimpse at the bottom of the stairs, by the faint light of a street lamp through net curtains, but that was enough for a man trained to recognise faces.

'But if he didn't follow you, what was he doing there?'

'Meeting somebody, probably. Somebody who didn't want to risk going there by daylight.'

Yellow Boater. Verona's older lover, the man with the little moustache. Rizzo and Toby had been right about the assignations, wrong about the lover.

'So what's it got to do with your cousin's daughter?'

A policeman walked past on his beat, gave us a curious glance, no more.

'Morning, officer,' Bobbie said, in a Cockney accent that wouldn't have fooled a dog.

He took no notice. I waited until his footsteps had faded in the distance before answering.

'I'm very much afraid that Verona was a spy.'

Chapter Twelve

⊗

WE FOUND THE COFFEE STALL. THE OTHER CUSTOMERS were a cab driver, a tramp and a couple of young men in evening dress trying to sober up on the way home, unsuccessfully. One of them decided to lecture the rest of us about war being inevitable – civil war this time, in Ireland. 'Ulster will fight and Ulster will be right.' Only he had a lisp, either from affectation or from drink, so it came out as 'Ulcer will fight'. We didn't argue. Bobbie was still absorbing what I'd told her on the way there and I was so angry that I couldn't trust myself to speak to anyone else. We finished our coffee. Bobbie said she was staying somewhere not far away. These days she was always cagey about where she was living, even with her best friends, and was never in one place long. We parted in Sloane Square. It was after three o'clock by then, not far off daylight, and I decided to walk the five miles or so home to Hampstead.

The sun was up by the time I was going through Regents Park, with squirrels scuttling, dew on the grass and all the signs of a fine day, but it was wasted on me. Partly, I was angry with myself for being duped. I thought of Verona, new to London, quizzing me about left-wing political groups like a student taking notes for an exam. The minute I'd gone, she'd have been scribbling it all down for transmission to Yellow

Boater in that odious room over the chart shop. Look what I've got for you – what a clever obedient little spy I am. Another blob or two on the map, a few more cards in the index. My friends, some of them. Harmless, idealistic men and women who'd committed no crimes and would no more think of betraying their country than these self-satisfied patriots who were snooping on them. Verona had used me. Even in my anger, I acquitted her of supplying the information on my own card. Special Branch or M-whatever-it-was could have managed that mixture of truth and lies without her help. But there were friends of mine who'd have been prepared to trust her because she was my relative and she'd cold-bloodedly set about betraying them. Even that shambolic household of students looked pathetic in this new light. I supposed she'd taken Rizzo and his rantings at his own evaluation – thought she'd unearthed a nest of dangerous anarchists. Stupid, treacherous girl!

Striding up Haverstock Hill, with the milk-carts on their rounds and a few housemaids up early sweeping steps, I moved on to being angry with the person who deserved it more. My dear cousin Commodore Benjamin North. He must have known. I'd been surprised that he'd let her go to London, but he must have been part of it from the start, even volunteered her services. The brave, loyal daughter who'd wanted to join the navy like her brother. The Roman father, offering his dearest treasure to his country's service – then blaming me when it went fatally wrong. Alexandra, I was sure, knew nothing about it. She'd been left to breed her cats, paint her watercolours and worry. This had been a secret between father and daughter – them and the men with the initials.

In Hampstead High Street the commercial day was just beginning. Smells of warm bread from the bakery, of strawberries from the pony cart delivering punnets of them to the greengrocer. Verona was dead. They'd used her courage and idealism in a dangerous game, and it had killed her. Somehow she'd stumbled on something that was really dangerous – far more so than any of the assorted idealists, political agitators and high-principled law breakers she could have discovered through me. Ironically, she must have found her way to people who really were a public danger. That was what was happening in the nineteen days of her life that were unaccounted for. Then the people she was spying on found her out and killed her. Killed her horribly on her father's doorstep as a sign to him that they knew what had been happening. Who 'they' were I had no idea. Up to that point, I'd laughed at the stories of German spies and lurking saboteurs, as the creations of the popular press and would-be popular politicians. But because the *Daily Mail* got itself into a frenzy, that didn't mean there weren't such things as foreign spies. If so Verona would, by the standards of her new profession, have scored a success. Except she'd been dragged way out of her depth, and it had killed her.

I got home, drew the curtains of the bedroom to shut out the sunlight and slept dreamlessly for six hours or so. The midday post crashing through the letterbox woke me. I got up, still feeling full of sleep, went down in my dressing-gown and put the kettle on the gas ring. One of the envelopes had a Teignmouth postmark and was addressed in careful schoolgirlish writing. There were three pages inside, the first a note from the doctor's daughter.

Dear Miss Bray,

I am enclosing copies of Verona's two letters, as you requested.

I have been thinking about her all the time. My father says I must forget her and won't discuss it, but I can't help it. I know what her family must be suffering and I pity them from my heart, but I will never have another friend who meant to me what Verona did. I won't believe what they said about her at the inquest. Surely even doctors can make mistakes, even though my father says they don't in things like that. I haven't said anything to him yet about going to train as a nurse, but I promise I will as soon as he has got over this, for Verona's sake.

Yours with respect and sympathy
Prudence Maidment

Then the two copies of Verona's letters. The first, dated 19 December 1913, was from the lodging where she'd stayed for her first months in London.

Dearest Prudence,

I'm sorry not to have written before, but as you can imagine, there are a world of things to do. Everything, even finding your way about, seems to take so much longer here than at home. But I am working hard and starting to meet people. Sometimes, quite often to be honest, I wish I were back in Devon, having our long talk-walks together and going up to the Ness to see the ships. But we all have to make sacrifices and I know it would be cowardly if I were to give up what I really want to do and come running home just because I get lonely sometimes and miss Daddy and Mummy and you and all the animals. I'm sorry I shan't be coming home for Christmas, but there is so much to learn, in such a short time. Please give my love to all the puppies. (Have you found homes for them yet?)

Happy Christmas to you and your family.

From your devoted friend
Verona

The second letter was dated 3 May – the same date as Verona's last note to her mother. It had the address of the student house at the top of it, though I knew from Toby and Rizzo that she'd left there the day before. Its tone, even down to the punctuation, was more hurried than the previous one.

Dear Prudence,

Sorry not to have written. Life here interesting – very. Lots to tell you one day – though goodness knows when that will be.

If you don't hear from me for a while, don't worry. I have some good friends and will be all right.

Your friend
Verona

Knowing what I knew now, that second letter didn't read as innocently as Prudence had taken it – Verona 'making a lot of friends and having an interesting time'. It was Verona about to plunge into whatever, before the month was out, would kill her. The good friends weren't there when she needed them and she hadn't been all right. I put the copies away in the only drawer of my desk that locked, made coffee and read my other mail while I drank it.

The mail was unremarkable, with one exception – a little paste-board card inviting me to attend an 'At Home.' Normally that would have gone straight into the wastepaper basket with a passing puzzlement as to how anybody had so much time to fritter away. The names on this one made it different. Mr and Mrs Vincent Hergest would be at home from 2.30 p.m. on Wednesday 24 June and would be delighted to have Miss Bray's company at Mill House, near Guildford, Surrey. I assumed that Mrs Hergest must have sent it, because Vincent wasn't due back from his researches in Paris till the weekend, which meant she must have picked up my message from the publisher. I'd never met her, but I'd heard that she acted as her husband's secretary so that he could concentrate on his books. I'd have preferred a more private chance to speak to him. In fact, knowing what I now knew about Verona, I'd have preferred not to talk to him about her at all. But it was only fair to give him some idea what she'd been doing in case she'd put him in the card index as well. I scribbled a note saying Miss Bray would be delighted to attend and went out and posted it.

There's a point, I suppose, when your mind has too much of grappling with serious things and flies to trivialities. That's the only reason I can think of why, as I was walking back from the postbox, I started worrying about shoes. I had a blue silk dress and a dark blue jacket that would just about do for an author's 'At Home', a straw hat that would pass muster once I'd steamed out a dent in the crown. The question was whether the blue shoes that were all I had for summer party wear would hold together through an afternoon. I was in no mood to go shopping. When I got home I started burrowing around and getting unreasonably angry when I couldn't find them. Then I remembered that I'd put them in a cupboard in the spare room along with some other summer things, flung open the door and found them on the floor with the rest of the clutter. The toes were scuffed and a button on one of the straps was coming loose, but with a bit of repair work, they'd do. Relieved that one thing at least was going right, I tried to close the cupboard door but couldn't. A small raffia work basket, stuffed full of mending things and other oddments, had toppled off a pile of boxes and blocked it. I picked it up, opened it in case there was any thread inside that would do for the button.

134

'Oh no.'

Thread, different colours all ravelled up together. Scraps of darning wool unwinding from cards, pins sticking out at all angles. That was normal, the way I'd most likely left it. What wasn't normal were the other things there, nestled comfortably in the soft stuff. Four things. A small glass cylinder with a measuring scale along the side, graduated from five to twenty-five, with a brass plunger at one end. A smaller cylinder, unmarked, that looked as if it would fit inside the first one. A silver needle. A small brown envelope, folded over. I knelt by the cupboard with the work basket on my lap. Even when I was asking myself what on earth it was, I knew. 'Yes, sir, a hypodermic syringe, in the bottom of the dinghy . . .' I heard the Devon policeman's voice saying it. Another one. I picked up the needle. It was hollow, sharp. It slipped neatly inside the smaller cylinder and stuck out from the end of it. Then if you pulled back the brass plunger on the larger cylinder, the smaller cylinder and the needle fitted inside. One syringe, clean, dry and ready for use. There'd been a trace of liquid in the one the police had found in the boathouse, none in this. But the brown envelope contained about two tablespoonfuls of white crystalline powder. I refolded the envelope, put it back in the work basket along with the assembled syringe and tried to make my mind work. All it was doing was screaming to throw the things away, now, before anyone saw them. Right, take it slowly. How did they get there? Not by my hand. I might not be domestically organised or house-proud, but I'd have remembered bringing this little lot into my home. Could it have been one of my visitors? The house was like Piccadilly Circus at times, but nobody I knew who'd been here was taking morphine – which is probably what the powder was – either medically or as an addict. Verona herself? She'd never

135

been to my house. Not as far as I knew, but what did I know? Then I remembered the searchers. Not Verona anyway, she was dead by then. Whoever the searchers were, they'd left no traces except a mark in the dust and a reversed postcard. Those, plus these things in my lap that would link me by implication to Verona's death. But what was the point? Unless I went running to the police with them, and I wasn't likely to do that, nobody would know. Then it came to me that whoever it was didn't need me to go running to the police, because sooner or later the police would come to me again. Easy enough to find an excuse. Suffragette homes were being raided all over London. This time they'd have been told what to look for, and they'd find it. When I thought of that, I started sweating. I got up in a hurry, intending to flush the powder down the lavatory, break the syringe with a hammer and throw away the pieces, before the police came back. It wasn't rational. The things must have been there for ten days if the searchers had put them there and could have stayed for days more if I hadn't needed the shoes.

I was standing over the lavatory with the envelope in my hand when some sort of sense came back. That and the syringe were evidence of something. Disposing of them would be like admitting my own guilt. But if I couldn't take them to the police and I couldn't just leave them around the house to be found, what *could* I do with them? In the end, I locked them in my desk with the copies of Verona's letters, sat down at my Underwood and wrote a long letter to Bill. I told him about everything, the syringe, the chart shop, the file cards. If anything happened, like another police raid and arrest, I wanted my version to be out there somewhere. I couldn't burden my suffragette friends or Max with it because they had enough problems. It did occur to me that Bill might have enough problems too, but he was a lawyer and I needed help from somewhere the way a person lost in a desert needs water. Once I'd got that sealed and posted I felt a little safer. Not much, though.

Chapter Thirteen

'I HAVEN'T READ HIS LATEST,' I SAID.
'But didn't you find the last chapters ever so slightly
déjà vu? I thought he'd handled the same theme more inci-
sively in *Midday Dancing*. Or don't you agree?'

'I haven't read it.'

'But then even his amazing vitality as a writer . . .'

I stopped listening. My blue shoes were planted on neatly
mown turf. A breeze off the North Downs was fluttering the
phlox and poppies in the borders, bending the plume of water
from the fountain in the lily pond so that it feathered out
over groups of guests. Their little exclamations and laughs
blended with the overture to *The Pirates of Penzance*, played
by a wind and string band on the lower terrace by the gazebo.
I had a bowl of strawberries and cream in my hand, a glass
of claret cup on the edge of the sundial beside me, a literary bore at my elbow. So far, I'd had no opportunity to get
Vincent Hergest on his own, and with around a hundred
people present, the chances looked as slim as the cucumber
slices in the sandwiches. The train I'd caught from London
had carried a dozen other people, obviously bound for the
Hergests' party. Two chauffeur-driven cars were waiting at
Guildford station and carried us in relays through the lanes,
joining a queue of other vehicles at the entrance to the drive

of Mill House. Some of the tens of thousands that Vincent's books earned him went on hospitality to his friends as well as on international peace. His socialism, he said, meant wanting everybody to enjoy life as much as he did and the 'At Home' was more of a private garden fête. He was waiting to meet us on the top terrace in a cream linen suit and soft collared shirt with a floppy purple bow tie. He was in his mid forties but his round freckled face, sandy hair and blue eyes gave him the look of a confident schoolboy. His handshake was warm.

'So glad you could come, Miss Bray. I got your note. We must talk later.'

As I was swept strawberrywards in the tide of guests I heard him welcoming the next in line.

'Johnny, glad they could spare you from the House. Imogen darling, such reviews! It will run for ever.'

There were quite a few people I knew in the throng and ordinarily I'd have been happy enough circulating and talking, but now I wished I hadn't bothered. I ate the last of my strawberries (they were sweet, I had to admit) put the empty bowl on the sundial, picked up the claret cup and set about losing the bore.

'I haven't said hello to our hostess yet. I've never met Mrs Hergest. Could you point her out to me?'

'Valerie? Down in the herb garden last I saw her. Green and white with feathers.'

By the sound of it, I should look for her perching in a tree. I was sure it wouldn't ruin her afternoon if she never saw me, but at least it set me free to stroll round the gardens. There were several acres of them, lawns and flowerbeds near the house with views southwards over farmland, then lower down a line of white-painted beehives, a vegetable garden planted for decoration as well as use, with beet, peas and lettuces set among

139

box hedges like a knot garden. Next to it, a wired enclosure with a few fruit trees and a muddy pond was home to a colony of Indian runner ducks. I watched them scuttling around, absurdly upright, like clockwork toys. The whole thing had a Marie Antoinette quality to it, since the Hergests could easily order their duck eggs and honey from Fortnums but I couldn't help liking it, and liking him more because of it. I wandered on. The band, still on *Pirates*, was up above me now. '. . . *Yet people say, I know not why, that we shall have a warm July . . .*' There was a low stone wall beyond the duck enclosure and a trellis with sweet peas. Chatter and laughter came from the other side of the trellis, glimpses of dresses in the same pastel colours as the flowers and a smell of crushed camomile. I went down a shallow flight of steps between lavender bushes and found my hostess, or at least the back view of her. The dress was white and mint green, draped in an oriental style that emphasised her slimness. Her dark hair was crowned with a cascade of white swan feathers. The effect, as with their garden, was odd but attractive. She was talking to a big bald man. I moved round to join them and do my social duty and waited for a gap in their conversation.

'Mrs Hergest? We haven't met but . . .'

I stopped, probably with mouth open and gaping, because what I was saying wasn't true. Or true only in the sense that we'd never been formally introduced. Our eyes, at any rate, had met – just a week ago across a coroner's court in Devon. The mystery woman sitting next to Bill had been Vincent Hergest's wife. Now she was looking at me, hand out, a little smile on her lips, the perfect hostess.

'Miss Bray, isn't it? Vincent was so glad you could come.'

Her self-possession was total. The big dark eyes gave nothing away. To be fair, she had the advantage. She'd known from the inquest who I was, but I'd had no way of knowing her identity. She put a light hand on my wrist and managed somehow to draw us away from the bald man, so that we couldn't be overheard. There was a rosemary bush beside us, humming with bees. Her voice was low and pleasant.

'I was so sorry to hear about your cousin's daughter. Vincent was quite devastated.'

'You knew her?'

My brain was working again, but only slowly. She could have commiserated back in Teignmouth if she'd wanted to. According to Bill she'd driven away so fast that people had to jump for their lives. She nodded, setting the swan feathers quivering.

'Yes. We met her when Vincent was researching his latest.'

'Where?'

She looked at me, head on one side.

'If I tell you, would you try to keep it quiet? Of course, I'd understand if you wanted to talk about it in the family, but we'd rather it didn't get around.'

'I assume we're talking about something political?'

So Verona had managed to burrow her way in here as well. I wondered how many of Hergest's idealistic schemes had found their way on to the file cards.

'No, not that.' She moved so close to me that a feather tickled my cheek and murmured, 'Ju-jitsu.'

'What?'

I must have yelped because several people looked in our direction. Valerie waved a don't-worry signal at them with her slim white-gloved fingers.

'There's an academy run by this amazing woman near Oxford Circus.'

'I know.'

'Vincent's decided that the girl in his next novel is going to be a ju-jitsu expert. He wants to explore how a love affair

141

develops when a woman is physically and intellectually stronger than a man. Only if word gets round what he's working on, by the time his book comes out half a dozen wretched scribblers will have rushed out *Ju-jitsu Jane* trash and his will look dated, even though he had the idea in the first place.'

She looked at me as if I should understand that this would be one of the world's great tragedies. She was, at a guess, about ten years younger than her husband, but her pride in him seemed more like a mother's than a wife's. There were little lines round her eyes and on her forehead, as if she did a lot of worrying.

'So you and he met Verona at Edith Garrud's place? When?'

'It would have been back in February. We were sitting in on some of the classes. I started talking to Verona and knew Vincent would be interested, so I made sure they met. Didn't she tell you about it?'

I said something about not seeing much of Verona. I was still off balance.

'His central character is a little like her – young, brave, wanting to change the world.'

She must have seen something in my face and misinterpreted it, because she started trying to reassure me.

'I don't mean that the girl in the book would be your cousin's daughter. Vincent creates, transmutes. You know, a look or a way of speaking from one person, something else from another. It's how he works.'

She made it sound like something holy. Her eyes were on mine, unblinking, almost commanding me to understand.

'As I said in my note, I think I saw your husband and Verona together at the Buckingham Palace deputation.'

'Yes, I'm sure you did. He mentioned seeing her there.'

'Did either of you see much of Verona, apart from the ju-jitsu classes?'

'Oh yes. We invited her down here for one of our youth weekends.'

'Was that your idea or hers?'

'Ours, naturally. It was obvious that she was interested in politics, but a little naïve. From the start, she was asking Vincent almost as many questions as he was asking her.'

'What sort of questions?'

'His ideas on world peace, the countries he visited, the people he met. She really was hungry for knowledge.'

'Yes, I'm sure she was.'

'Anyway, from time to time we cram this house with young people from all over the place, from as many different countries as possible, from all classes of society. They enjoy themselves together and talk in an entirely informal way about what concerns them and how they see the future.'

'When was the one Verona came to?'

'The last weekend in April.'

'Can you remember who else was there?'

'We had about twenty people. I've got a list somewhere. I remember there was a young man who'd been imprisoned in St Petersburg, a couple of German pacifists, a rather quiet Sinn Feiner and some Communist musicians from Paris.'

'Tell me, was there anybody there she seemed particularly interested in?'

'Why do you ask?'

'A few days after that weekend she disappeared. I can't find anybody who knows where she was until your husband saw her outside Buckingham Palace. Then she just disappeared again, until I found her in the boathouse.'

'Are you suggesting that it was something to do with our weekend?'

'Not directly, but I'm wondering if there was somebody she met there that explains it.'

143

'I honestly don't think so.'

'It's possible that your husband noticed something. I'd like to ask him.'

A bee from the rosemary had settled on her gloved hand. She was looking at it as if she'd never seen one before.

'Do you really need to talk to Vincent? All this is upsetting for him and he's been working so hard on the book.'

'Yes. I think I do.'

She opened her lips to ask why, decided against it and wafted her hand gently in the air to make the bee fly.

'There's a bench in the vegetable garden, near the water tank. If you wait there, I'll get him to come to you.'

She started moving away.

I said, 'Why did you come to the inquest?'

'Vincent couldn't go. You know, the press . . .' She took a step. 'I'm so sorry for her parents. It must be awful, wondering . . .' Another step. 'Please be careful with him. He's so much more sensitive than people think.'

She walked slowly past her guests, up the steps towards the house. I went back to the vegetable garden and found a stone bench between the water tank and rows of carrots. After ten minutes or so there were quick footsteps on the path and Vincent Hergest appeared and sat down beside me.

'I can't tell you how sorry I was to hear about it.'

The words were conventional enough, but he seemed genuinely disturbed. His fingers were kneading away at his kneecaps, doing no good to the cream-coloured linen.

'How did you hear?'

'The place in Chelsea where she used to live. I hadn't seen her for some time so I went round there. The fellow with the red beard told me. I should have written, I suppose, to you or somebody. But I didn't know what to . . .'

Probably a literary first. If only the bore up by the sundial

144

could have heard it – Vincent Hergest admitting he didn't know what to write. He sighed and shook his head. 'Valerie tells me you want to know about the weekend she was here.'

'Yes, mostly whether she seemed particularly interested in any of your other guests.'

'You haven't been to one of our weekends, or you'd know. Everybody's interested in everybody. You should see – no, you should *feel* this place when we have our young people here. They're making connections that are going to change the world, I really believe that. How can you think of waging war on people, whether it's class war or war between countries, when you've swum with them and had pillow fights with them, and sat up half the night talking music and books and politics?'

You could tell he was on a favourite theme, trying to cheer himself up by talking about it.

'Did Verona talk much about herself?'

'No. She did more listening than talking, as far as I remember.'

'Not just at that weekend, at other times. Your wife said you were interested in her for your book.'

'Aspects of her, yes. A young woman from a conventional background, seeing the wrongs of the world for the first time, wanting to put them right in one great heroic charge.'

'So she told you about her background?'

He stared at his rows of carrots. 'She said her father was a doctor in Devon.'

'I'm afraid she lied about that.'

He darted up, grabbed a carrot by its ferny top and pulled it out of the ground. 'Yes, I know. Valerie told me from the inquest. Naval officer, isn't he?'

'Yes.'

He sat down, still holding his carrot. 'Perhaps she was

145

ashamed to admit it, poor girl, meeting pacifists and so on.'

'Why did you want Valerie to go to the inquest?'

He looked at me. The blue eyes had a glaze of tears over them.

'I wanted to know what had happened.'

'For the book?'

He stared at me for a moment, mouth open, as if I'd hit him unfairly.

Then, 'What sort of a monster do you think I am? Do you think I have no feelings, just because I'm a writer? A young woman hangs herself and I'm only interested for my book?'

He hurled the carrot away. It went skittering through the air like a vegetable comet, trailing green, landed somewhere among the marrow plants. 'Carrot fly, damn them.'

'I'm sorry to have to tell you this, but I'm afraid there was something more important she deceived you about. All of us in fact.'

He stared. 'What?'

'I'm very much afraid Verona was a government spy.'

He rocked back on the seat as if I'd hit him. 'No! What do you mean? I don't believe it!'

I told him as much as he needed to know. I had to, not just for him but for the assorted people she'd met through him. At first he was angry, trying to interrupt, but when I got to the room with the filing cabinets and the map his head went down in his hands. From what seemed like a long way off, the band he'd hired was playing something from *The Dollar Princess*.

He said through his fingers, 'I was beginning to be afraid there was something. When Valerie told me about her father being a commodore I was afraid there was something. But this . . .'

146

I waited. When he looked up at last his eyes were damp and the muscles round his mouth were quivering.

'They must have wanted to get me very badly. Sending her where they knew I'd meet her.'

It's one of the funny things about being spied on – knowing you're being watched is like appearing on stage all the time and however much people may hate that, nobody will admit to having just a walk-on part.

'You might not have been the main target.'

'Why else would they go to all this trouble?'

'You know a lot of people the War Office might think of as potential enemies.'

'For God's sake, we create our own enemies out of our fears and weaknesses.'

'It's a good quote, but I'm not sure it would convince the men in the Secret Service Bureau.'

'Is that who she was working for?'

'I don't know who exactly. People with money and resources behind them, that's certain. They must have been pleased when you invited her down here.'

He brushed a cream linen cuff over his eyes.

'I still can't believe this.'

'Didn't you wonder about all those questions she was asking?'

'Why should I?' He shook his head, honestly puzzled. He expected people to be interested in him. 'Do you . . . do you think that might be why she killed herself? Because she was ashamed of what she was doing?'

'If she did kill herself.'

'But the inquest . . .'

'The jury didn't have much choice. They didn't know anything about this.'

'You could have told them.'

'I didn't know then either.'

'What are you going to do?'

'Find out. Which is why I want to know whether she took a particular interest in anybody on your weekend.'

'They're not like that – none of them.'

'Can you be sure of that?'

'I don't think I'll be sure of anything ever again.' He sat there for some time, staring at the dirt on his fingers. 'I'll get Valerie to send the list to you. I expect she's still got it.' He sounded subdued now, reality breaking in.

'Was it Verona at that Buckingham Palace deputation on the twenty-first?'

'Yes.'

'Did she say anything about where she'd been?'

'No. We came across each other in the crowd and I said we'd better get out of the way of the police horses. I helped her over the railings by the Memorial.'

'And afterwards?'

'We got separated. I never saw her again.'

'It's a pity. That's the first we know of anybody seeing her for nineteen days. Did you ever know her to inject morphine?'

'No, definitely not. I'd have stopped her.'

'So that surprised you from the inquest?'

'Everything surprises me. I just don't know where I am.'

Little boy lost. I felt sorry for him, but wondered if he ever stopped listening to the sound of his own voice.

'If anything occurs to you about what she was doing in those missing days, you will let me know, won't you?'

He nodded, head bent.

'Vincent are you there?'

Valerie's soft but carrying voice came floating down the garden, then she was with us in a flutter of white and green.

'Vincent darling, I think you'd better come. Kitty Dulcie's

thrown the man from your publishers into the lily pond and he thinks he's broken his elbow.'

She was flustered, as any hostess might be, but I guessed she wasn't sorry to have an excuse to get him away from me. One glimpse of his tear-washed eyes and rumpled hair was enough to convince her that I'd disobeyed instructions to be careful with him.

'Not poor little Robbie?'

At least the news seemed to cheer him up, or perhaps it was relief at being rescued.

'No, the big one from accounts.'

They hurried together back up the lawn. A few words from Valerie drifted back, '. . . told you we shouldn't invite her . . .' I followed and found that most of the party had congregated round the pond. A plump man, wet as a frog, in a pink-and-maroon-striped blazer was sitting on a bench dripping water onto the gravel. Somebody was making a sling by knotting table napkins together and people were twittering around the flowerbeds asking each other if they'd seen it and if anybody had called a doctor. At some distance from the rest a small woman with dark hair cut very short stood frowning over the lawn. Valerie went up to her, touched her on the arm and said something then they went together into the house. If the woman was meant to be in social disgrace, she didn't seem to feel it. She walked in a jaunty athletic way, with a swing of the shoulders. Vincent, meanwhile, had gone up to the man in the striped blazer and was trying to pacify him.

'I'm sure she didn't mean any harm, Rodney. Doesn't know her own strength, that's all.'

'Well, she damned well should. Ju-jitsu be blowed. The woman's a homicidal lunatic.'

A small man in a quieter blazer, Robbie possibly, said, 'After all, Rodders, you *did* challenge her.'

'No I didn't. All I asked her was whether she really thought she could throw a normal athletic man and – whoomph!'

'That was when you grabbed hold of her, um, upper body, Rodders.'

'Only after she got hold of my wrist.'

A woman in the crowd, trying not too hard to hide her amusement, said, 'But she was only demonstrating how she'd do it theoretically—'

'Theoretically, be blowed! She was determined to get somebody in that pond.'

While somebody fixed the sling, Vincent suggested that the victim should come inside with him for a stiff whisky and a change of clothing. They went, Rodney still grumbling but not moving like a man with any bones broken. I noticed that Vincent had given Valerie plenty of time to get Kitty Dulcie out of the way. Those two worked well as a team. After a few minutes I went up to the house myself and found Valerie on the steps, waving off one of the chauffeur-driven cars with a single passenger in the back of it.

'Was that Kitty Dulcie?'

She turned, and I had the distinct impression that I'd outstayed my welcome too. Still, she was polite.

'Yes. She has to catch the train back to town for a demonstration she's giving this evening.'

'I'd hoped for a word with her.'

She looked alarmed. 'You're not *writing* about this, are you?'

'No, but I've seen her at Edith Garrud's gymnasium. I wondered if she might be a friend of Verona's.'

'I expect they would have known each other but Kitty . . . well it has to be admitted that Kitty is in some ways a rather peculiar young woman.'

I thought, but didn't say, so was Verona. Soon afterwards,

when the party was breaking up and we were sorting ourselves into carloads to be driven back the station, Valerie said how nice it had been to meet me and handed me an envelope. I opened it in the train back to London. It was the list of their guests at the young peace-makers' house-party in April. Verona's name was there, along with a dozen others I didn't recognise, though with luck some of them might mean something to Max. In spite of what I'd said to Vincent, I still found it hard to believe that whatever had killed Verona had started there among the ducks and the high-mindedness.

Somebody in the train said, 'Wish I'd seen the ju-jitsu girl throwing the fat man in the fountain.'

Although I bore the man no grudges, so did I. It would at least have been some reward for an afternoon's work.

Chapter Fourteen

⌘

SOMETHING WAS WORRYING ME ON THE WAY HOME. It had been worrying me for five days. As far as I could tell, nobody was following me. In the way that even the most outlandish things become commonplace, I'd adapted over the past month to the fact that the watchers were there unless I made a determined attempt to lose them, and it wasn't usually worth the bother. At first I'd dated their persistence from the Bobbie escape episode. Then, more chillingly, from when Verona died. But five days ago in raiding their office over the chart shop, I'd done something they should find unforgivable. Yellow Boater must have recognised me. At the very least, they could have me charged with breaking into the place. So where were they? I was worried when they started following me, scared now they weren't. It meant they were trying different tactics, hollowing out the ground under me. Some day soon a pit would open up and there was no way of telling where or when.

I searched the house routinely when I got home. There was no sign that anybody had been there. The letters and the syringe were still locked in my desk, the inch of black silk thread I'd closed in the drawer was still in place. I picked up the mail and the sight of a Manchester postmark and Bill's handwriting was as reassuring as a landmark when you're lost. His letter was dated Monday, two days ago.

152

Dear Nell,

I have received your letter with great concern. I wish you had consulted me, or even told me, about what you were planning to do. There's a lot I can't say in this letter, because if you're right, or even halfway right, there may be other people apart from you reading it. But please, please promise me that you won't think of doing anything remotely like that again. Whatever's going on, that can only make things worse.

I'm also, as you may imagine, seriously worried about this business of the work basket. I think you're mistaken in keeping the objects in the house and the only sensible course is to hand them over to the police, with an explanation. If you like, I will get one of my friends who is a solicitor in London to handle the matter for you, but of course I can't approach him until I have your permission. As to how they got there, I have my ideas on that.

I've been giving all this a lot of thought since last week and I'm becoming convinced that you are tackling all this from the wrong end. I can't say more about that until we're together but I'll be making my own enquiries and will let you know the result. Until then, please, *please* lie low, do as little as you can even in suffragette activities and do nothing at all to attract the attention of the police or anybody else.

I suppose you won't like this letter. I can see you biting your lip in that way you have and cursing me for a cautious, conventional, passive lawyer. Well, I am a lawyer and so I suppose I am, by your standards, cautious and conventional (but so, my dear whirlwind, is the greater part of the known world). But I'm not, I hope, passive and – with luck – may be able to prove that to

153

you the next time we meet. If I am lecturing you like an elder brother, please put it down to the fact that I do care about you very much, more than I've been able to say to you when we've been together, and that I hope and believe you've given me a right to be concerned about what happens to you.

Oh my dear, do please for once – for my sake if not for yours – be patient and be careful.

Yours
Bill

I was furious. Let your defences down for an hour or two, and a man assumes that you're simply waiting for him to gallop into view on a white charger – or in this case a bicycle – and start running your life for you. I'd thought that Bill was different and I'd been wrong. How dare he lecture me about not attracting the attention of the police when I'd been playing cat-and-mouse with them for months. What right had he to tell me to cut down suffragette activities, even temporarily? As for giving him a *right* to be concerned . . . I grabbed a postcard, addressed it to his private address and wrote: 'I already have an elder brother. I don't need another, thank you.' Then I tore it up and threw it at the overflowing wastepaper basket. He didn't deserve even that. He didn't deserve anything except being ignored. I changed out of my party things and broke the strap on the shoe I'd repaired, cursed a bit, put down fish for the cats. They ate while shooting sidelong nervy looks at me. I made tea and toasted cheese for supper and burned the toast. The rest of my mail was routine, including a polite but pained letter from the London Library asking if it might be convenient to return some of the German fairy-tale books because other people were wanting them. Trying to work off the black mood, I

154

sorted out business letters from the pending pile that deserved uncivil replies, banged away on the Underwood until the keys started sticking then lost a hairpin in the works trying to clear them. At ten o'clock it was still light enough for children to be playing in the street outside, but I'd had enough. I went to bed and, amazingly, went straight to sleep. At four in the morning, with the first light coming in through the gap in the curtains and sparrows making a racket on the sill, I woke up, still angry, but thinking more clearly.

There was one thing in Bill's letter that was worth considering. He thought I was tackling things from the wrong end. I didn't know what he meant by that and certainly wasn't going to ask him but there was a glimmer of sense in the words. Whatever caused Verona's death probably had its origins in those lost nineteen days. I wasn't investing too much hope in Vincent Hergest's house-party. His instinctive reaction that there were no desperate characters on the guest list was probably right. He was too careful of his reputation to take serious risks and I was prepared to bet that Valerie was even more careful on his behalf. I'd show the list to Max in case he recognised any of the names, but even with his encyclopaedic knowledge of the left, that was betting on an outsider. So if that was no good, start at the other end. The people who'd know where Verona was and who she was spying on in those lost days would be her employers, the initials. All I had to do was ask. I laughed out loud, imagining myself walking into the imposing building on Whitehall that housed the War Office and up to the doorman.

'I want to speak to somebody from a department called MO5 or possibly from SSB. I gather they're fairly new and very secretive. Purpose of visit? To ask them about one of their spies who died. My name? They'll know me as card number 191 on their index.'

Well, it wouldn't be the first time I'd hit the pavement in Whitehall but it wouldn't be much help either. I could hardly put an advertisement on the front of *The Times*. 'North London woman wishes to meet gentleman from the Secret Service for exchange of information.' The ironic thing seemed to be that there was never a secret service man around when you wanted one. A few days ago I'd been over-supplied with them. Now when I wanted to ask some questions they'd all deserted me.

Then it struck me that I could do something about it. Since we broke into the chart shop I'd been waiting for them to take the initiative and they hadn't. Either I could wait patiently or I could do something to provoke them into showing themselves again. At the best of times I'm not good at being patient and with Bill's unwanted advice to lie low still rankling, this wasn't the best of times. So provocation it was. The only question was, what would work best? I thought of my file card: 'Travels frequently on Continent. Fluent in most European languages.' (They flattered me there, by the way. I'd only rate myself really fluent in French and German.) If speaking foreign languages and travelling abroad were suspicious activities, then I'd give them something to worry about.

First it was only fair to give the London Library its books back so I took the underground to Charing Cross and walked to St James's Square. I handed them in, then started discussing something or other with the man at the returns counter. There was a little queue of people waiting to have books checked out at the counter next door, but it wasn't until I turned to go that I noticed the man at the back of it. He had one book tucked under his arm, and was reading another while he waited, his neat little grey beard angled down at the page. Even then, I only gave him a casual glance but it was the scar that made me stop dead. A pink shiny line down the left side of his face from hairline to beard, dragging down the corner of his eye. I don't know why I was so surprised to see Archie Pritty there. After all, there's no rule that retired rear admirals can't use libraries, and Prudence had told me he spent some time in London. Seeing him unexpectedly brought back all the raw hurt of the inquest and I hesitated, thinking meanly he hadn't seen me and that I might get out before a meeting that could be embarrassing for both of us. Perhaps I thought better of it and made some sound or move, or perhaps he sensed me there. Anyway, he looked up from his book and our eyes met. He seemed startled at first, as if trying to place me, then was courteous.

'Miss Bray, isn't it? I'm glad to see you again.'

'How's Alex?'

'Being brave, as one would expect. If you'd be kind enough to wait a minute while I sign these out, perhaps we could go outside and talk.'

I waited for him to deal with the books and collect his bowler hat from a peg, then we walked together down the steps and into the square. He tucked the books under his arm. 'An ancestor of mine, involved in the Napoleonic Wars in the West Indies. I'm working on a biography of him, on and off. God knows if I'll ever finish it.'

We walked across the road and along the pavement under the plane trees. He'd suggested talking but he didn't find it easy to start.

'So you've seen Alex since the inquest?'

'Oh yes, several times. The fact is, Ben's had to go back to sea . . .'

'Already?'

'Demands of the service, Miss Bray. The best thing for him in the circumstances, though probably not for her. I promised Ben I'd look in on her, do what I could. Probably shouldn't have come to London and left her, but she insisted she'll be all right.'

'And will she?'

He shook his head. 'Lord knows. I said in there she was being brave. Kind of thing you do say. Frozen more like.' The sun was out and there were leaf shadows lying on the pavement, flitting over the highly polished toes of his shoes. 'What's hit her is not understanding.'

'I think that's hit all of us.'

'Yes. I gather you didn't know Verona very well.'

'No.'

'I knew that girl from the time she was a few days old. I can promise you there wasn't a cleaner, straighter, more honourable girl in the whole country. She wasn't capable of telling or implying a lie – even of thinking one.'

I suppose I nodded or murmured something. I seemed doomed to have people telling me about her saintly qualities.

'As for the opposite sex, she simply wasn't interested, not in that way.'

'Surely that's unlikely – a healthy young woman.'

There were limits after all. He gave me an annoyed look. 'Very well, Miss Bray, there are things we might not agree on and I'm sure I'm quite out of step with a lot of modern ideas. I'm not saying Verona wouldn't have made a first-class wife and mother for some lucky man in the fullness of time, I'm not saying that at all. Oh, she'd go sailing with the young men, picnics with them and so on, but it was all as innocent as brother and sister. She'd rather beat them in a dinghy race than get up to any kind of nonsense with them.'

'Her best friend Prudence would have agreed with that. She and Verona weren't going to get silly about men until they'd done something in the world.'

A smile, or it might have been a grimace, made the scar writhe across his cheek. 'You've met little Prudence, have you? A nice child, but not a patch on Verona.'

'She's missing her.'

'We all are.' We finished one circuit of the square and started the next. 'Or rather, we're all missing the Verona we thought we knew. How can a girl change so much in such a short time? That's what's making things so hard for Alexandra.'

I guessed now why he'd wanted to talk to me, both for Alex's sake and his own.

'I promise you, if I knew anything that would help her, I'd tell her.'

But what I knew wouldn't help her at all. He was quick enough to pick me up on it.

'You mean you do know something, but it won't help?'

'Nothing for certain. Nothing to tell her.'

Alex dear, your daughter went to London to learn to be a spy. Your husband knew and didn't tell you. It was possible that Pritty had been in Ben's confidence, in which case it was a hypocritical game he was playing. Still, the concern for Alex was in his favour.

'If there is anything ever . . .'

He was holding out a card to me. I took it and put it in my pocket.

'There's one thing I have wondered,' I said, 'and that is why she went home to kill herself.'

'Where she was happy. Where she was innocent.'

I thought, but didn't say, that nobody in the world was ever as happy or as innocent as they wanted Verona to have been.

159

'That's all?'

'She loved the sea. You know, even after she was dead the local fishermen . . .' He hesitated, took a few steps and looked sideways at me. 'I don't suppose you know much about West Country fishermen.'

'No.'

'They're the best men and the best seamen on the face of the earth, but superstitious. All of us sailors are superstitious, but they beat the lot.'

Another sideways look.

'You're not trying to tell me people have seen Verona's ghost around the estuary?'

He could tell from my voice I was a sceptic. I could feel him clamming up, but I had enough on my hands without ghost stories.

'Not her ghost, no. A story about a boat that rowed itself. As I say, Miss Bray, they're a superstitious lot. I'm sorry to have taken your time. It was kind of you to talk to me.'

Then he raised his bowler hat and was gone, not into thin air but round the corner into Duke of York Street.

By midday, I was back at the Archimedes J. Stuggs Chess Forum. Max took the list of the Hergests' guests, didn't recognise any of the names but promised, without much optimism, to make some enquiries. Then at my request he introduced me to their resident lepidoptericide. He turned out to be Dr Hassler, born in Prague about seventy years before, qualified as a medical doctor but passionate about chess and butterflies. Max left us alone because he knew I wanted as few people involved in this as possible. Dr Hassler had a manner of old-fashioned courtesy but couldn't help showing his surprise at what I wanted of him.

'My dear lady, it is a very long time since one of the

160

fairer sex has asked me to lunch with her, but I shall be delighted.'

He collected his ebony cane and a white panama with a black band round it and we walked up the street together, quite slowly because he was lame in one foot. A little accident while on a collecting trip to the Amazon, he explained. I was glad of the slowness. I could see Dr Hassler's personal shadow, the man with the greasy hair and drooping moustache known to the chess club as Weaver, keeping pace with us on the other side of the street. To make it easier for him I'd already picked out a café where the tables were conveniently close together. It had a big window on to the street and looked like the sort of place where office workers would come to eat. Dr Hassler and I took a table near the window and studied the menu. Over the top of it, I watched Weaver on the opposite pavement. He was taking a close interest in a row of boots and shoes in a cobbler's widow. After a while he crossed the road, did what was probably a regulation saunter into our café and stood just inside the doorway looking round, but carefully not in our direction.

'There's steak-and-kidney pudding with stout,' I said to Dr Hassler, keeping his attention on the menu. I wanted to make things easy for Weaver.

'Also liver and onions.'

Weaver settled at a table near the wall about ten yards away from us and immediately buried his face in a newspaper.

I said to Dr Hassler: 'You know we're being followed?'

'Yes, of course. My chess apprentice. I'm glad. From his complexion he smokes too many cigarettes and doesn't eat enough of the right things. Should I go over and recommend the steak-and-kidney, do you think?' His eyes sparkled. If he hadn't guessed exactly what was going on, he had a good idea of it.

161

'Dr Hassler, I should warn you I'm doing something that may cause trouble. Not for you, I hope. But I asked you here hoping he'd follow us.'

I switched into German when I said this. He didn't turn a hair and replied in the same language.

'Such a pity. I was hoping it was for the charm of my company and conversation.' He grinned. He was obviously enjoying himself.

'That too. If you don't want to be involved in this, we can have a pleasant lunch I hope and talk about other things.'

'I know about you from our friend Max, Miss Bray. He said I might have doubts about your methods but I need have none about your motives.' He switched to English for that, then back into German. 'So your unbeautiful butterfly has settled. What do you intend to do with it?'

'I hope it's more of a pigeon than a butterfly. I want it to fly back where it came from with a message.'

The waitress arrived and we ordered. Liver, onions and mashed potato for Dr Hassler, a poached egg on toast for me.

'You should eat more meat, Miss Bray. You wish me to creep under the tables and tie a little message to his ankle?'

We laughed. Weaver's newspaper quivered. The waitress was on her way towards him.

'For a start, it would be useful if you could get him to acknowledge you. At the moment he's pretending not to know you're here.'

When the waitress got to his table Weaver performed a kind of fan dance with the newspaper, trying to give his order while keeping his face screened from us. Dr Hassler leaned out, waving like a passenger from a train.

'Hello, Mr Weaver. We recommend the pie.'

Weaver glanced at Dr Hassler, gave a twisted smile of acknowledgement and went back behind the newspaper.

'That's done. What now?'

'I take it you'll be seeing him this afternoon?'

'We have an appointment to play chess.'

'Now that he's had to admit he's seen you, it would be natural for him to ask who you were lunching with.'

'Ill-mannered.'

'But professional. All these hours at the chess forum and he's got something to report at last. You might make it easy for him by pretending to be in a bad temper and explaining it was because of something that happened at lunch.'

Our meals arrived, along with a plate of bread and butter and a big pot of tea. Dr Hassler ate with an enthusiasm you wouldn't have guessed at from his spare build, carrying on the conversation between mouthfuls.

'One can't play chess in a bad temper. Am I supposed to explain what put me in this unusual state of mind?'

'I was trying to persuade you to do something for me. This is the first time we've met. I was introduced to you by Max and promptly insisted on taking you out to lunch.'

'Which has the merit of being true.'

'So far, and if you'd like to leave it at that you'd already have done me a great kindness.'

'That would be a small message for a large pigeon.'

'There is more, only it wouldn't be true.'

'Go on.'

'I wanted you to post a package for me to somewhere in Switzerland or Germany. Zurich might do well. I'd heard that you post butterfly specimens all over the place so wondered if you be very kind and slip this in with your next batch.'

I took a brown paper package the size of a small book out of my bag. In fact, it was a small book, a pocket edition of *Three Men in a Boat*. I'd chosen it because it was about the

163

same size and shape as the batch of file cards Bobbie had taken from the office at World's End. I didn't look Weaver's way, but held it up so that he could hardly miss it. Dr Hassler got the point immediately and looked surprised, a little annoyed.

'I think I'd ask you why you don't put it in the post yourself.'

'Because I don't trust the post. I think all my mail is intercepted. For some reason, they think I'm a suspicious person.'

'I wonder why. So do I perform this little favour for you?'

'You don't. In fact, you're getting quite worried about it all.'

He waved the parcel away. I put it back in my bag, reluctantly.

'I think we probably argue about it a bit. I try to insist and you get angry.'

'By all means. Tell me, what do you think is more dangerous in politicians, hypocrisy or stupidity?'

I chose hypocrisy, leaving him with stupidity and we went at it hammer and tongs in German, over treacle pudding with custard for him and more tea for me. We let our voices rise enough for Weaver to know we were speaking German, throwing in the occasional reference to Asquith, Churchill and Carson to keep him interested. He couldn't have heard all of our conversation from where we were sitting, but must have got the point that we were disagreeing. I signalled to the waitress for the bill, paid it. Dr Hassler tried a genuine protest.

'Don't worry, that's part of it. You can let him know I was flashing money around.'

I risked a look at Weaver. He was smoking a cigarette and had the newspaper folded on the table beside him, apparently intent on it.

164

'Dr Hassler, would you be kind enough to walk with me as far as the corner?'

'Are we still angry with each other?'

'Let's try frozen politeness. Less tiring.'

I made a long business of sorting out change for a tip, giving Weaver time to get organised. He was intent on the paper when we passed his table. We walked slowly down the street, not looking back, and paused on the corner.

'What now?'

'You go back to the club. I'm going to the station to book a ticket.'

'Good luck,' Dr Hassler said quietly in German, 'and may the Reisengott be with you.' He added in English, loud and very formal, 'I'll wish you good afternoon then, Miss Bray,' raised his hat stiffly and walked away.

I didn't look to see if Weaver followed me on the way to the station and the booking hall was so crowded that even a mediocre watcher would have no trouble keeping out of sight. I joined a long queue at a second-class ticket window and paid 19s6d for a single on the overnight service from Liverpool Street to the Hook of Holland via Harwich the following evening, Friday. I harassed the poor clerk and set the queue behind me fidgeting with a lot of questions about the steamer, tides and the precise time we docked at the Hook to make sure he remembered me when the initials came to enquire.

A telegram arrived soon after I got home.

PLEASE TELEPHONE, ANY TIME 4 TO 6. NEED TALK. BILL MUSGRAVE.

It gave a number. I knew it belonged to the tea importer on the ground floor of the building where Bill had his chambers. Bill had no telephone of his own but used that one in emergencies. Or what he thought were emergencies. I'd no intention of finding a coin-box or walking a mile to my nearest friend who possessed a telephone, just to be told all over again to lie low and be cautious. Besides, he'd have wanted to know what I was doing and that would have worried him even more. So that got thrown at the waste-paper basket as well.

Chapter Fifteen

THE BOAT TRAIN DIDN'T LEAVE UNTIL 8.30 ON Friday evening. With the day to fill and in no mood for hobgoblins and fairy-tale forests I decided to try to talk to Kitty Dulcie. 'A rather peculiar young woman,' Valerie had called her. Ju-jitsuing fellow guests into ponds was unconventional, but not necessarily a bad thing. She'd met Verona and was around the same age. It was just possible she'd picked up things other people had missed. But when I went to the ju-jitsu school in Argyll Place to enquire after her, the response wasn't encouraging.

'Miss Dulcie won't be coming here again,' Edith Garrud told me.

I'd caught her between classes. There was a smell of sweat in the air, sounds of people changing behind curtains at the far end of the room.

'Why not?'

'Because I threw her out.'

'Literally?' I had visions of bodies flying across Oxford Circus.

'No, though I was sorely tempted.'

'What had she done?'

'Quite a lot of things. For one thing, I found she'd been giving private lessons here in the evening after I'd gone home.'

'Was that so bad?'

Edith gave me a look. 'Mostly to gentlemen.'

'You mean . . .'

'I don't mean anything, but there's enough prejudice against physical women in any case. I'm not giving anybody a chance to gossip.'

'What else?'

'I tolerated the music-hall demonstrations but I never cared for them. She does a double act with her brother. I told her, ju-jitsu's not a circus act, it's a sacred art developed by monks centuries back, not something to get the gallery whistling at the Metropolitan.'

'She sounds enterprising at any rate.'

'Too enterprising.' Edith took hold of her ankle with one hand and bent her leg up behind her back. 'The last straw was, I found she and her brother had opened a so-called martial arts academy without saying a word to me about it. That young woman's altogether too fond of money.'

'Perhaps she's always been short of it.'

'Not recently, judging by the clothes she's been buying.'

'This martial arts academy, do you know where it is?'

Unwillingly, she gave me an address near the Elephant and Castle.

'But I'd leave her alone if I were you, Nell. There's something not straight about Kitty Dulcie.'

As far as I could tell the watchers weren't following me but I made no efforts to check that on my way out to Elephant and Castle, not wanting to discourage them if they were. Elephant and Castle isn't an area I know well and once out of the underground I had to ask for directions. It was a little street off Walworth Road, or rather half a little street because all one side of it was being knocked down and rebuilt. The surviving side was a gappy mixture of terraced houses, small workshops and locked wooden gates, with no numbers on any of them. There was a smell of brick dust from the demolished houses and of bad drains, with a lot of flies zigzagging around and a dog tearing at a bone in the gutter. As I stood looking for somebody to ask for more directions, a wooden gate opened from the inside and a man came out trundling an empty handcart. Through the gate I got a glimpse of a scrap metal yard.

'Excuse me,' I said, 'do you know where the martial arts academy is?'

He jerked a thumb into the yard behind him and rolled on his way. I went through the gate, shutting it behind me. It was an ordinary enough scrapyard, quite tidy as these things go, with bits of corrugated iron and railings, wheel rims, cooking pots, even the crushed carcass of a motorcar piled into heaps against walls of old railway sleepers. A black-and-white notice, newly painted, was nailed to one of the sleepers: 'Dulcie's Academy of Martial Arts'. An arrow pointed to a newish single-storey red-brick building at the far end of the yard. It had big uncurtained windows and when I got near it I heard the patter of steps from inside and saw two figures moving in what looked like an angular kind of dance.

The door was round the side. There was another notice beside it. 'D. and M. Dulcie. Lessons in Fencing, Shooting and Ju-jitsu for Ladies and Gentlemen'. I knocked and waited. When there was no reply I opened the door and walked in. At the far end of the bare room a man and woman, both barefoot and wearing suits like white flannel pyjamas, were performing a cross between a fight and a ballet. The man lunged forward, like a fencer but empty-handed, with a sideways chopping movement that seemed to be making straight for his partner's head until she pivoted sideways on the ball of her foot and aimed the other foot in a kick that could have taken his kneecap off if it had connected. Only it didn't because his knee moved back and his hand came round in a scything arc that would have caught her across the eyes, except she ducked below it so that the edge of his hand did no more than ruffle her short dark hair like a dragonfly wing over a pond. It wasn't like ju-jitsu or anything else I'd ever seen but it took the breath away just watching. Part of the beauty was the intense concentration the two of them gave it, like Max's chess players. I don't think they even noticed I was there until by mutual agreement but without a word said they stopped, looked at each other and laughed the way people do when something's satisfied them. Then the woman, Kitty Dulcie, glanced in my direction, said something to the man and disappeared behind a screen. He came walking towards me, light as a lizard on his bare feet. Her brother, the other half of the music-hall act. He was a few inches taller and a few years older than Kitty but had the same dark hair and eyes, and an intensity about him that made the air hum. When he spoke, it was a North-of-Ireland voice like hers, quiet but hard-edged.

'Good morning. Were you wanting lessons?'

From the way he said it, embattled already, he knew I wasn't. Whatever she'd said to him had been a warning.

'I'd like to speak to Kitty Dulcie.'

'What do you want with her?'

'I believe she knew a relative of mine, Verona North.'

Something happened in those dark eyes. I wasn't sure what it was, but I didn't like it.

'Is that so?'

He just stood there, not moving. It was like trying to talk to a slab of slate.

'So, if you'll excuse me, please . . .'

170

I stepped past him, towards the screen. He probably knew a dozen different ways of sending me flying through the window and when I heard his bare footsteps padding behind me I thought it might happen. But I made it to the screen.

'Miss Dulcie, could you spare me a few minutes, please.'

She'd taken off the trousers of her pyjama suit and replaced them with a white pleated skirt. When she came out from behind the screen her face was expressionless and she gave no sign she'd seen me before.

'Do you remember a pupil at Argyll Place named Verona North?'

'Why are you asking?'

'She was my cousin's daughter. She's dead.'

Surely Edith Garrud would have told her that after my visit, but there was no reaction.

'I don't remember any of their names.'

'About your age, red-brown hair, a beginner.'

'They mostly were.'

'She was one of the people Vincent Hergest talked to.'

'He talked to a lot of people.'

No sign there of being impressed by the great man.

'You went to his party on Wednesday.'

'So did a lot of people.'

Her voice stopped just short of being insulting, the way that her brother, standing a few steps behind me, stopped just short of being threatening.

'She stopped going to classes in April. Do you know why?'

She shrugged. 'A lot of them give up when they're afraid they might get hurt.'

'That doesn't sound like Verona.'

'I told you, I don't remember her.'

'I think you do.' Silence. 'Well, if you do remember anything at all, I'd be grateful if you'd get in touch with

171

me.' I gave her my card and, remembering what Edith had said about her liking money, added, 'I'd pay you for your time.'

'She's told you, she doesn't remember.'

The brother, from behind me. Kitty had taken my card between her fingertips. Now she opened them and let it fall to the floor. I turned and walked over what felt like a long expanse of bare boards to the door, opened it and stepped out into the yard. Why should Kitty bother to lie about somebody who should have been no more than a passing acquaintance? Some people panicked at the thought of being associated with an inquiry into a suspicious death, but that didn't apply here. Kitty had no reason to think Verona's death was suspicious and she didn't strike me as a type who panicked. She liked money, but she'd thrown away the chance of earning some. If she'd known . . . A bang and a crash of metal stopped me in my tracks. I was in the middle of the scrapyard, alongside the remains of what looked like a corrugated-iron chapel. At first I thought a piece of metal had fallen against another, and stopped and looked around, simply curious. Another bang. It's funny how the mind can be so reluctant to acknowledge that inexplicable things are happening. Probably a workman dropping something on a building site, lots of them round here. But an instinct quicker than the mind made me turn and, as I turned, something flew past my ear and punched a hole through a rusty corrugated-iron sheet, so close to me that little flakes of rust landed on my jacket. The brother was standing outside the red-brick building, with what looked like a Winchester rifle on his shoulder.

I shouted, 'Are you shooting at me?' Which was admittedly not one of the more intelligent questions of my career, but my mind was still trying to catch up. For answer he sent

172

another shot into the corrugated iron, this time about an arm's length above my head.

'Leave my sister alone. Kitty doesn't want to talk to you, understood?'

The voice wasn't loud, but it carried.

I said, 'If this is meant to be an advertisement for your music-hall act, I'm not interested.'

The gate at the end of the yard opened and the man I'd asked for directions came through it. He looked at me, then at Kitty's brother standing there with the rifle and went back through the gate before I could ask him for help. I couldn't blame him. I was capable, just, of standing there, even talking to Kitty's brother without my voice shaking. What I couldn't do was turn my back on him and walk to the open gate. Then there was a rumbling of wheels and the man came back through the gate, this time pushing his handcart loaded with bits of broken guttering. If they'd been gold bullion I couldn't have been happier to see him. He trundled the cart towards me, seemingly not in the least put out.

'Found them then, miss? He been showing you his trick shooting?'

'Yes, something like that.'

'Good shot, he is. Put a hole through a cigarette card blindfold.'

'Good thing I'm not a cigarette card.'

'What was that, miss?'

I glanced round. The brother and his rifle had disappeared, presumably back into the studio.

'Nothing.'

'Lucky, you were.'

'Lucky?'

'I mean, most people have to pay to see him, don't they?'

I agreed I was lucky, wished him good morning and walked

to the gate. The dog was still worrying its bone. The work-men opposite were unloading scaffolding poles from a cart with a noise very like rifle shots. And that was meant to be the easy bit of the day.

Chapter Sixteen

LIVERPOOL STREET HAS NEVER BEEN ONE OF MY favourite places to start a journey. Stations seem to take on the characters of their destinations. At Victoria, for instance, you can almost catch the whiff of coffee from the street cafés in Paris or pines by the Mediterranean. Liverpool Street, even on summer evenings, always feels to me as if a blast from the cold and foggy North Sea has found its way down the lines and into London to mix with soot and pigeon droppings. All it can promise you on the journey are views of the flatlands and slow rivers crawling between muddy banks to a grey sea. The boat connections link to serious northern places – The Hook, Rotterdam, Antwerp – nowhere to make your heart beat faster. The passengers too have a grey, dour look to them. You know they're mostly travelling for business or, if not, then for a very sober kind of pleasure.

I got there soon after seven, nearly an hour and a half before the train left, with no luggage but a shoulder bag, and my mind still going round in circles. I was at least half-persuaded that Bill was right, that the answers I wanted were somewhere else and I was wasting my time. When in doubt, go on. The smell of cheap pies from the buffet made me glad I wasn't hungry but I went in, sat at a conspicuous table in the middle of the room and lingered over a coffee. As far as I could see, nobody was at all interested. I strolled over to the W.H. Smith stall and collected an armful of papers and magazines. When I paid and stowed them away in my bag, I made a point of letting it flap open to show the brown paper package inside because there was a man in a trilby hat loitering near the counter. He didn't react which wasn't surprising because a few minutes later a plump woman with three children, a porter and about a dozen suitcases collected him and took him away. I was already feeling like the girl in the song who took her harp to a party and nobody asked her to play.

By that time a queue was already forming at the barrier. There were a group on a weekend excursion to Holland in the care of a Thomas Cook courier; two or three families with armfuls of babies; an invalid in a Bath chair with uniformed nurse and valet in attendance; a German husband and wife with what looked like all their worldly goods, down to kettle, cushions and a picture in a frame almost as tall as they were; and a few young sailors in uniform, probably on their way to join their ships at Harwich and Ipswich. Apart from them, the queue included just six men on their own. Two of them were elderly so I ruled those out, as most of the watchers had been in their thirties or forties. One was plump and too prosperous, with a rolled umbrella and dispatch case, another in his early twenties, so thin and languid that it seemed only a matter of time before somebody came and grew beans round him. The two remaining were both possibles, although I'd seen neither of them before. One, in his late forties, had a retired sergeant-major look and a waxed moustache. The other was dark, in his twenties and twitchy, definitely waiting for something besides the train. I joined the back of the queue and kept an eye on both of them. A couple more sailors and a pale girl who'd been crying arrived just after me. We all of us waited glumly while the babies yelled, the girl gave an occasional sniff and pigeons scavenged round our feet for non-existent crumbs. I thought how nice it would be to see someone I knew, like Weaver or Yellow Boater or even our homely Detective Constable Gradey.

A quarter of an hour before the train was due out a ticket collector opened the barrier and started grudgingly letting us through. As we shuffled forward a beautiful girl came flying up to the twitchy man and they hugged as if they'd been apart for years. The sailors behind me whistled, a few older women tut-tutted and I mentally crossed another one off my list. When I got to the barrier the inspector took my ticket, punched it and handed it back without a second glance. I'd considered going first class to be easier to find, but all that open space round me wouldn't give them the cover they needed. You had to understand their habits, like rearing pheasants. I walked halfway down the platform, got in at the door of a second-class coach and went along the corridor looking for an empty compartment. It turned out to be too much to ask. Although the train was going to be far from crowded, every compartment had at least one person in it. I glimpsed the sergeant-major sitting back smoking a pipe, looking uncurious and at ease with the world. A little way on from him was a compartment with only a man and woman sitting face to face in the window seats. I opened the door, said good afternoon and settled into one of the seats by the corridor with my bag on my knees. From there, I watched people as they came hurrying along the platform behind their porters, steam from the engine wafting round them. Then, a few minutes to half past, the late arrivals came sprinting, outdistancing the porters who refused to do anything as undignified as break into a run. Doors all along the train slammed like . . . like rifle shots into corrugated iron. Don't think about that now. Concentrate on what's happening out there. Only a minute to go. The guard stood with his green flag furled, whistle in mouth. A man and his suitcases were bundled in at the door nearest to the barrier. Then the green flag went up, the whistle blew. The couplings made their groaning, wincing sound as the strain came on them and we started moving, first at walking pace then picking up speed. Our carriage must have been nearly at the end of the platform when the brakes came on with a suddenness that sent us rocking forward in our seats and brought a bag thumping off the overhead rack. There was shouting from the platform at the barrier end.

'It's all wrong,' the woman in the window seat said. 'If people can't get here on time they shouldn't let them on.'

The man said nothing. I could see he was trying to wedge his false teeth back and looked away to let him get on with it. After a minute or two we started moving again. The platform fell away and there was only an expanse of rails shining in the sun, sooty brick walls on either side. The door from the corridor opened.

'Excuse me, would you mind if I took one of these seats?'

A clergyman, quite young, curate probably. Surely even the watchers wouldn't . . .

'I was in one of the compartments back there but there was a man with a most dreadful pipe and it does so aggravate my chest.'

He smiled and settled on the seat opposite me, considerately halfway between the window and the corridor to give us as much space as possible. The other man anchored his false teeth and stowed the bag back on the rack.

'My sister's got a weak chest too,' the woman said. 'Can't stand even the sniff of a pipe.'

You could tell she felt that even a junior clergyman raised

the tone of the compartment. We were moving faster now, the grey-and-yellow-brick terraced houses of Bethnal Green flicking past the window. I got a magazine out of my bag and skimmed through it. There was a photograph of the Archduke Franz Ferdinand, linked to a forthcoming visit to Sarajevo. I looked up and found the curate staring in my direction. He gave an apologetic little grimace and looked away.

'You're welcome to a look at the magazine,' I said. 'I've got plenty of other things.'

He thanked me and took it clumsily, committed to trying to read it whether that was what he wanted or not. We rattled past small factories and a few grimy rivers, then into open country after Brentwood with the fields managing to heave themselves into the corrugations that pass for hills in these parts and sheep grazing. We stopped at Chelmsford where a lot of people got out, including the couple in the window seats, leaving me and the curate alone in the carriage. When the train started again he gave me back the magazine.

'Thank you. Very interesting.' Again, the apologetic little grimace.

'Are you going all the way to Harwich?' I said.

'Oh no, I'm getting out at Colchester.' Slightly shocked, as if I'd suggested some form of dissipation. Then, 'Are you going to Harwich?'

'I'm booked through to the Hook of Holland.'

'Do you know people over there?'

'A few.'

By now I was sure he wasn't my fish, so I threw him back into silence and hid behind *The Times*. I'd told him I was booked through to the Hook of Holland, as I try not to lie unless people deserve it. The ticket was in my bag, but that wasn't the same thing as going there. I was almost certain

179

that the initials would move in on me before the boat sailed. On one hand, they might think it useful to follow me on to foreign soil and catch me delivering a package to my supposed accomplices. On the other, what could they do about it in Holland, Germany or Switzerland? Evidence of an intention to go abroad would be enough for them and they'd have that as soon as I walked through the customs shed at Harwich. There'd been an outside chance that they'd confront me at Liverpool Street but that hadn't suited them. If they were on the train with me they must deliberately be keeping their distance. It would be easy enough to find me if they wanted me. From their point of view, it might be easier to wait until Harwich.

We stopped for a long time at Colchester and took on water. The curate wished me *bon voyage* and left. I saw the sergeant-major figure marching along the platform towards the exit, which meant every one of my guesses had been wrong so far. When we pulled away from the platform I still had the compartment to myself. By now the heat was making me drowsy. I got up and walked along the corridor, peering shamelessly into compartments as I passed, but I knew I'd entirely lost faith in my ability to spot them. A few of the compartments had blinds drawn on the corridor side against the sun that was already well down in the west. It was quarter past nine by my watch. We were due into Parkeston Quay at Harwich at five to ten. My stomach churned. I was in for it now, with no stops scheduled between Colchester and Harwich. Even if you've been running around inviting the beast to pounce, it's hard to look forward to it. I went over in my mind for the hundredth time what I'd say, what I had to do to make them understand. We started slowing down. Surely not there already? I let down the window, smelt salt in the air and heard seagulls. There were fields of long grass stroked sideways by the breeze off the sea, gleaming like a lion's mane in the setting sun. We stopped alongside a platform. The sign said 'Manningtree'. Nearly journey's end, but we weren't meant to stop there. We were on the estuary of the River Stour with Harwich Harbour at the end of it. I hung out of the window, trying to see if there was anything happening. A few heads were looking out of other windows. Nobody got in or out. There was nothing but the seagulls and the bumps and clanks of machinery cooling. I went back in the compartment and waited, wondering why we'd stopped there, looking out of the window on to the track. After a while there were steps along the corridor, loud and heavy, breaking the hush that settles inside a stopped train. The steps came to a halt at the open doorway of my compartment.

'Excuse me, madam, are you for Harwich?'

A middle-aged ticket inspector, forehead sweating from his heavy uniform, a hat several sizes too small for him balanced on top of his head like a pat of butter on a teacake.

'Yes.'

'Train splits here, madam. This half goes on to Ipswich. Back half goes to Harwich.'

'They didn't say anything about this at Liverpool Street.'

'I'm sorry, madam.'

The regulation satchel slung at his waist was new, with a powerful smell of leather coming off it. He looked at me and waited. His face was surprisingly tanned for a man who worked inside but it had a blank, official look as if he always did what he was told. In his schooldays he'd probably been the ink monitor.

'May I take your luggage, madam?'

The hand he stretched towards my bag was tanned like

his face and looked stronger than it needed to be for punching tickets.

'No thank you. I'll carry it myself.'

He stood back to let me out then followed me along the corridor. A door to the platform stood open.

'That way, madam.'

'Can't we just walk along the corridor?' It's such a suffocating feeling, handing yourself over to other people, that I was already kicking against it.

'They've already uncoupled the carriages, madam.'

He said 'madam' with a gulping sound. I was getting tired of it. We walked side by side down the platform. A few people inside the train looked at us curiously.

'What about these other people?'

'All going on to Ipswich, madam.'

He was right about the carriages being uncoupled. There was a gap between the main body of the train and the last two, both first class. The back one of the two had blinds pulled down over the windows. I looked up the line to the north and saw a cloud of steam and under it an engine shunting backwards towards us.

'That's the one for Harwich, is it?'

'Yes, madam.'

I nearly undid all the work there and then because I was so angry at being taken for a fool. My geography for this part of the world wasn't the strongest, but I did know which way the sea was. Off to my right, to the east. If the engine backed on to the last two carriages of this train we'd be pointing at right angles to it, northwards. I tightened my grip on my bag, ready to whirl round and run back into the part of the train I'd just left. He wasn't holding me. He couldn't wrestle with me on the platform with a dozen or so people leaning out of windows to watch. Only sanity said at the last minute: 'Well, you wanted them and you've got them.' I walked on. He opened the nearest door in the two severed carriages and held it for me. When I went inside he climbed after me, opened the door to a compartment and again held it for me.

I said, 'My ticket's only second class.'

'That doesn't matter, madam.'

The last shred of doubt went. I tried to look as if I believed him.

'We'll be going in a minute or two, madam.'

Then he went away down the corridor. A whistle blew and I watched through my stationary window as the rest of the train moved away from the platform, turned right at a junction and headed for Harwich and the Hook of Holland ferry that would steam into the North Sea minus at least one passenger. Then steam from the backward-shunting engine clouded the window and there were the usual jolts and clankings as our two carriages were joined on to it. The ink monitor hadn't been far out. We moved off in just over five minutes.

It was a conventionally luxurious first-class carriage, highly polished dark wood panels, three broad seats on either side with comfortable armrests in between and framed photographs of Clacton and Great Yarmouth above them, silver-grey upholstery that smelled only very faintly of soot. We drew slowly out of Manningtree then picked up speed quickly, which wasn't surprising as the engine had only two carriages to draw. At first we went alongside the estuary with its salt flats and flocks of swans in water turned to a sheet of copper by the setting sun, then inland through deep cuttings between birch woods with the dusk gathering. It was an easy run on a summer evening. All that was wrong with it was that there was no sign of any other passengers. I got up and walked along the corridor to the front of the carriage and there wasn't a man, woman or dog anywhere. When I walked back to where the two carriages joined, intending to check the other one, I found the ink monitor standing there in the shadows, blocking my way. If I'd asked him he might have moved but I doubted it.

'Everything all right, madam?'

He was less anxious now, rather pleased with himself in fact.

'When do we arrive?'

'Soon be there, madam.'

I went back to my seat. The fields were giving way to houses, first just a scattering of them, then terraces. The train started slowing down. We were coming into somewhere, Ipswich probably, where a reception committee would be waiting. What I couldn't understand was why they were going to so much trouble. If they'd wanted to arrest me they could have done it at any time from Liverpool Street onwards. The expense and trouble of this – the Harwich express halted, this train to ourselves – was far out of proportion to anything I'd started, like walking through an ordinary doorway and finding yourself in the ogre's castle. We stopped for a few minutes on a raised piece of track with sidings to the left and a row of terraced houses below, soft gas-light glowing in their windows. Half past ten, the sun down, trees and buildings turning into dark shapes against the afterglow of a long summer's day. When we started moving again we took a turn to the left and crawled slowly across a dark river on a single-track metal bridge then into a large siding with expanses of rails gleaming on either side and mountains of coal where the rails ended. We moved alongside a rough platform made of old railway sleepers that looked as if it was meant for

184

railway mechanics rather than passengers and stopped there with a long sigh of steam from the engine. I went out to the corridor. The ink monitor was standing there and I could smell the sweat coming off him.

'Any minute now, madam.'

He heaved the words out painfully. I moved towards the door and put my hand on the leather strap that let the window down, knowing very well I wouldn't be allowed to get out but wanting to make something happen. There were heavy footsteps from the carriage I hadn't been allowed to go into and when I looked round reinforcements had arrived. Two men in plain clothes were standing behind the ink monitor. One of them was Yellow Boater, dressed today in pinstripes and bowler and carrying a lamp that sent shadows darting and diving along the corridor. The other man I hadn't seen before. He was older than the other two, tall and thin, with hair more grey than dark, and the look of a senior civil servant or a university don. He didn't stand up straight enough to be a retired military man but crouched slightly, heron-like, looking down his nose over half-glasses.

He said to Yellow Boater, 'Do you identify her?'

Yellow Boater nodded. 'She's the one. Will you leave that door alone and hand over your bag, please, Miss Bray.'

'Who are you?'

Yellow Boater glanced at the heron, who nodded him permission to answer.

'I'm Sergeant Stone.'

'Police or Army?'

He didn't reply. The heron said, 'And my name's Burton, from the War Office. Shall we sit down?'

He nodded towards the compartment behind me. I went in and sat down, and the two new arrivals followed. The invitation obviously didn't apply to the ink monitor, who stayed

185

outside in the corridor. Burton sat down opposite me, looking at me through his glasses as if I were a new sub-species of something and nodded to Sergeant Stone, alias Yellow Boater. He put down his lamp on one of the armrests opposite so that it was shining mostly on my face, pulled down the blinds on both sides of the compartment then came to sit alongside me, nearly touching.

'Your bag, please.'

I handed it over. Stone glanced again at Burton and got another nod. It was clear that the older man was in charge. Stone took everything out of it slowly, putting each item down on the seat beside him – the papers and magazines, a purse with some small change, a notebook and pencil, a comb (I'd wondered where that comb had got to). Burton held his hand out for the notebook and looked through it. I could have told him that it contained nothing more interesting than notes from a talk I'd been to about the first eight years of women's franchise in Finland but I let him puzzle it out for himself.

'What's this?'

He was frowning at a page with a scrawled pencil diagram. I held out my hand to take the book but he snatched it away and let me look from a safe distance.

'Oh, that. I was trying to explain the printing press to somebody.'

He gave me a look as if he didn't believe me. Oddly, I didn't quite believe myself when I said it, though it was quite true. The business of the empty train, of keeping me isolated in a siding, was making me feel as if I had an infectious disease and that disease was guilt. Burton put my notebook in his pocket.

'Then there's this, sir.'

Stone was holding out the brown-paper packet, away from me at arm's length as if scared I might make a grab for it.

Burton took it in his fingertips as if picking up a soiled hand-kerchief and turned it over.

'Is this your property?'

'Of course.'

He unknotted the string, folded back the paper. It was oddly reassuring to see *Three Men in a Boat* with the squashed peach stain on the cover from the day I took it punting, but he didn't seem pleased at all. He looked at me.

'Some kind of joke, Miss Bray?'

'Quite a lot of jokes. Haven't you read it?'

He riffled through the pages.

'If you're looking for pinpricks or words underlined I don't think you'll find them.'

He ignored me, looked at Stone and commanded, 'Jacket pockets.'

Even Yellow Boater seemed startled. He stood up. I stood up too, took my jacket off, handed it to him, sat down again. I thought he looked a little shame-faced but he rummaged through the pockets. Result, one handkerchief, a stub of pencil, a wallet with two five-pound notes and my ticket. Burton pounced on it.

'I see you're booked through to the Hook of Holland.'

'I think you knew that already.'

'With what purpose?'

'Meeting somebody.'

'Who?'

'You.'

Up to then Burton had been cool. Now he was angry or perhaps he'd been angry all along and was just letting it show.

'So you think spying's a joking matter.'

'If you're accusing me of spying, yes it is a joke.'

'Sergeant Stone has identified you as a person who broke into certain premises a week ago.'

'If you mean the room over the chart shop, yes I did.'

The two men looked at each other. I wasn't supposed to admit it so easily.

'And you also admit that you're now travelling to meet somebody on the Continent. I'm asking you again, who is it?'

'And I'm telling you again, you. It didn't have to be on the Continent and you needn't have bothered with the private train. I'd have been happy to see you at your office in London if I'd known where to find you.'

'How did you know about me?'

Just a touch of conceit there, so perhaps even people whose work is secrecy like to be famous. I had to disappoint him.

'I didn't even know you existed until you walked in here. When I say "you" I mean anybody who knows what's going on. I don't care if you call yourself Special Branch or the Secret Service or MO5. I just want to talk to whoever Verona North was working for.'

The name hung in the air. Neither of them gave any sign they'd heard it before.

'Let's call a truce,' I said. 'I'm not a spy. If you want to waste your time having me followed, that's your decision. I want to know who killed Verona. Whoever she was working for should want to know too.'

Burton looked at me for a long time and I couldn't read anything in his eyes. They were strange-coloured eyes, bright metallic grey like a new galvanised bath tub. He stood up.

'Stay here.'

He was talking to Stone, not me. Then he opened the door and went out, stepping past the ink monitor, closing the door behind him. Stone too looked surprised at the suddenness of it. I stood up and put my jacket back on to prove to myself I had that much freedom at least and listened

188

to Burton's footsteps going along the corridor. No sound of an outside door opening, so whoever he was going to consult must be in the second carriage with the blinds drawn. Experimentally, I put my hand on the door of the compartment.

Stone jumped up. 'Where are you going?'

'I thought I might take a walk outside.'

'I'd rather you didn't.'

'Why not?'

'I just shouldn't advise it.'

I sat down. Whatever Bill might think, I could take advice sometimes.

Chapter Seventeen

I HATE BEING CLOSED IN. ONE WAY AND another I've had quite
a lot of it but it still makes me jumpy and when the minutes
dragged out into half an hour it was hard not to let Stone,
alias Yellow Boater, see my uneasiness. We were a parody of
any delay on any rail journey. There was I, re-reading by lamplight a magazine feature I'd read twice already. Stone was sitting
opposite me with a little black-covered notebook open on his
knee and fountain pen in hand like a man composing a letter
of complaint to the rail company board of directors. He'd
drawn up the blind enough to show the back of the ink monitor standing conscientiously outside in his railway uniform. I
wished somebody would tell him he could get rid of the satchel
and ridiculous cap. I wished too that I could get a closer look
at Stone's notebook. At first I thought it might be intended
to unsettle me, letting me know I was under observation all
the time, but when I did manage a sideways glance I saw only
a column of figures before he scowled and tilted it away. Our
siding between the coal heaps was peaceful but from a distance
you could hear the town going on with its normal life – trains
whistling from the station on the other side of the river, motor-
lorries on our side, a cow mooing not far away. The cow
surprised me because we were almost certainly somewhere in
the middle of town, then I thought that there were docks at
Ipswich, probably with cattle lairage and our sidings might be

near them. After forty minutes footsteps came back along the corridor, slow and deliberate. I didn't know why, but something told me the person on his way wasn't in a negotiating mood. One look at Burton's face when he came back in proved I was right. The metallic eyes were colder than ever. He sat down next to Stone, putting them both opposite me. Stone must have sensed the atmosphere had changed too because he flipped over his notebook to a clean page.

'Not yet,' Burton said to him, without taking his eyes off me. Then, to me, 'You mentioned Verona North. What do you know about her?'

'She was the daughter of my cousin, Commodore Benjamin North. She came to London about six months ago to work for the secret services. I think her task was to identify students, especially foreign ones, who might be spies or dangers to the public in some way, but you'd know more about that than I do.'

'Go on.'

'Am I right, so far?'

'You're not here to ask the questions.'

'As far as I'm concerned that's the main point of being here. That – and suggesting we might work together.'

Stone opened his eyes wide and looked at Burton, but the older man's expression hadn't changed.

'Work together?'

'Yes. I want to know who killed her and I assume you do too. I might know things you don't and I'm sure you know things I don't. Doesn't it make sense to pool resources rather than your wasting time following me?'

It had seemed reasonable when I planned this. It even sounded reasonable to me as I said it, but when I looked at Burton I knew I might as well be preaching vegetarianism to tigers.

191

'I understand the verdict of the inquest was suicide while the balance of mind was disturbed.'

So he – or the unseen person he'd gone to consult – had known something about Verona before I mentioned her.

'Yes, but there were things the inquest jury didn't know.'

'Such as?'

'Less than a month before she died she wrote to an old schoolfriend. She said she had a lot to tell her but the friend was not to worry if she didn't hear from her for some time. For more than two weeks after that she was missing. Her friends and family still don't know where she was. Only the people she was working for would know that.'

'And who, in your opinion, was Miss North working for?'

'I told you. You. Some part of Special Branch or the secret services. For goodness sake, even if there are a lot of you, somebody must know what everybody's doing.'

Burton smiled, though it looked more like a crack in the metalwork than a smile. 'I wonder about that sometimes, don't you, Sergeant Stone?' It was Stone's turn not to react and Burton's smile had been welded over by the time he turned back to me.

'So you have no idea what she was doing in the weeks before her death?'

'I don't know, but I can guess. She thought she'd discovered a person or a group of people who were foreign spies or dangerous revolutionaries. You, or somebody like you, let her take the risk of trying to join them to find out more. And she was right – so right that they killed her.'

Silence, except for a steam engine not far away. It sounded as if this one were on our side of the river, probably coming from the docks towards these sidings. As an exchange of information this wasn't going well. At least, that was my impression until Burton sighed, leaned forward and started talking.

192

'Very well, Miss Bray. You want to know what happened to Verona North. I can't tell you with certainty, because there's probably only one person on earth who knows with certainty, but I'll tell you what I think happened and you can tell me where I've gone wrong.'

I stared at him. This was too easy. Stone was looking surprised too.

'Let's take it that you're right, that your cousin's daughter was a brave and patriotic young woman who, young as she was, wanted to play a part in defending her country, as her father and brother were doing.'

I nodded. Verona deserved that tribute at least.

'Let's take it that you might even be right that she came to London and became a student for that purpose. After all, many anarchists and revolutionaries are young people. They're more likely to trust somebody of their own age than a person like Sergeant Stone here.'

He waited. I said nothing. In spite of his reasonable tone I had a feeling that things were going wrong.

'And, of course, Miss North would have an advantage. She has a relative who is already well known among – what shall we say – people who are not exactly friendly to this country's government.'

'What are you implying? Am I supposed to be a dangerous revolutionary, a traitor?'

'I'm not implying anything, but you must agree you have a record that speaks for itself.'

'I'm not a revolutionary, unless wanting the Vote and not wanting a war make me one. And if you're thinking of that bomb in Lloyd George's house last year, I had nothing to do with planting it.'

Which was true but I shouldn't have said it. It was an acknowledgement I was on the defensive. I heard my voice

193

rising, felt sweat trickling and knew he was aware of it. He raised his eyebrows and went on in the same level voice.

'So it would be quite likely that Miss North, on coming to London, would make some contact with her father's cousin.'

'As you almost certainly know already we did meet and she did ask me about various political groups. None of them was dangerous and I'm sure all the details are on your wretched file cards.'

'Ah yes, those file cards. You've admitted to breaking into the premises. Why?'

'Verona had been seen going in, not by me, by one of her friends. I wanted to know what she'd been doing there in case it had any bearing on why she died.'

'Any other reason?'

'No.'

'Are you sure of that?'

'I said no.'

'It wasn't because you wanted to know what we had on record about yourself and some of your friends?'

I wanted to shout at him, but managed to keep my voice down. 'No. I didn't even know what the place was until I got inside.'

'But you were angry, weren't you, Miss Bray, when you found out what she'd been doing?'

'Yes.'

'Did you let her know how angry you were?'

'What?'

I stared, at a loss. The two of them stared back.

'How could I? By the time I knew what she'd been doing, she was dead.'

'You're sure of that?'

I started shouting at him that of course I was sure, then

I saw where this was heading and went quiet. My silence sounded even more guilty than shouting.

Burton said, with a cog-wheel purr in his voice, 'Yes, Miss Bray?'

I said nothing. He went on talking, but this time there was a horrible confidence about him, like a chess player seeing the end of the game in his opponent's first mistake.

'I was telling you my theory about what happened to Verona North. I'll go on. She came to London. The two of you met and talked. Foolishly, from your point of view, you told her more than you should have done about the activities of some of your friends. Perhaps, who knows, you were trying to impress her. Then somehow, and this is a part of the story you'll know much better than I do, you find out that she's not on your side, as you'd assumed. That she is, in fact, on what you'd think of as the other side. In your place, Miss Bray, I'd have felt very angry about that.'

I'd stopped sweating. I was cold now with shock and fear, not believing that I'd actually gone looking for this. From his expression, I guessed the shock and fear were showing but couldn't do anything about it.

'You felt angry. Guilty too, probably, at betraying your friends. It was too late to do anything about that, but there was one thing you could do. I don't suppose it was too difficult to decoy Miss North down to Devon. Some message about a family emergency, perhaps. You met her off the train. You had a syringe of morphine in your bag, probably that same bag you're holding now. Perhaps you borrowed a boat and rowed her up the estuary to the boathouse. Can you row, by the way? I'm sure you can.'

He was observant. I was clutching the bag like a lifebelt. He stopped talking and stared at me with the cold analytical kindness of a doctor looking down at a patient after an

195

operation. My fingers were rummaging in my bag, looking for the tear in the lining. I found what I was looking for, raised a hand to my mouth, bit and swallowed.

'Stop her.'

Stone grabbed my wrist, but he was too late. I slumped to the floor.

'Oh God, you should have been watching her!'

One of them trod on me in the hurry to get the door to the corridor open. Burton shouted, presumably to the ink monitor.

'Doctor! Get a doctor!'

The ink monitor started to ask where he'd get one, a reasonable question in the circumstances.

'A police station. Run.'

Stone was kneeling over me, trying to force my mouth open. Too many bad memories there from forcible feeding. His rotten luck. I let him get his fingers over my lower jaw then bit down as hard as I could. I heard and felt bone scrunch. He yelled and let go. I struggled to my feet – I think my knee made contact with his jaw but that wasn't intentional because he was out of the fight in any case. My bag and his black notebook were on the floor. I grabbed them, turned and found Burton standing in the doorway of the compartment and simply hurled myself at him. We both went down but I was up first, into the corridor then out of the door to the platform that the ink monitor had left open when he went for the doctor. I sat on the platform edge and slid down into the darkness under the train. There were shouting and running feet up above me and the sharp taste of peppermint in my mouth.

Chapter Eighteen

A LOT OF SHOUTING, BUT ONLY ONE MAN doing it. I recognised Burton's voice, gone high and sharp – from pain, I hoped. A pair of feet was thundering along the corridor over my head.

'Outside! She's outside!' Burton, out of the train now, yelling to Stone, still inside. Then, more loudly, 'Come back! Come back here!'

He couldn't be stupid enough to think I'd come when he called. It must be the ink monitor he wanted back, presumably sticking to the original order and running for a doctor. He hadn't seen me slipping under the train. It gave me the advantage for a little while but I couldn't see how I could use it, with Burton waiting for me on the platform. I was crouching between two sets of wheel axles, looking out at an expanse of rails between me and the coal heaps. If the sidings had been completely dark it would have improved the odds in my favour, but there was enough light coming from somewhere – possibly street lamps outside – to put a shine on the rails and make objects visible as dark shapes. I turned towards the platform, not worrying too much about making noise because the machinery was cooling with a troll orchestra of clanks, bumps and and little wheezing sounds, then I almost yelled when my shoulder came into contact with a pipe that

197

was scalding hot, even through clothes. There was a smell of hot oil or grease. Everything I touched or that touched me was sticky and something was clotted in my hair. Yet it was, in its clamorous way, almost peaceful under there, like being in a sea cave, as if you could let the world go by and rejoin it or not as you fancied. It was a pity some people had other ideas. Squinting up through the gap between train and platform edge I could see two dark columns that must be the legs of Burton on guard. Somebody was walking along the platform, so that meant two of them at least were outside and watching. Then somebody from inside the train shouted. I jumped and came into contact with the hot pipe again because it seemed to come from right overhead. It sounded like the voice of a man used to giving orders.

'Underneath. Look underneath.'

The man Burton had gone to consult. The man who sent him back to accuse me of murder. I dropped down on all fours and wriggled under the wheel axle and further down the train with no plan, just an instinctive urge to get away from the voice. It made things worse because on the other side of the axle was the gap between the two carriages with a metal step placed very conveniently for anybody coming down from the platform. I wriggled back under the axle, catching my hair on something, yanking it free and had hardly got clear of the gap before a foot came down on the step. Then Stone's voice, so close I could feel it vibrating in my head.

'Could you get the lantern, sir?'

With a badly bitten finger and probably an aching jaw, no wonder he was hesitating. He was facing away from me. I wriggled backwards in the direction I'd come from, making for the higher part where I could get back into a crouch at least, not wanting to be dragged out like a ferret from a rabbit hole. I'd been aware for some time of another noise, but with no attention to spare for it. Now it was getting louder and unmistakeable. Another train was coming into the siding.

It was moving slowly. I couldn't see it but I could smell the smoke and see the red glow from its firebox reflected in the rails. At first I cursed because it would stop me hearing what Stone and Burton were doing, but then I realised it might give me just the ghost of a chance. I got on hands and knees and put my head out on the side away from the platform. The back of a goods wagon was coming towards me, not much faster than walking pace. I made myself wait until it was almost on me, not wanting to give the driver a chance to brake if he happened to be leaning out of the cab and looking back, then pushed myself upright and half-ran, half-dived across the tracks in front of the wagon. I landed with my face on ballast, shins against the rail and an arm, still with the bag hanging on it, crushed under me. What got me upright, shaking and gasping, wasn't even Stone and the rest but the fear of my feet being sliced off by the train's wheels. It was a goods train, rusty with a lot of high-sided open carriages. Perhaps I could have got into one of them if I tried, but it was too much like a trap. With the goods train now screening me from the men on the platform I went running and stumbling across the tracks. If they'd seen what happened, the only start I'd have would be the time it took them to run behind the goods train. What I was counting on was that with Stone under the train and Burton and the mystery man looking out on the platform side they might not have seen.
At first I was tempted to make for the coal heaps, but that would be the first place they'd look and I would waste any advantage I might have. I looked along the tracks and saw

to my right tall brick warehouses and the glow of lamplight on open water. It was like seeing an open window instead of cage bars and I changed direction and went running along the tracks towards the glint of water, fearing at any moment to hear shouting, but the blessed goods train, still slowly shunting backwards, was screening me. The tracks went across a docks road. There were two motor-lorries parked on it, headlights on, loaded with flour sacks. I dodged in between them. A driver called out something. It sounded like a joke, certainly not an alarm, but I didn't wait to make sure. There was a wharf in front of me, ship masts to the right, sheds and warehouses to the left, new sounds and smells. One smell was especially strong. I put my foot on something that squished and recognised what it was. Cowpat. There was disturbed mooing in the air coming from one of the sheds, wisps of straw floating about. I walked along the wharf in the direction of the smell and the mooing, slowing down and trying to look as if I had a right to be there. Even at night men were working on the wharf, doing things with the boats or stacking crates by lamplight in the warehouses, all too busy to take any notice of a stranger. Still no tumult from the sidings. If my luck held, Burton and the rest would be hunting me through the coal heaps. I wondered if the mystery man in the train would be getting his hands dirty too and somehow didn't think so. I could see the cows now, black and white Friesians, heads poked over the rails that penned them into the shed. I stroked warm, muscular necks, made a narrow gap between a couple of rails and slipped inside the welcoming cow-smelling dimness.

The cows were remarkably tolerant. There was the occasional fresh outbreak of mooing as I stroked and shoved my way through them, but nothing loud enough to attract attention.

The far side of the shed, like the front, was open with only metal rails to keep the cows inside. Beyond was a concreted yard lit by a couple of gas lamps with a single-rail track running across it and half a dozen cattle wagons in position, then walls and a broad wooden gate closing off the yard on the far side. I leaned on the rails with white and black necks on either side, thinking. On the other side of the yard there might be a road. If there was a road I could get to the station. I had money in my pocket. Thanks to Stone and Burton I'd even re-discovered my comb. I could tidy myself up, go to the ticket office like any respectable passenger, take a ticket to . . . where? Not so easy. Burton was no fool and the unseen man who gave him orders even less so. They'd have men watching the station. I still had a ticket to the Hook of Holland in my pocket but they'd be watching the docks and the boats. Even if I did, by some miracle, manage to get on a train back to London, they'd be waiting for me at Liverpool Street. Things had changed in the train. I knew now that I'd stirred up something that was better left unstirred. Until this evening, in some odd misguided way, I'd *trusted* the watchers to stick to the rules. We had our differences but deep down I'd thought there were decencies we all accepted. If the initials had made a bad mistake and sent Verona to spy on people who killed her they'd want to know what happened, just as I did. It was only a matter of making them understand that and we'd be on the same side. I'd been wrong, so wrong that it looked as if I'd be marooned on the other side for all time. The world had changed in that siding by the docks. Some people – including the unseen man in the train – must know what really happened, who really killed Verona, and yet if it suited their purposes they'd hang me for it all the same. So I wouldn't be stepping into their welcoming arms at Liverpool Street, which left the question of where in the world I went from here. Certainly not into the town. Wandering around at getting on for midnight in a place I didn't know would be a sure way of getting arrested. The word would have gone out by now: dangerous female spy on the loose. They could be searching the docks in a matter of minutes, especially if they happened to speak to one of the lorry drivers who'd seen me heading there. Stowing away on one of the ships by the quay had its attractions if I could discover where it was heading. But I might easily end up in a German or Baltic port facing permanent exile, no friends, not much money, no hope of walking into a consulate and getting help.

Which left the cattle wagons. I shoved a couple of cows aside, squeezed between the railings and walked across the yard. The wagons smelt of clean straw, which was a good sign. The cows must have arrived by sea and would be travelling on somewhere in the morning, early probably. If I could get through the next six hours or so I could steal a ride with them – hoping for all our sakes that it wasn't to an abattoir. The wide doors were all open and the ramps down ready for loading. The wagon at the end was a different design, divided into three wide stalls inside, for horses not cattle. I walked up the ramp into the rustling darkness. There were worse places to sleep than on straw in a nice solid horsebox. I chose the stall at the far end, shuffled a pile of straw up against the wall and lay down with my jacket for a pillow. The doorway faced the cattle lairage and the quayside. There were still some lights on over by the ships, slow footsteps on the quay, a man in the distance whistling *Won't you come home Bill Bailey?*. For some reason that struck me as funny and I joined in under my breath. *I'll do the cooking, darling, I'll pay the rent, I know I've done you wro-o-ong*. Reaction, I suppose. I didn't sleep; I was expecting any moment to see a policeman's lantern coming from the direction of the quay or hear footsteps on the other side of the wagons. At around four the rectangle of sky through the doorway was light and the cattle in the lairage were getting restless, shifting about and mooing. Later buckets clanked and I supposed somebody was bringing them water. By that time there were other sounds, men calling good morning to each other, a machine starting up. Quite soon they'd be loading up the cows and, presumably, horses although I hadn't seen any so far. All night I'd wondered how not to be discovered while that was going on. The question was urgent now and I still had no answer. I was combing straw out of my hair – though goodness knows why I was bothering – when the gate in the wall on the far side of the yard opened. I heard it dragging back, then a man's voice shouting. He sounded angry. I jumped up and looked out through a ventilation slit.

'Will you stop that, you daft bitch. Stop that!'

The voice, in a strong Suffolk accent, was coming from outside the gate. Then the man came through the gate, wearing a tweed jacket, gaiters and flat cap, leading a grey cob by the reins. She was behaving sedately enough, so the problem must be whatever was on the end of the halter rope in his other hand. He tugged, swore some more and a thing about the size of a German Shepherd dog came bucking and whinnying through the gateway. If I'd any sympathy to spare the man would have had it. Shetland ponies can be little devils.

A voice very near me, from somewhere along the line of wagons, said, 'Shall I take the other one then?'

He must have come from the direction of the cattle lairage while I was watching the first man. I ducked down behind the partition. No chance of running for it now. The man with the cob and pony had to cross the tracks to get to the side with the loading ramp and the second man walked over to help him. There was a skittering of hooves on ballast, some calming words, more cursing. Only the cob and the Shetland as far as I could make out and three stalls in the wagon. If I were the groom, I'd put a horse at either end and leave the middle stall empty as a buffer between them. I grabbed my bag and burrowed under the straw in the middle stall. The hooves came to a halt by the ramp.

'We'll get her in first, then the little bugger might go in quietly. Hold on while I loosen the girth.'

'You travelling with them?'

'Nah, thank god. They're only going as far as Shenfield and being met there.'

Two lots of good news. Shenfield had a railway station and was back in the direction of London. A heavy hoof hit the bottom of the ramp. Squinting through the straw I saw four feathery grey fetlocks, a pair of dusty boots and the bottoms of trousers tied with binder twine.

'Put her at the end, shall I?'

They went past me into the far stall. A ring clinked as the man tied a halter rope to it then the boots went away and down the ramp. The grey cob whinnied then urinated in a steady ammoniac stream that ran under the partition and over the floor where I was lying. The sounds from outside suggested that the Shetland wasn't coming quietly. It took the two of them to haul it up the ramp then, blessedly, into the stall at the other end. By that time, I don't think they'd have bothered if a baby rhinoceros were in the middle stall. The boots and the gaiters went back down the ramp, the ramp went up, the horizontal bars that held it in place banged home. As the two walked away the one who'd brought the horses into the yard was asking where a man could get a drink at this time of the morning because he reckoned he bloody well deserved it. So did I.

Soon after that the cows were loaded into the cattle wagons. The jolting and mooing made even the quiet cob fidget and sent the Shetland diving backwards and forwards on its halter rope like a horizontal yo-yo.

'All right, Molly. All right, Devil.'

I had to call them something. More to the point I'd found some more mints inside the torn lining of my bag. I offered them one each. They took them and crunched, the cob delicately, the pony with a snatch that nearly had the skin off my palm.

'That will have to do as my fare,' I told them. 'I shan't be in your way.'

Nobody would hear me over the noise the cows were making. I found some dry straw and settled down on it feeling boneless with relief. Some light came through ventilation slats on both sides. There was a feeling of security, closed there in the dimness with the animals. My breathing and heartbeats slowed down and for a while I didn't think about anything. Bars clanged into place on the cattle wagons. The train rocked as an engine was shunted into us and coupled on. The mooing rose to a crescendo and we were moving slowly, past the backs of the warehouses, jolting across the road then clattering back over the river on the metal bridge into sidings on the other side. We stayed there some time, more than half an hour, and from the sounds outside and occasional juddering and bumpings I guessed that other wagons were being added to our train. It was hot and the air was heavy with the smell of cow and horse dung, straw and coal dust. I'd have given pounds for a glass of water. At every shout or crunch of steps outside I expected the door to fly open, and ended up quivering and sweating worse than the pony. A lurch, a blast of steam and we were moving again. I looked out through the ventilation slats then ducked

205

down. There was a policeman in uniform standing on the edge of the sidings. He had his back to us, but it was an odd place for a policeman to be unless they were hunting somebody. I stayed crouched in the straw until the train settled to a speed and rhythm that suggested we were back on a main line. When I looked out we were heading south through a wooded cutting that opened out on to fields, and my heart started to slow down. I should be safe now until Shenfield, which as far as I remembered was about two-thirds of the way down Essex.

It was a short but slow journey. We seemed to be a goods train of lowly status, because we went past stations but had long waits in between them to let faster trains through. Fields and creeks slid past. The horses dozed and nodded, shifting their weight with the jolting of the train. We passed Manningtree with no incident this time, picked up more wagons at Colchester and went on our unhurried way through Chelmsford. The calm was a mixed blessing though, because it gave me time to think about how much worse things had got since I'd travelled up this line yesterday evening. I was a murder suspect on the run. I couldn't go home, or make contact with my friends or even get money out of a bank. It was partly my own stupidity to blame, but only partly. That syringe and morphine had been planted in my work basket before I took it into my head to turn the tables on the initials. The idea that it might be useful to accuse me of Verona's murder must have been in somebody's mind almost from the start. As long as the verdict of suicide was unchallenged, that wasn't necessary. But I was challenging that verdict by asking questions, so the plan was coming into effect. Somebody in all this had a cold tactician's mind. I didn't know who that somebody was, but I guessed I'd been just one railway carriage away from him last night in the sidings. The puzzle was, why hadn't he accepted my offer? If Verona had been killed by spies, surely it was in his interest to find them rather than plant the guilt on me? The only answer must be that the stakes of the game were so high that her death, or mine come to that, didn't matter.

'What have I got into? And how do I get out of it?'

The cob turned a sympathetic eye on me. I rummaged in my bag for more mints and found an unexpected shape. It wasn't until then that I remembered that I'd come away with one pathetic trophy – the notebook of Yellow Boater, otherwise known as Sergeant Stone. I delivered the mints then sat down on the straw for a look at it. There were stubs of pages at the front, showing that quite a lot had been torn out. The remaining ones were blank, except yesterday's date, 26 June 1914, on the front page. I remembered Burton had stopped him taking notes of our conversation, so that made sense. Only it didn't. While Burton was out of the compartment consulting the mystery man, I'd watched Stone writing in the notebook. I flipped to the back and found several pages covered in neat columns of dates, words and figures.

Fri. 19 June	Bus fares	1s2d
	Lunch (sandwich)	6d
	To boot boy	
	(as approved)	5s0d
Sat. 20 June	Woolwich	9d
	Lunch	1s3d
	Entrance to meeting	6d

And so on. No more than the wretched man's expenses from days of snooping. I stuffed it back in my bag because the train was slowing down again and I guessed we couldn't be far from Shenfield. This was the next danger point.

Somebody would be meeting the horses there. The ramp would be let down and I couldn't rely on burrowing in the straw to save me, particularly with the condition the straw was in by now. There was no reason to think the watchers would expect me to get out at a little country station, but a stowaway in a horse wagon would attract attention, possibly police action. The obvious solution was to leave the train by the groom's door as it was slowing down before it got to the station. It had done so much slowing down and stopping in the course of the journey that I thought I could rely on it for a dawdling approach, but it let me down. Before I could get the door open we were coming alongside a platform and the sign said Shenfield, Change here for the Southend Line. Too late.

There were heavy steps outside. A man's voice said, 'Here's the horse wagon, ma'am.' Then a child's excited babbling, 'Is she in there? Can I ride her out?' A woman's voice, 'No, darling. Giles will bring them out for us. You can ride Angelica later.'

I looked at the Shetland. She avoided my eye. Angelica! Whether she liked it or not, for the next few minutes we were a sister act. I brushed straw off my jacket, ran a hand over my hair. My hat was probably somewhere back in Ipswich, but the lack of it would help the appearance of eccentricity. Somebody slid back the bars and started bringing the ramp down. I unhitched the Shetland's rope from the ring and when Giles the groom walked in, there I was standing at her head. He blinked.

'She's very nervous,' I told him. 'I'll lead her out if you'll see to the cob.'

Angelica helped by lifting her front legs off the straw and pawing the air. He left me to it.

208

'Mummy, she's here!'

The child, a boy of about five, wouldn't have noticed if it had been King George himself on the end of the halter rope. His mother was another matter. She was a pleasant-looking woman, rather too elegantly dressed for meeting horses. When she saw me leading the pony down the ramp her jaw dropped and her eyes widened. I got in quickly.

'I do hope you'll excuse me but I happened to notice them loading her. I could see she was nervous so as I was travelling this way, I offered to go in with her. She's such a *sweet* little thing.'

I stroked Angelica's nose. She tried to bite me but I was expecting that and her teeth only grazed my sleeve. Goodness knows what I looked like, all over straw and axle grease.

'You . . . you came all the way from Ipswich in a horse wagon?'

Clearly she thought I was mad. Was I dangerous too?

'I do hope you'll excuse the liberty, only I am *so* fond of all animals, especially horses. I just couldn't *bear* to think of this little one shut up in a horrid dark wagon with nobody to comfort her.'

All the time the boy was dancing round in delight at seeing the creature. That decided her. I was daft but not dangerous and the main thing in her mind was getting the whole equipage home. Giles and the cob had joined us on the platform now, ready to move off.

'Really you shouldn't have, but I'm sure we're all very grateful to you. Do we owe you . . . ?'

She had coins in her hand. I waved them away grandly. I knew I might need every penny before I was through, but it would have spoiled the act.

'Not at all. Only too delighted to be of help.'

I gave the Shetland a last loving pat and handed the rope

to Giles. All the time this was going on I'd been glancing round the platform. There were quite a few people coming and going, but no police and nobody I recognised. The train was getting ready to draw out. As I'd guessed, it was a hugger-mugger collection of wagons and trucks but there was one thing about it that made my blood run cold. Sandwiched between trucks were two lonely first-class passenger carriages. There was nobody at the windows and several compartments had blinds pulled right down. I had a suspicion amounting to certainty that those were the carriages used by the initials on their way back to London. Whether there was anybody on board I didn't know. Perhaps Burton and the rest of them had stayed in Ipswich to lead the hunt. Even so, it was a reminder to be cautious. I skulked behind some cycle racks, watched the train draw out and my family group with the horses walk across the yard and out of sight down the road, the cob plodding along, the boy and the pony skipping rings round each other. There were still quite a few people around, probably waiting for the next passenger train to London. It would be easy enough to walk across to the booking office, buy a ticket and join them, but no point in that if I got straight off the train at Liverpool Street into the arms of the police. Then I remembered 'Change here for the Southend Line'. Southend-on-Sea was out of the way to anywhere, stuck out among the mudflats at the mouth of the River Thames. I could go there, and work out some roundabout way of getting back to London. I waited until there was a queue at the ticket office and bought a second-class single to Southend from a bored clerk who hardly gave me a glance.

There was plenty of room in the carriage, possibly because of the smell of me by now, so I had another look at Yellow Boater's columns of expenses. There were seven pages of them and all but the last two were scored through with a diagonal line, meaning presumably that the claims had been submitted and his money repaid. I read through the cancelled pages more from curiosity than anything, wondering if I could identify the days when he'd been following me.

A clutch of dates struck me, in that meticulous writing in the left-hand column: Mon. 4 May, Tues. 5 May and Wed. 6 May. Then a few lines further down: Sat. 23 May and Sun. 24 May. I noticed the first three because they were at the start of the period that was haunting me – Verona's missing nineteen days. Stone's entries for all three days were identical: Epping ret. 3rd class 3s2d, Lunch 1s3d. The later two were similar, with two exceptions. Lunch had cost him 1s6d on the Saturday and Sunday. And, beside the Saturday entry, there were some intials in brackets (VG/YTC). It was the V that made me look twice. VN would have been neater, but that was expecting too much. I looked back over the other entries. Quite a few had other initials against them. It looked as if it might be Stone's way of reminding himself who the quarry had been that day. VG. Not, surely, 'very good'. There was nothing in the way of comment in any of the other entries. Then YTC. Yvonne somebody? Yacht Training Club (surely not in landlocked Epping)? One of the things that kept me worrying away at it was that the pair of entries for 23 and 24 May were during the period of Verona's second disappearance, from when she'd been with Hergest outside Buckingham Palace to when I found her dead in the boathouse. But why, for goodness sake, a quiet little town twenty or so miles out of London like Epping? Let's take it that my guess was right and that Verona had been spying on somebody dangerous in that lost period. For serious spies or trouble-makers, not the posturing kind, the very unlikeliness of Epping would be an attraction. If Verona joined them there, wouldn't it be reasonable that her employers, the initials, would want to watch over her from a distance? Perhaps not even from a distance all the time because she'd have to get messages out to them somehow. Was that what Yellow Boater was doing in his five trips out to Epping? I decided to go there and have a look. With no more than five initials and a hunch to follow it didn't make much sense, but nothing else made any sense at all. I was hunted. I couldn't go home. Epping would do as well as anywhere.

Meanwhile, Southend-on-Sea on a warm Saturday in June had its advantages, the main one for me being that there were crowds of happy people in such an assortment of holiday clothes that I attracted no attention at all. A lot of East Enders had come out for the day on the London Tilbury and Southend Line and even though it was still only mid-morning the promenade was already the scene of a great open-air party. A band on the pier played *O dem Golden Slippers* and lines of young men and girls were doing the cakewalk, arms linked together, paper hats with fluttering streamers dipping and rising as they bowed their heads and advanced towards each other's lines then threw them back and danced away, cheerfully sweeping up pedestrians as they went, swaying round stalls selling pies, ice cream, paper windmills on sticks and vases plastered with sea shells. Wafts of warm beer mingled with the smell of hot sugar from toffee-apple booths, a tripper steamer blew blasts on its siren alongside the pier and the more decorous holiday-makers watched from the balconies of seafront hotels that were as sparkling white in the sun as the yacht sails out at sea. I found a stall selling lemonade and gulped down two glasses of it then bought a shilling's-worth of fish and chips and strolled along eating them from the paper with my fingers, adding cheap fat and vinegar to the odours of horse and the under-side of railway train already clinging to me.

I was starting to feel better, realising I'd accidentally done something clever in coming to Southend. The Tilbury and Southend line that had brought the day-trippers out from the East End had its terminus at that most obscure of London stations, Fenchurch Street. The initials might have men waiting at Liverpool Street but they'd have no reason to expect me there. I strolled to the station, sorry to leave the security and cheerfulness of the crowds on the promenade, bought a single ticket and dozed all the way back to London.

Near Fenchurch Street station I found a second-hand clothes shop and spent eight shillings and sixpence on a complete outfit, navy blue skirt and jacket, matching straw hat and white cotton blouse. The shop owner let me change in her back room. The skirt was on the short side and the hat was beginning to unravel a bit round the brim but the general effect was more or less respectable. I left my old clothes in the shop for the rag bundle.

Chapter Nineteen

⊗

I GOT ON A TRAM TO HACKNEY, THEN another tram and then the train to Epping. Probably I convinced myself that this eccentric progress was to confuse the initials, but that was no more than superstition because they must have lost track of me a long way back. The truth is, I was half-dazed from all that had happened the day before and more than half-asleep. Several times I dozed and woke up when the tram or train stopped, without any idea where I was and in no hurry to get anywhere. In spite of the notebook in my bag, I wasn't greedy to go on finding things out. So far it had only brought more problems and no answers. Meanwhile it was soothing, this slow progress through a warm Saturday lunchtime, with people about their normal business, shopping or chatting, men going home in clerks' dark suits and stiff collars after their half-day's work in banks and offices. I was letting it drift me, in there but not quite part of it, watching myself from a distance. Then it struck me that this was, in its smaller way, like Bill's description of the effect of morphine '. . .watching yourself from a distance, calm and easy as if it had nothing to do with you'. I hadn't wanted to think about morphine, or Verona or Bill, but that made me wake up and think. Not that thinking did much good. By the time the train drew into the station at Epping, I still had no clear idea where to start or much hope that I was doing anything that made sense.

Step one, walk out of station. Stone would have had to do that, at any rate. I got his notebook out of my bag and had another look at it. He'd kept his expenses carefully and on the rare occasions that he took a cab he wrote it down. There was no record of bus or cab from Epping, so he'd probably travelled to wherever he was going on foot. In his job he'd have to be a good walker, but he was there to observe, not to hike. If his target was more than an hour's walk away he'd probably have found some other way of getting to it. That put it, possibly, within a three-mile radius of the station. I strolled uphill to the centre of the little town. Most of its life was going on in the High Street. Some elegant buildings and a couple of comfortable-looking inns held memories of a time when this had been the first coaching stop out of London and highwaymen roamed in Epping Forest. It wasn't a big place, so new arrivals there would be noticed, whether Verona and a group of revolutionaries or Yellow Boater in pursuit of them.

When I bought a local paper and a map at a grocer's and general store and sat down on a bench under a chestnut tree to look at them, it became clear that Epping itself was only part of the picture. The area round the town, edging on to the Forest or farmland, was sprinkled with villages or clusters of houses – Great Gregories, Ivychimneys, Copthall Green and so on – and any of them could have been full of spies, anarchists or secret police. Still, even spies and anarchists have to buy their groceries somewhere. I could have gone into the shops and asked if they remembered anybody of Verona's description, but that would draw attention to myself. For whatever reason the initials had sent somebody here five times at least and there was no guarantee that they

215

wouldn't come again. I looked at the advertisement page in the paper and found the half column that advertised properties to rent, reasoning that my hypothetical group of suspicious people would have to live somewhere as well as buy groceries. They'd hardly have stayed there after Verona's death, so if they'd rented a property it would have become vacant again in the past month. Pinpoint a recently vacated property within a three-mile walk of the station and I just might have the place that Stone had been watching.

I found a pencil and started working my way down the column. I ruled out furnished rooms because they tended to have landlords and landladies on the premises which would be the last thing you'd want if you were involved in suspicious activities. That left seven properties, and in the cases of four of those you were invited to contact Mr Cyril Jones at a local address and telephone number for more information. I asked a boy for directions and found he operated from a little office just off the High Street. The window was hung with net curtains and a sign painted on the front of it said Cyril Jones, Building and Architectural Services, High-class Properties for Long or Short Rentals. Surprisingly on a Saturday afternoon the office was open. A bell on the door tinged when I went in and a bald middle-aged man at the desk looked up with a hopeful smile that faded a little when he saw my clothes.

I said, 'I'm enquiring for my brother. He's thinking of moving to the area and I wonder if you have anything that might suit him.'

I don't like lying but the truth would have made him very unhappy. As it was he cheered up again, probably hoping that my brother would be more prosperous than I looked.

'Has your brother a family?'

'A wife and three children.'

216

True, at least, though a long way from Epping. Mr Jones cheered up even more.

'What kind of thing has he in mind?'

'I was wondering about these.' I showed him the properties I'd marked in the paper.

'Yes indeed. Four of those I can thoroughly recommend for a family and there's another one come in since we put the advertisement in.'

'My brother's quite particular about some things. It must be no more than three miles away from the station and reasonably private. He does so hate nosy neighbours.'

'I'm sure he wouldn't have any trouble with those in our class of property.'

'And he wouldn't want to take anywhere that's been standing vacant for a long time. Places do deteriorate if they're left empty, don't they?'

'Our properties never get the chance to try it, ma'am. They're snapped up very quickly. If your brother is seriously interested in any of these, I'd advise him to move quickly.'

Not half so quickly as I might be moving. 'I thought I might walk round and look at some of them – draw up a short list for him.'

'Certainly, certainly.'

He took a piece of paper from his desk and started drawing a sketch map of the area, putting crosses where the houses were.

'Rosedene, Rosebank and Rosemount are all completely new properties in the same road within two minutes' walk of the station. They're very high-class family developments and I'm sure they'd suit your brother down to the ground.'

'Not lived in at all?'

'Not at all. The builders are just out of them.'

That ruled them out.

217

'The Firs is about a mile out towards Epping Bury, very secluded with a nice garden for the children to play in.'

'I like the sound of that one.' True again.

'Then there's the one only just come in, Tomintoul. That's a mile out on the edge of Wintry Wood, backing on to the Forest. Very secluded, but the garden is a little overgrown.'

'I think I'll look at the Firs and Tomintoul.'

'Not our nice new Roses?'

He was disappointed and went on for some time about fireplaces, fully fitted gas appliances and plumbing, but gave in at last.

'Would you like to borrow the keys to the two you're interested in? You could post them through the letter box if the office is closed when you get back.'

Feeling mean because he was being so helpful, I said yes please to the keys. As he was looking for them in a desk drawer I said, 'I don't suppose my cousin has been to you. She was helping him look too, but that would have been a few weeks ago. Young, quite tall with red-brown hair.'

'Nobody of that description, ma'am. Most of our clients tend to be more mature ladies.'

I left with the two sets of keys, the sketch plan and a headful of directions. I chose the lane leading to The Firs first because it looked shadier and the afternoon was hot. The house turned out to be medium-sized with a lot of fancy brickwork, a gravel drive almost as wide as it was long, rhododendrons in the front. There was a similar house next door to it with enough shrubbery in between to make things difficult for nosy neighbours, then nothing else but fields and some buildings half a mile away that looked like a farmhouse and barns. I used the keys and wandered upstairs and downstairs through empty rooms, footsteps echoing on bare boards. The place had been thoroughly cleaned out and there wasn't as much as a hairpin to show who had lived there or what they'd done. I wasn't even sure what I was looking for, only that whatever it was, it wasn't there. As I let myself out and was bending to lock up a man's voice said, 'Good afternoon, ma'am. I'm from next door. I wondered if you needed any help.'

So much for shrubbery deterring them. He was an elderly brown-faced man in a Panama hat, leaning on a stick. I explained I'd got the key from the agent and was looking on behalf of my brother.

'What does your brother do for a living?'

By the sound of it, you'd have to pass a viva voce examination before they let you come and live here.

'He's a doctor.'

A nod, conceding that doctors might be acceptable. 'It was a professor who had it before.'

'What kind of professor?'

'A retired one. Classics, I think it was, but retired a long time.'

It didn't sound like a nest of anarchists.

'Did he have a big family?'

'Only a daughter who kept house for him.'

'What happened to them?'

'He died two months ago. His daughter's gone to live with her sister's family in Crawley.'

'And nobody's been living there since?'

'No. I keep an eye on it of course, make sure that everything's as it should be.'

'I'm sure you do.'

No need of the watchers, with this one around. He raised his Panama to me, I wished him good afternoon and walked back to where I started.

* * *

219

The way to the other place, Tomintoul, was along the main road northwards. The scenery was nice enough, a wide expanse of town green, then the cool forest on the right. I looked at it longingly as I trudged because the sun was hot and the road dusty and infested with motorcars. Five of the brutes swept past me before I got to the opening of the lane that Mr Jones had marked on my map – one of them close enough to send me diving into the hedge. The lane at least was too narrow to attract them, no more than a track between the trees, rutted by carts and dented with hoofprints. After a few hundred yards it broadened out into a little clearing with three houses in it and forest all round, like a set for *Babes in the Wood*.

Tomintoul would have been trundled in from a different stage set. It was a rambling bungalow in the style of the Indian Raj, behind a green-painted fence brimming over with climbing roses and honeysuckle. A path led from the rickety gate through a front garden so overgrown that I had to unwind myself from trails of perennial sweet peas fighting a losing battle with rampaging brambles. There was a wide verandah at the front of the house. The back garden was a space carved out of the forest, with an expanse of overgrown lawn, a children's sandpit with an abandoned tin bucket in the middle of it, a swing with a broken seat, all framed in tree branches hanging over a sagging fence. I went back to the verandah and unlocked the door. Like the other house, it had been well tidied, but there were indications that its last inhabitants had been a large and easy-going family. The wallpaper was scuffed, the skirting boards scratched and dented. A room that looked as if it had been the nursery had a line of horizontal pencil marks on the walls, probably recording the family's growth, and grooves in the linoleum that might have been made by a rocking horse. All disappointingly innocent.

I locked the door behind me, chalking it up as another blank, and walked back up the path. Opposite Tomintoul was a less ambitious bungalow with a tidier garden. Next to it, the top of a thatched roof was just visible behind a high yew hedge. I was being watched again, or rather the young woman dead-heading roses in the garden of the bungalow was trying hard not to watch. The child with her, holding a garden trug for the rose heads, was less polite and I could see she was telling him it was rude to stare. We exchanged good mornings over her neat hedge and I explained I was house-hunting and felt mean again when I saw how pleased she was.

'We'd love to see it lived in again. There's been nobody for Jimmy to play with since the Hayworths went.'

'A big family?'

'Six children. We were so sorry when they left, but he was offered a headmaster's job in Yorkshire.'

'How long's it been empty?'

'Two months, nearly.'

Which disposed of Tomintoul. I was resigned to going back to the town and starting again, but didn't want to tramp along the main road again and asked if there was a footpath through the Forest. The woman said yes, of course there was and came out of her gate to show me. She was ready to stop and talk, perhaps grateful for any adult conversation after a day with the child. She told me what a nice area it was, peaceful and healthy.

'Do you get many strangers round here?'

'Not many. A few walkers now and then.'

The child meanwhile had wandered off. She called, 'Jimmy, where are you?', and his voice came back from the garden of the thatched cottage next door telling her he'd found an enormous butterfly. She gave me a mock despairing look.

221

'I don't care how enormous it is, darling. That's not our garden.'

She unlatched next door's gate and went in under an arch of neatly clipped yew hedge to fetch the boy back. I stood outside by the gate, listening to the bees buzzing and admiring the little cottage that dozed behind its cushiony yew hedges like a cat in a basket. It was newly thatched and cream painted, with apricot-coloured roses over the porch and rows of beans at the side. The woman brought the boy back and I opened the gate for her, glancing at the carved wooden nameplate under my hand: Yew Tree Cottage. Fair enough name. Then something sparked – YTC.

'Oh God.'

She glanced at me.

'What a pretty cottage,' I said. 'I suppose that one's not for rent?'

'Oh no. That belongs to our writer.'

'Writer?'

She was occupied with the child who was grizzling at being dragged away from the butterfly.

'It's supposed to be his hideaway, but of course we all know round here.'

'Hideaway from what?'

'There are plenty of other butterflies, darling, look. Just somewhere he can come and work in private when he's starting a new book.'

Something knotted up inside me. I wanted to walk away before this took me somewhere I'd rather not go.

'He must be a successful writer if he can afford this.'

'Oh yes. He and his wife lived here just after they were married. He was a teacher. Then when his books did so well they moved to somewhere larger in Surrey but they loved Yew Tree Cottage so much they kept it on. That was long before we moved here, but of course the local people do gossip and we're all very proud of him.'

'Are we talking about Vincent Hergest by any chance?'

'Yes.' She smiled, pleased I'd guessed. 'I love his books, don't you? Have you read his latest?'

'Does he come here very much?'

'Not very often. We've only seen him a few times. We just say good morning, the way you would to any neighbour. After all, if he comes here for privacy we should respect it, shouldn't we?'

'Has he been here recently?'

'I last saw him about two months ago. He came to call on Mrs Grey when she was staying there.'

'Mrs Grey?'

'He's very generous about letting his friends use it.'

VG. Verona Grey? I tried to keep my voice on the same conversational level.

'Was she staying on her own?'

'While her husband was away working in France. She had a woman friend with her sometimes, but the friend had to go up to London a lot, so Vera was left on her own. I think she must have been lonely sometimes but she was very brave about it. We got quite friendly.'

'An elderly woman?'

'Oh no, very young, younger than I am. My husband said to me she hardly looked old enough to be married, let alone . . .'

'Expecting?'

She gave a little nod and a significant glance at the child. 'I must have said something when we were talking and I could see her blushing and she looked at me in a way that, you know – well, you just know, don't you?'

'Was Vera Grey slim with red-brown hair?'

223

'You know her?'

'I think perhaps I do. What was the friend like?'

An anxious look came over her face. 'Well, different. I must admit I was quite surprised that she and Vera . . . I mean, you know . . . although she was always perfectly polite when we happened to speak, which we didn't often because she always seemed to be dashing off somewhere, but . . .'

I thought I recognised the source of the anxiety. She was trying to convey without saying so that the friend was socially a step down from Vera.

'What did she look like?'

'Small, with dark hair cut short, like a pageboy's.'

'A northern Irish accent?'

'To be honest, I thought it was Glaswegian, but they do sound alike if you're not used to them, don't they?'

I didn't answer, staring down the path of lavender bushes to the cottage. A few minutes ago it had looked a pleasant place. Now I wanted to drive a fist into its plump, self-satisfied face. The woman was chattering on happily.

'Anyway, her husband must be back now.'

'Vera's? How do you know?'

'We haven't seen her for about a month, so we assumed that's what must have happened.'

'You didn't see her go?'

'No, but we were away visiting relatives around the end of May, so that must be when she went. I'd have liked to see her again, but it's nice to think of her being back with her husband.'

I suppose I said yes, very nice, or something along those lines. She walked with me to the start of the path through the Forest, the boy trailing beside us, still mourning his missed butterfly. They waved me off through the trees. Her parting words were, 'I do hope you find the house you're looking for.'

I wished I hadn't.

Chapter Twenty

IT DIDN'T EVEN FEEL LIKE ANGER. ANGER FLARES up and down, with sulks and smoulders in between the outbursts. The feeling that came over me didn't change at all on the way back to London. It was as if a diver's helmet had closed over my head and all I could see through the visor was a world that had changed and would never change back again. This new world felt and looked in some ways like the old world, but there wasn't a single thing in it you could rely on to be the same. The train tracks might, if they chose, end in mid-field. Things that looked like doors might refuse to open, things that looked like walls might melt away to mist. When I talked to people, as I had to for the simple business of buying tickets and checking platforms, it was a surprise that they seemed to understand and answer me. I must have managed. I'm pretty sure I remembered to put the two sets of keys through the door of the estate agent before I left Epping.

I got myself out to Elephant and Castle by underground and found the half-demolished street off Walworth Road. It was after seven o'clock by then, all work on the sites over for the weekend, but the smell of brick dust and drains was still hanging in the warm air. The gate to the scrapyard was unlocked. I went inside and pulled it up after me, not taking much trouble to be quiet. Kitty's brother couldn't be permanently on guard and with luck on a Saturday evening he'd be trick shooting at some music hall. It was possible that she'd be with him doing their double act, but there were figures moving inside the uncurtained windows of the martial arts academy so somebody had been left to look after the business. I got behind the remains of an old copper boiler and watched from a distance. It was fencing this time and, as far as I could see, three people there. The small one might be Kitty, but it was imposible to tell for sure because I could only see the top halves of their bodies and they were wearing masks and padded waistcoats. The sound of thudding feet and the occasional male gulp of triumph or frustration drifted out through an open window. After twenty minutes or so everything went quiet and there were no moving figures. Ten minutes after that two young men came round the side of the studio in flannels and jackets, hatless. They were carrying canvas sports bags and looked well exercised, pleased with themselves.

'Fierce little filly, isn't she,' one of them said.

They went past me without noticing and out of the gate. I walked over and looked through a window, standing to the side. There was only one person in the studio. She was sitting on a bench in the changing area at the far end of the room with the heavy curtain half-drawn back. The fencing mask was off, but she was still wearing the padded waistcoat. Even from a distance you could see that her short dark hair was spiky with sweat and her usually taut body slumped with tiredness or depression. The bench and the floor round it were strewn with foils, Indian clubs, shoes. The end of a long, hard day – only it wasn't the end and it was going to get worse. I walked round the corner of the building, in at the door, smelling the beeswax odour of dry sweat.

'Good evening, Kitty Dulcie.'

She'd started putting things away and spun round, a shoe in each hand.

'What are you doing here?'

'Come to talk to you.'

'He told you, we don't want you.'

'How much were you paid?'

'Get out, will you. Get out.'

She dropped the shoes and started walking towards me, eyes on my face, arms a few inches out from her sides, hands at hip level.

'Going to throw me out, are you? I shouldn't try.'

There are rules and courtesies in ju-jitsu and if I kept to them, she could probably get me on the floor. But I was around six inches taller, at least a stone heavier and in no mood for keeping rules. She stopped just beyond arm's reach.

'These are private premises. We don't want you.'

'Call a policeman, then.' Her eyes changed. She wasn't to know what a disaster it would be for me if she did. 'But you don't want to, do you, Kitty? You're afraid they might have some questions to ask you about why Verona was murdered.'

Her hands were on her thighs now, pressing down the pleats of her white fencing skirt.

'Who says she was murdered?'

'The police do. I've been talking to them.' She deserved a lie.

'I don't know anything about it.'

'No? When you were one of the last people to see her alive? When you were keeping her hidden away in Yew Tree Cottage?'

She turned and walked away from me. 'Get out.'

But this time she didn't expect it to work. There was no confidence in her movements as she walked to the end of

228

the room and started sorting out shoes again. I followed and sat down on the bench, watching as she stowed them away in open lockers. The lockers were made of unvarnished pinewood, so new that the knots of it were still bleeding sap.

'You've spent money setting up this place, haven't you? Did it all come from Vincent Hergest?' She picked up a foil and slid it into a long canvas bag. 'I asked you how much he paid you.'

'What's that got to do with you?'

'I suppose I'm curious what the current rate is for assisting a kidnap.'

That got to her. She turned round, furious. 'What the hell are you talking about? Kidnapping, murdering, just what the hell are you accusing me of?'

'Of knowing a lot more than most people about the last few weeks of Verona North's life – or Vera Grey if you like that better. You and Hergest kept her tucked away in that cottage . . .'

'She wasn't bloody kidnapped! She wanted to be there. She could have walked away anytime if she didn't.'

'So what were you doing there?'

'Protecting her, for Christ's sake. I was there to protect her.'

'Against what?'

'She'd got it into her head that she was being watched. She thought there were people out in the trees watching her. She didn't like being alone there at nights.'

She sat down on the bench, elbows on her knees, head in her hands. 'You're mad, you are. Coming in here, accusing me of kidnapping and murdering people. I was helping her.'

She looked and sounded much younger than before. Her fingernails were bitten to the quick, like a nervous child's.

'You didn't do it very well then, did you?'

229

She glared. 'Yes, I did. She was all right the last time I saw her.'

'When was that?'

'I can't remember days. Late May.'

'She was dead by May the twenty-eighth.'

'Are you trying to make out that I killed her?'

'No. Where did you see her last?'

'Are you going to the police with this?' She was scared, ready to bargain.

'Not unless I have to.' Not in a thousand years.

'So what are you playing at?'

'I want to know what happened to her. If I can do that without bringing the police into it, I will.'

'If you tell the police about me, I'll kill you.'

'Where did you see her last?'

'I mean it.'

'All right, you mean it. Where did you see her last?'

'At the cottage.'

'What was she doing?'

'Eating breakfast, quite normal. I left early because I had to take some classes in town. She was all right. When I got back, there was a note for me saying she'd gone away for a few days and she'd let me know when she got back. She never did.'

'A note in her handwriting?'

'Yes.'

'Did she say where she was going?'

'No.'

'Or why?'

'No.'

'Have you still got the note?'

'No.'

'How long had she been living at Yew Tree Cottage?'

230

'I don't know. I'd been there with her about three weeks.'

That was most of the missing time. 'Did she ask you to stay with her there?'

'She wanted somebody she knew. I knew her a bit from the ju-jitsu classes.'

'So she asked you to stay with her?'

'No, he did.'

'He being Vincent Hergest?'

'Yes. I knew him because of helping with his book. He came to me one day and said would I spend the nights down there because she was nervous on her own. So I said I would.'

'Was Verona happy about that?'

She shrugged. 'Yes, she seemed to be.'

'How did you get on together?'

'All right. I was away in London some of the time. When we were there together she was mostly reading or writing. I'd bring food in and we'd cook it. We'd talk a bit, sit out in the garden. We got on all right.'

'What did you talk about?'

'The kind of things you do talk about. What food to buy, next door's cat, the baby.'

'Her baby? The one she was expecting?'

'Yes.'

'She was quite open about that?'

'Yes.'

'How did she feel about it?'

Kitty hesitated, looked at me. 'To be quite honest with you, she got on my nerves.'

'Why?'

'You'd have thought no woman in the history of the world had fallen pregnant before.'

'Pleased, you mean?'

'As if she'd won an Olympic medal.'

'Did you ever know her to take drugs, like morphine?'

'No. She even gave up tea because she'd read somewhere it wasn't good for babies.'

'There was morphine in her body when she died.'

'Well, I didn't put it there and I don't know who did, so don't blame me.'

That was a mistake on my part. She'd started talking more easily, but now the fear and hostility were back.

'These people she thought were watching her – did she say who they were?'

'No.'

'You must have asked her.'

'We didn't talk much about it.'

'Why not? That's why you were there, wasn't it?' Silence. 'Well, wasn't it?'

'That was why she wanted someone there.'

'So you talked about it?'

'At first I did. I asked her why she thought she was being watched.'

'What did she say?'

'To be honest, she didn't make a lot of sense. She didn't know why anybody would be watching her, she didn't know who they were and she didn't even know what they looked like.'

'So how did she know she was being watched?'

Kitty's shoulders gave an exasperated little shudder. 'God knows. One day, I got back and she said there'd been this walker come out of the Forest, looking over the hedge. Young man with dark hair. But you get walkers all over the place, don't you, and everybody stares over hedges.'

'So you didn't believe her?'

'Not really, no. I thought maybe it was the sort of idea women get into their heads when they're expecting.'

'But you were content to take the money.'

'Why not? If there had been anybody, I'd have dealt with him. Besides, I think she quite liked having me there.'

'Did you report to Vincent Hergest?'

'What do you mean?'

'Tell him how she was getting on.'

'I'd see him every week at Argyll Place, yes.'

'Why was he doing this? Why was he keeping her out of the way in his cottage, paying you to be with her?'

She stared at me, honestly puzzled. 'Well, what else was he supposed to do? He could hardly walk down Piccadilly with her on one arm and his wife on the other, could he? He was just doing what everybody else does in the circumstances if they've got the money.'

'Circumstances?'

'Well, it was his baby she was expecting after all.'

Chapter Twenty-one

WATERLOO STATION IS TWO STOPS UP ON THE underground from Elephant and Castle. I got there in time to jump on a train for Guildford just as it was leaving. Another set of London suburbs, another lot of woods and fields, went past in the evening light. Just twenty-four hours, almost exactly, since the boat-train had pulled out of Liverpool Street and so many things turned upside-down since then that I was beyond giddiness. The one thing that mattered was getting to the house facing the North Downs with its lily-pond and its ducks and its neat little knots of vegetables. As far as I had any plans, I'd intended to start walking from the station but it was after nine by the time I got there and the Hergests' house was around half an hour by motorcar out of town, which probably meant seven miles or so along country lanes. No cabs, of course, and with my money down to seven pounds and some small change that was probably just as well. I was tempted to press on but had just enough sense left to see that there was no point in getting lost in country lanes in the dusk.

The landlady of a mean-looking boarding house near the station gave me an odd look when I asked for a room but landladies tend to do that to single women without luggage arriving as they're about to lock up. She charged me over the odds and agreed to leave the key on the inside of the front door so that I could leave early in the morning. Seven days after midsummer, it hardly got dark at all. I lay there with the net curtains pulled back and watched the sky change from gold to blue-black, then to the near transparent white of pre-dawn. The stairs creaked as I went down in stockinged feet and the first sparrows were chirping as I put my shoes on outside. Nobody about, but it was only just after five. I walked out of town and found the road southwards towards the Downs. There were wild roses in the hedges, a lark overhead, all the trimmings of an early summer morning and I wanted to tell them they were in the wrong play. I'd thought that the walk would give me time to think what to say to him, but my mind wouldn't work and, after all, it didn't seem to matter. I remembered the way well enough from being driven out there in his motorcar and by eight o'clock I was in the lane that led to the gates of Mill House. There was a church not far away, sending out the first peal of a peaceful Sunday morning, a smell of honeysuckle in the air, their ducks quacking behind the mellow brick walls. I guessed he'd be at breakfast already, although it was a Sunday. He wasn't a man to waste time. Whether Valerie would be with him I couldn't guess, but I hoped so. She'd been at the inquest; she'd known.

The gates were open, the gravel newly raked. I ignored the front door, with its neat columns of bay bushes on both sides, and went up the steps to the terrace, between urns of pink geraniums and blue-flowered sage. The doors of a French window were opened on to the terrace and there they were, just the two of them, having breakfast inside. It was a perfect picture. They were sitting opposite each other, sideways on to me. He had two brown eggs in a double egg cup in front of him but had paused with his spoon in the air to

235

read her something from a magazine. She was sipping coffee as she listened, barefoot in a wonderful Chinese silk dressing-gown with red and blue dragons, hair as tidy as if she'd just come from the salon. For a moment, I almost pitied them. I took another step. He was the first to see me. In a few seconds his expression ran through surprise and annoyance then settled in the little-boy smile that his admirers found so attractive.

'Well, if it isn't Nell Bray. Have you come to join us for breakfast?'

She turned and saw me as he spoke. Her expression started annoyed and stayed that way. I took another step and stopped just outside the French windows, so that I could talk to them without raising my voice.

'I was at Yew Tree Cottage yesterday,' I said.

The smile stayed on his face but the light died away from behind it. He said 'Oh'. The sound was gentle and regret-ful, as if a child had punched him in the stomach or an animal he'd been petting had bitten him. Valerie stood up and put a hand on his arm.

'I think you should disappear into your study, darling. I'll talk to Miss Bray.'

From the tone of her voice I might have come to sell clothes pegs, and not particularly good ones at that. At first I thought he might do as she told him. He looked at the egg spoon that he was still holding poised in the air, then down at his two brown eggs and seemed to despair of the mental effort of bringing it into contact with them. The spoon clattered on the table and his head went down in his hands.

Valerie said, 'You might have warned us.'

'What about? This isn't a social visit.'

'You'd better come in.' Vincent said it from behind his

hands, small square hands with clean neat nails. The hair at the back of his neck, freshly trimmed, looked as soft as a boy's. I walked in and Valerie shifted so that she was protecting him from me.

'You needed to come to the inquest to see how much evidence would come out,' I said.

'Yes.'

'Did he tell you what he'd done?'

'I'm not answering any questions until I'm ready. You must give us time to think.'

'Why? You're a quick thinker.'

Vincent had raised his head and was watching us. His expression was different now, with nothing of the little boy in it. He looked ten years older than when I'd walked in and his face was grey.

'We'll tell her, Val. It's all we can do.'

'I want an undertaking from her first that she won't tell anybody else.'

'You won't get it. I might have gone to the police without talking to you first. I could still do that.'

'Police?' He sounded bewildered, fighting to get a grip on what was happening. 'Let's . . . let's go and sit down, over there.'

It was a big, sunny room, with cream fleece rugs on a pale parquet floor. There were comfortable chairs arranged round the hearth and a big copper jug full of Shirley poppies in the fireplace. Vincent sank into an armchair, she sat beside him and I chose a chair opposite them.

I said, 'It was your baby Verona was expecting, wasn't it?'

He nodded.

'She was two months pregnant when she died, so you were lovers before the end of March.'

Another nod.

'You pretended you didn't know what she was doing in those missing days in May. She was at your cottage in Epping all the time.'

He didn't answer.

'I suppose you put her there while you decided what to do about her. You seduce a girl nearly young enough to be your daughter and she's flattered because a famous man is taking notice of her. You make notes on her for your wretched book then when she tells you she's expecting your baby you hide her away so that she can't tell her friends and spoil your precious do-gooding reputation.'

'No.'

The protest came from Valerie, not Vincent. He was staring at me as if I'd been speaking a language he didn't understand. I'd been so angry that I'd forgotten what this might be doing to her feelings, but her face and her voice were terribly calm.

'I'm trying to make allowances for you being grieved and angry, Miss Bray, but you're as wrong as you can be.'

'Wrong about Verona being pregnant by your husband?'

'No, that's true. Wrong about everything else. I don't suppose you have any idea of the attitude of young girls to my husband. You've accused him of seducing her. I've known about this almost from the start and I can tell you almost the reverse was true.'

'That she seduced him? She was hardly out of school.'

'Believe me, she wasn't the only one. I've sat there at public occasions and seen girls no older than she was going to almost any lengths to get him to notice them. Vincent enjoys the company of young people. He's a kind and generous-hearted man, and I'm afraid there's a certain type of girl who'll take advantage of that.'

'And I suppose he's not taking advantage of them?'

'No, I'm not denying that. He's a man with normal feelings. If a young woman makes it clear that she is, let's say, available to him and understands what she's doing – well, is it so surprising?'

She looked me in the face. I hated them both but couldn't help respecting her toughness. He was staring at the poppies, head bent.

'And if we're talking about taking advantage, Miss Bray, your young woman scarcely out of school was doing one of the most cruel and cynical things I've ever heard. Vincent's told me what you said at the garden party. She was spying on him. Every moment they were together, when she was letting him think she cared for him, she was going home and writing down what he'd said in her nasty little notebook and selling it to a government department that's got nothing better to do than spy on people who are trying to make this a slightly less awful world. I've talked to women who were selling themselves for five shillings in public houses who had more morals than your precious Verona.'

'Are you saying she deserved to be killed?'

'She deserved something. It almost destroyed Vincent when you told him how she'd been using him. He hasn't written a word since then.'

She said it as if it were the worst calamity of all and put her hand protectively over his, lying inert on the chair arm.

He said, 'Thank you, Val,' on a long sighing note. Then he pushed himself upright in the chair and looked at me. 'Valerie's nearly right, but there are some things even she doesn't understand. Forgive me, darling.' He raised his hand with hers on top of it to his lips, kissed her fingers then, very gently, disengaged his hand from hers. 'I'm going to be completely honest with you, Miss Bray. I'm going to try to make you understand things that I haven't even explained to Valerie.'

She shifted her position slightly in the chair so that neither of us could see her face. She'd clasped her other hand over the fingers he'd kissed. He looked at her, took a deep breath and turned to me.

'Miss Bray, have you any idea of the desperation of young women these days?'

'Of course I have.' Our movement was full of women ten years younger than I was who couldn't wait to get out with matches and cans of paraffin.

'I don't mean politically. I mean desperate to catch up with life. Maybe it used to be easier for them when all their world consisted of was looking after their parents or marrying the curate. Now the doors are opening all over the place – perhaps you and I have even helped open some of them – and suddenly there's a big world out there. They're like children in a magic toy shop, desperately afraid it will all disappear again before they can grab everything they want.'

It sounded like a passage from one of his books, and possibly it was and yet there was real sadness in his voice. I reminded myself that he was successful at both story-telling and seduction.

'Are you claiming that Verona grabbed you off the toy shelf?'

'Please, please, *please*, stop being so angry for a minute and just listen to me. I'm not trying to make you understand what attracted her to me. I'm telling you why I was attracted to her.'

Valerie didn't move perceptibly, and yet there was a change in the quality of her silence as if she were spreading some invisible membrane to catch the slightest change in his tone.

'Valerie was telling the truth when she talked about impressionable young women wanting to attract my attention. I

240

know it sounds conceited, but it's just a fact. She may be right, too, when she implies that I'm a pathetic middle-aged man, deceived by an unscrupulous young woman who happened to be a spy.'

That wasn't quite what Valerie had said, but she made no attempt to correct him.

'What I want you both to see is that I wasn't so unscrupulous, or even as stupid, as you both think. All right, I was attracted to her, I was flattered that she wanted my opinion on things, wanted to see the world through my eyes. But I sensed there was something there I didn't understand, some reserve I couldn't break through. Oh, she had all the headlong, desperate courage of those other young girls, but there was something else besides and it puzzled me, intrigued me. Perhaps that's why I let what happened happen – because I thought it might help me understand her.'

I said, 'You mean making love to her?'

He looked at me, his eyes shining with tears. 'Yes, although if you want the truth, she was the one who suggested it.'

We both glanced at Valerie, although she'd made no sound. Her head was still bent, the hand still clasped over her fingers.

'And then she came to you and told you she was pregnant. That must have worried you.'

'No!' The word came out explosively. 'No. It didn't worry me, it didn't worry Verona and, if you want to know, it didn't worry Valerie.'

'I don't believe you.'

We stared at each other. He sighed and looked away.

'You tell her, Val.'

Slowly she unclasped her hands and ran them over her tidy, shining hair. When she looked at me her face was hard and she talked as if she were already giving evidence in court.

'I knew about Verona from the start. Vincent and I have

241

always been completely honest with each other. Completely, in everything. Sometime in April he told me that Verona was sure she was expecting his baby. We discussed what to do. Vincent was in favour of acknowledging the relationship and the baby and having them here to live with us. I argued, rightly or wrongly, that the public attitude to that might reduce the amount of good he could do for the various causes we support. Also, there was the question of what Verona herself wanted. I suggested we should invite her here for one of our regular weekends with other young people present so that it didn't start gossip.'

'The peace weekend?'

'Yes. She came that weekend in April and the three of us had a long talk. The decision we came to was that Verona should live quietly at our cottage in Epping and have the baby there. Once it was born Vincent and I would adopt it, set Verona up in a flat of her own and support her to train for whatever career she wanted.'

'Verona agreed to that?'

'Yes. There was never any question of doing anything without her agreement.'

'And you?'

'I was happy.'

Vincent hadn't taken his eyes off her while she was talking. Now he burst out, 'Happy! That's the point! I know it sounds ridiculous after all that's happened, but you've got to understand this. Back in the spring, when Verona was fulfilled and in love with everything and there was the baby to look forward to, we were all so happy. It was life, life, life! Life for the baby, a new life for Verona, this little life to guide for Val and me. It was all turning out so well, so very, very well for all of us.'

I said, 'So when did it start going wrong?'

242

'It didn't.'

'She's dead.'

'It didn't go wrong. She went down to the cottage. I visited her now and then, took books for her. We'd discuss what she was reading – our tutorials, we called them.'

'She was willing to be hidden away there?'

'Yes. It was what she wanted. Just now and then, she'd get impatient about being out of things. She insisted on going with me to the Buckingham Palace deputation where you saw us. Val was angry with me about that. She was worried about the risk to the baby, but it was all right.'

'So everything was still all right and she was happy and you were happy and Valerie was happy, but just a week after that she was dead. I'm asking you again, when did it start going wrong?' There was a long silence. 'She was worried that people were watching her, wasn't she? Hiding in the Forest and watching her.'

He flinched. 'Did she tell you that?'

'Of course not. None of us had any idea where she was in all that time.'

Valerie interrupted. 'I suppose she's been talking to Kitty Dulcie.'

'Did you believe Verona about the watchers?'

He looked at Valerie before answering. 'I . . . we discussed it. You do get strange people in the Forest and even if she was imagining things . . . well, it showed it was wrong to leave her there on her own at nights. So Val suggested we should ask Kitty to keep an eye on her.'

'So Kitty was watching Verona for you?'

'No, helping us look after her.' Valerie glared. 'You've got such a brutal way of looking at things. Vincent saw Kitty once a week at the ju-jitsu place and they'd naturally discuss how Verona was, that's all.'

'And Kitty concluded that the watchers were a figment of Verona's imagination?'

Vincent burst out, 'That's what I'll never forgive myself for! If we'd taken it more seriously – talked to her more about it.'

'You think now they were real?'

He hesitated. Valerie was looking at him intently, as if she was as interested in the answer as I was. 'Yes . . . that is . . . after what you told me about what she was doing, I just don't know what was real and what wasn't any more. Even the happiness. Oh, I know she was happy about the three of us and the baby – I'm as sure of that as the sun rising. But the reserve was still there. I could feel there was something worrying her she wouldn't talk about – only . . .' His voice trailed away.

'When did you last see her?'

'That deputation outside the Palace. After that, I put her on the train for Epping and we arranged I'd come and see her the next Thursday.'

The day I found her dead.

'Did you go?'

A long silence. He and Valerie looked at each other.

'We got a letter two days before that, on the Tuesday.'

'From Verona?'

'Yes. It was dated from Epping the day before. What it said worried me. I showed it to Val and we agreed that I should go straight to Epping and see her.'

'Have you got the letter?'

'Yes.'

'May I see it?'

He got up and went out, moving like an old man. While he was out of the room, Valerie didn't move or look at me.

'Here you are.'

244

It was in Verona's handwriting, the date and postmark as he'd said.

Dearest Tutor,

I told you I was scared sometimes. It helps a little when Kitty's here, but not enough. I know you both think I'm imagining things, but I meant it. I am being watched. I know who and I know why. It scares me, especially at nights when the trees make odd noises in the wind. Oh dearest, there are things you don't know about me. It has grieved me so much in the last few weeks having any secret from you and from Val, my more-than-sister. Before I see either of you again, there is something I must put right. I shall have to go away for a few days soon to do it, but don't worry. Tell Val I shall be careful of myself and even more careful of our little Hero.

My love,

Your devoted pupil
Verona

'So you went to the cottage?'

'Yes. She wasn't there. I went to the place in Chelsea where she'd been living before. They had no idea where she was.'

'So what did you do?'

'What could we do? We waited for her to come back, waited to hear from her. Then . . .'

He stared at me as if I could somehow make the end of the story come out differently.

Valerie said, quietly, 'We saw a paragraph in one of the papers about her being found hanging in Devon.'

'Why did you go to the inquest?'

'I wanted to know what had happened to her.' Valerie's calm was sliding away.

Tears came into her eyes. 'To her and to our baby.'

'And the verdict was suicide. Did that come as a relief to you?'

'No. Why should it have?'

Vincent said, 'Because Miss Bray thinks we murdered her.'

She stared, eyes huge and face colourless. 'No! No!'

'You went to a lot of trouble to hide what had happened. You were paying Kitty Dulcie to keep quiet.'

'That was me. Vincent didn't know about it till this moment. Verona was dead, the baby was dead. There was only Vincent to think about then. Why should he suffer – have people pointing at him, blaming him, saying that shows what happens to men and women who are brave and clear-minded and don't let other people dictate their morals to them?'

She was furious with me, with everybody.

He put a hand on her arm. 'Easy, Val.'

'I thought things were as bad as they could be, then *she* came here and made them worse and she's doing it again.'

'Did you really not know that Verona was spying until I told Mr Hergest?'

'No. I'd no idea and nor had he.'

'That's true,' Vincent said. 'You know, I think it was one of the worst moments of my life, sitting there among the vegetables, hearing you say it.'

'You knew it was true though.'

He nodded. It explained everything, including that last letter of hers. He picked up the letter from the chair arm where I'd put it and read '. . . *there is something I must put right. I shall have to go away for a few days soon to do it* . . .'

'You think that was what she meant?'

'I've been thinking about almost nothing else since you told me, and I'm sure of it. It was real, what she'd found with Val and me. Whatever she'd been before, this was what she wanted. She knew . . .' He turned away and when he spoke again he was crying, '. . . knew we loved her.'

There was so much pain in Valerie's face that I had to look away, but her voice was as calm as ever. 'Well, Miss Bray, do you still think we killed her?'

I must have shaken my head because when I looked back at her there was relief on her face as well as pain. No point in explaining that the head-shake wasn't her answer, only my confusion because all I'd done was make my burden of anger heavier, and I still couldn't put it down where it belonged.

'Will you have some coffee? I'll ring for a fresh pot.'

She did too, and for the chauffeur to take me back to Guildford. I saw Vincent from a distance as I left, staring at the flower border, not moving.

Chapter Twenty-two

I HAD TO GO BACK HOME, EVEN IF all the watchers in the world were waiting. I needed the ten pounds I keep tucked away for emergencies, the hem of the second-hand skirt had come adrift and there was more travelling to do. The streets of Hampstead had a Sunday slack-tide feel, with most people gone to take the air on the Heath or dozing indoors, and only a few children playing hopscotch in the sun. There was nothing and nobody waiting for me when I opened the front door except two cats and a pile of post. I'd just changed and was looking for the train timetable when there was a knock on the back door and my neighbour came in with a little brown envelope.

'The post office boy brought this on Friday afternoon. I'd no idea where you were.'

It was a telegram from Bill.

SHALL BE AWAY FOR WEEKEND. PLEASE TELE-PHONE MONDAY, USUAL NUMBER. MEAN-WHILE, DO NOTHING. PLEASE.

'Bad news?'

'No, just a friend. Thank you for taking it in. Would you mind seeing to the cats for another day or two? There's some milk and fish money on the table.'

A few days ago I'd been angry with Bill for trying to inter-
fere. Now so much had happened that I'd have liked to talk
to him, even listen to him. For one thing, it was possible
he'd been right all along. I rummaged the wastepaper basket
for his letter, unscrunched it and read, '. . . *a right to be
concerned about what happens to you . . .*' No, not that bit.
'*I've been giving all this a lot of thought since last week and
I'm becoming convinced that you are tackling all this from the
wrong end . . . I'll be making my own enquiries and will let
you know the result . . .*' He'd thought all along that the trail
started further back in Verona's life. If Verona's last known
letter could be taken at its face value, it pointed that way
too. '. . . *something I must put right. I shall have to go away
for a few days . . .*' And if I didn't take it at face value, then
Valerie meant me to think it pointed there. Clever, resource-
ful Valerie with her motorcar and all those useful acquain-
tances in strange places she'd made researching Vincent's
books. Loyal, sad, lying Valerie who'd do anything to protect
her husband. Whether the trail was true or false, there was
only one ending to it – the boathouse on the river estuary.

I put Bill's letter in my bag along with a notebook and a
change of underwear, locked up and walked down the hill
to the underground station, not bothering to check for watchers on street corners. As far as I was concerned they could
be three deep behind every chimney stack. The game had
gone beyond that now. I got to Paddington, bought a return
and had a cup of tea and a dried-up cheese sandwich in the
buffet, not because I was hungry but because I couldn't
remember whether I'd eaten anything since the fish and chips
at Southend. Heading south-westwards in the train – more
fields, wider rivers – I started thinking again about Bill and
the telegram. I guessed he was spending the weekend walking in the Pennines with his deerhound, Roswal, for company

then called myself a fool for imagining just him and the dog. Why not another woman? Fool again because what did I mean, *another* woman? That implied there was a first one and a few hours on the moors didn't mean I'd accepted that vacancy, or even that it had been offered to me. '. . . *a right to be concerned* . . .' I got the letter out, re-read it and, for the first time, began to wonder if Bill's weekend away might be connected with all of this. Surely he couldn't have known about Verona and Vincent Hergest and Yew Tree Cottage. Or was it just possible he'd drawn conclusions from the two of them being together at the deputation, gone to confront Hergest and . . . There was a smear of something sticky on the armrest of the seat – jam, ice cream? A fly had settled on it, proboscis spearing into the stickiness, its whole body throbbing with sucking it in. I remembered the flies in the boathouse and felt sick and terrified. He wouldn't do that. He was methodical, cautious in his way. '. . . *I suppose I am, by your standards cautious and conventional . . . But I'm not, I hope, passive and – with luck – may be able to prove that to you* . . .' When I re-read that I tried in my head to send him back to the Pennines, with a whole bevy of other women if he wanted them, but he wouldn't go.

The journey seemed endless – the sun hardly moving down the sky, long waits at stations where nobody got off or on, the last Sunday in the month of longest days and nobody in a hurry but me. That was until we got to Exeter. I had to change there and was standing by the door as the train slowed down alongside the platform. There were purposeful crowds around and an air of bustle you wouldn't expect on a Sunday evening. A pile of what looked like rolled-up mattresses was stacked on the end of the opposite platform, a man with a clipboard watching them and, of all things, an Army officer in riding boots, cap and Sam Browne belt watching the man with the clipboard. There were more soldiers around on our platform, officers and men, plus civilians in Sunday suits, Boy Scouts and women with a tea urn on a trolley. A young man standing by the tea trolley had a bandage wound thickly round his head like a turban, but the stain had soaked through and the back of the turban was more red than white. The lad beside him had one arm in a fresh white sling and was drinking tea with the other hand. I got out before the train had properly stopped and the whole platform was full of walking wounded, with slings and bandages and crutches, all of them standing there quite stoically talking to each other as if nothing had happened, not even looking at a train on another platform and the team of men carrying empty stretchers inside, stretcher after stretcher, dozens of them. I grabbed a porter who was standing watching.

'What in the world has happened?'

'It's all right, miss. Nearly finished now they have.'

He moved off in response to a signal at the other end of the platform. A whistle blew. The wounded men started forming up in rows on the platform. I grabbed a passing Boy Scout and repeated the question.

'Blueland invaded us at Bridport, ma'am. Thirteen hundred casualties, eleven hundred of them hospital cases.'

He'd learned it by heart.

'Invaded? Why? What's Blueland?' The feeling of unreality that had been there for days became panic, heart thumping, throat dry. 'What do you mean? What's happening?'

The wounded men – not even men, most of them looked no older than schoolboys – had lined up now and an officer was making a speech to them, thanking them. At the end of his speech they started laughing and shouting, tearing off slings and bandages and throwing them at each other. A word from the officer and they were quiet and orderly again. Boy

Scouts went along the platform, collecting up crutches and soiled dressings. On the far platform the empty stretchers were all loaded and the train was pulling out. My Boy Scout had gone, chasing bandages with the rest. I found a young man in civilian clothes, watching the lines of wounded boys, and asked for the third time what had happened.

'An exercise. The War Office is running them all over the country.'

'War Office?'

'To test our readiness for dealing with casualties if we're invaded by a foreign army. They've been sending them to hospitals all over the place – Exmouth, Budleigh Salterton and so on. Our boys were asked to volunteer to play casualties.'

'Your boys?'

'I'm a schoolmaster, waiting to collect our lot and take them home to supper. By the look of them, they've been having the time of their lives.'

He was right. Outside the station there were rows of horse-drawn charabancs waiting for the boys. They were driven away laughing and singing, highly pleased with themselves. Back on the platform, the man with the clipboard and the officer were still watching their mattresses. There was no reason to think that anybody would be looking for me among all the excitement, but if there were War Office people around I couldn't risk trying to get a train connection for Teignmouth that evening.

I found lodgings near the cathedral, got woken by the bells in the morning and caught a local train from a platform as clear of soldiers, stretchers and mattresses as if the exercise had never happened. As the train ran along the estuary of the River Exe a man and a woman in my compartment were tut-tutting over a newspaper, saying something

252

was terrible. I'd bought a paper at the station, unfolded it to see what they were talking about and read that the Archduke Franz Ferdinand, heir to the throne of Austro-Hungary, had been assassinated in Sarajevo.

We'd turned the corner of the estuary by then and were running in and out of tunnels in the red rock along the coast. In a few minutes I'd be back on Verona's home territory and still wasn't sure where to start. Fact, Verona had been in Epping. Further fact, she was found dead about two hundred miles away in Devon. Conclusion, she'd gone from Epping to Devon. So how and why? I wished I'd asked the Hergests to let me take away the letter Vincent had shown me, or at least made a copy of it. She'd written about a secret and going away for a few days to put things right. One secret at least I'd known about and one interpretation of the letter was that she was ashamed of having been a spy and was going to resign or retire, or however people in her profession put it. Surely, though, she wouldn't have to go away for a few days to do that. She'd have contacts in London, might even have been meeting Yellow Boater out at Epping. So, if the letter could be taken at face value, that would point to some other secret. A former lover, or perhaps somebody who thought of himself as her fiancé back at home? That would fit, only nobody had mentioned there was anything of the kind and her best friend, Prudence, had implied quite the reverse. She and Verona had promised each other not to get married or 'silly over men' until they'd done something in the world. Only there had been a lot poor Prudence didn't know. Verona had grown up quite suddenly and left her behind with the puppies. The other passengers were still talking about the assassination.

'His poor wife too, such a lovely woman.'

253

'Austria will have to do something. Bound to do something.'

'I wish the Tories were back in. You can't trust the Liberals with foreigners.'

Normally I'd have been interested, even joined the discussion, but I was in the state where anything happening outside my own problems seemed frivolous and irrelevant, like having toothache on a grand scale. The discarded fiancé theory might make sense after a fashion – leaving aside that there wasn't a shred of evidence for him so far – but it involved one big and possibly wrong assumption. It assumed that the letter Vincent showed me could be taken at its face value. I ruled out forgery. I was almost certain that the handwriting was Verona's and it had the over-excited style of her earlier letter to Prudence. Verona had written it, but the question was, in what circumstances? Was it dictated to her? Could it even have been suggested to her as some kind of literary exercise? She'd called him 'Dearest Tutor' after all. It had read to me as artless and genuine, but then I'd been wrong about Verona nearly all along the line and there was no guarantee I'd stopped being wrong now. Assume it wasn't genuine – then what? The first thing was that there was no proof that Verona had made the last journey of her own free will – or even conscious. The Hergests had several motorcars and Valerie had proved she was capable of driving herself to Devon. '*Val, my more-than-sister*' at the steering wheel with a girl, morphine-doped, curled up in the back seat. The train came alongside the platform at Teignmouth.

At one stage in my varied education, I was taught by a schoolmistress who said that when you were in doubt about what to do, you should choose the option you least wanted and get on with it. It didn't stop my friend and me getting into serious trouble when we climbed the bell tower to put a bedpan on top of a gargoyle and claimed in defence that it was what we'd least wanted to do on a frosty midnight. She was stronger on morality than logic, but in fairness to her we still had ten years of Queen Victoria's reign ahead at the time. The memory of that schoolmistress came back to me for the first time in years as I was walking between my cousin Ben's white gateposts at the top of the drive leading to his house. Of all the things that I might have wanted to do, confronting Ben and Alexandra came at the bottom of the list, which would have made it the right thing by her standards, but there was logic to it as well. Either Verona had come home of her own free will, or she hadn't. If she had, then the letter to Vincent Hergest was probably genuine and she'd gone to put something right, and if there had been something that needed putting right at home, surely her father or mother – especially her mother – would have known or guessed.

The gateposts gleamed white, newly painted. The fuchsia bushes on either side of the drive with their dazzle of red-and-purple flowers were the kind you can find growing wild in the West Country but these specimens were disciplined and well drilled and the yellow gravel as bright as if it had been holystoned at dawn. There was a flagpole to the right of the gateway from which Ben had the irritating habit of flying the Union Jack when in residence but today there was no flag. It wasn't till then I remembered Ben wouldn't be at home. In that talk with Admiral Pritty, which seemed like weeks ago but could only be a matter of days, he'd told me Ben was back at sea already. I profaned his gravel with my footsteps, walked up the three granite steps into the porch. There was a tall wickerwork basket to the side of the royal-blue front door, stuffed with golf putters and croquet mallets.

255

My knock echoed hollow and empty inside and I more than half-hoped Alex had gone away.

'Good morning, ma'am.'

The maid who opened the door was very young, no more than fifteen or sixteen. She looked worried. A Siamese cat rubbed against her calves and gave me a go-away look from its blue eyes.

'Good morning. Is Mrs North at home?'

'I don't know if she's seeing anybody, ma'am.'

Then, from inside, Alexandra's voice, sounding weary, 'Who is it, Jenny?'

I gave my name. The maid disappeared inside and came back, still with the cat following her.

'Mrs North says to please come in.' She gathered up the cat, draped it over her shoulder. 'Drive you mad, they would.'

I followed her down the corridor and she nudged open a door at the end of it on the right. I knew the room from some family occasion, a lounge with a relaxed and floating feel that probably had more to do with Alexandra's taste than Ben's. The floor was polished wood with a scattering of rugs in bright jewel colours – garnet, amethyst and topaz – with cushions and drapes in the same colours flung over an assortment of unmatched but comfortable chairs. Even so, Ben's taste had barged its way there, with models of every ship he'd served in or commanded lording it on shelves, tables and windowsills. The room was built for the view over the estuary with a huge window taking up most of the outside wall. The tide must have been nearly full, because there was a great sweep of blue water with a few white sails.

Alexandra said, 'Good morning. Did you find your way here all right?'

It was as if she'd learned the words carefully in a foreign language. Although the maid had told her my name, it hadn't registered. The room was awash with pitiless light. It looked as if she'd tried to keep it out because she'd drawn up a tall screen on her right. The screen was covered with cut-out pictures of flowers, animals and sailing ships, the kind of work that good children are encouraged to amuse themselves with on rainy holidays. In the early morning it would have given some shade but now the sun was high and beat through the big window on to the armchair where she was sitting, the table beside it covered with cards and papers, the sherry decanter and half-full glass. Her hair was tidy, her white blouse and black skirt pressed and neat, her eyes desperate.

I said, 'I gather Ben's away.'

She nodded. 'On his ship, in the Bay of Biscay.'

'I'm sorry.' I wasn't, but she seemed so desperately lonely, marooned in all that sunshine.

'It's his duty, you see.' She'd had a sherry or two, but she wasn't drunk, just absent. I still didn't think she'd registered who I was, but she was being polite.

'Do sit down. You'll excuse my not getting up, but if I do they'll be all over the place and I'll forget which ones I've done and which I haven't.'

There were a few black-bordered cards on her lap and some more letters. I settled on a big footstool, opposite her.

'Condolences?'

She nodded. 'We should have replied to them by now. It's more than a month.'

'I'm sure people don't expect replies.'

'Ben says they do. These things have to be done properly, don't they?'

'Why?'

She stared at me. I hadn't expected her to take any notice of what I'd said, but her mind was working on it.

'Why properly?'

'I don't see that it matters either way. If it helps you . . .'

Without taking her eyes off me she picked up a black-bordered letter from her lap and held it by its corner between finger and thumb. She tore it just a little at the edge, then waited like a child expecting somebody to shout at her. When nothing happened she tore a strip carefully down the edge, then round the corner, along another edge and round another corner, slowly converting it into a spiral that trailed down her skirt. Silence, except for the sound of paper tearing and a shut-out Siamese complaining from the corridor. She concentrated hard on ending the spiral in a neat disc of paper, then held it up at arm's length and let it go. We both watched as it landed in a tangle on the floor and quivered gently.

'Is that right?'

'Yes, I think so.'

'Only I don't know what's supposed to be right, any more.' She started on one of the cards, then dropped it and picked up another letter. 'Would you like a sherry? There's a glass over on the sideboard.'

I fetched it, poured from the decanter. She signalled with her eyes that I should top up her glass as well.

'Thank you – Nell. It's very nice of you to call.'

She'd registered who I was then, but she didn't mean it about being nice. The last time she'd seen me was when I came up from the boathouse after finding Verona's body. She was in no state to notice me when she left the inquest.

'Are you on your own here?'

'Apart from Jenny and Mrs Tell. Adam had to go back to Dartmouth to get ready for the war.'

She said it matter-of-factly, watching as another spiral quivered to the floor, then took a sip of sherry and started tearing another letter.

'War?'

258

'Ireland or the Balkans or somewhere. Adam will be killed and Ben will be probably be killed too and then it will be all over.'

I could have argued about Ireland, pointed out that naval officers and cadets would hardly be at risk in the Balkans, but there was a mad, blank certainty about her.

'I'm sure they'll come back to you.'

'Verona didn't.'

The spirals were piling up now. She was working faster and faster. I wondered whether I should stay for a polite time, then go without asking any questions.

'Verona didn't, did she?' More urgently, looking at me as if she wanted an answer.

'I think perhaps she did.'

'To hang herself, yes. Home to hang herself.'

Over the last few days I'd come round so firmly to the belief that Verona had been murdered that it was a shock to remember she was still officially a suicide. Tread carefully.

'I think there might have been more to it than that. I think she came back here for another reason.'

Alex dropped a half-torn letter and stared at me. 'What do you mean?' Her voice was harsh, quite different from the dazed tone so far.

'I've seen a letter she wrote, to friends near London. She said she was going away for a few days because there was something she must put right.'

'The baby. She must have meant she was going to get rid of the baby.'

'No! No, I'm sure it wasn't that. She was happy about the baby.'

Even if the Hergests had been lying about other things, the evidence of Kitty Dulcie and the neighbour at Yew Tree Cottage was on their side in that respect.

'You knew that, did you? She talked to you?'

'No.'

'You knew her better than I did. Everybody knew her better than I did.'

'No. Listen, I hardly knew her at all, but I've been talking to people who did. It wasn't the baby, I promise you that.'

'Put right. What did she mean?'

'I don't know. I thought you might.'

'She was nineteen. She was expecting a baby. She was doping – my daughter was. How could she put that right?'

'I don't think she was doping.'

'Ben said the doctor at the inquest—'

'She had morphine in her body. We don't know she injected it *herself*.'

Alex took a long gulp of sherry and looked at me. I still didn't know if what I was doing would help her but it had gone beyond drawing back.

'If she didn't—'

'She came here. This was probably the place where she had to put things right. Have you any idea what it was? Was there anyone here she was close to?'

'Outside the family? A lot of friends. Prudence of course, the families we sailed and picnicked with.'

'Anybody special? Anybody she might think she'd . . . well . . . done wrong to by loving somebody else?'

She looked angry at first, then shook her head. 'There were plenty of young men who wanted to be special, mostly young officers – danced with her, sent her flowers. We'd . . . we'd laugh about them sometimes, the two of us. She didn't love anybody yet – not like that. She wasn't ready.'

More or less what Admiral Pritty had said. Alex picked a letter off the table, read a few sentences then started another spiral.

260

I said, 'There was an older man.'

'In London?'

'Yes.'

'The baby?'

'Yes.'

'I hope he rots in hell.'

No careful spiral this time. The letter went to the floor in jagged pieces. She grabbed a handful and wrenched at them together. She must have ripped a fingernail because there were smears of blood on the paper.

'I trusted you to look after her, Nell. I didn't want her to go to London, but I thought you'd look after her.'

'I don't think Verona wanted to be looked after in that way.'

'She was no more than a child.'

'She was quite a lot more.'

'What do you mean?'

All the way down in the train I'd wondered if I could tell her about Verona's spying activities. I'd have to put a patriotic gloss on it if I did, hide some of the nastier details like how she used me to find out about my friends.

'Alex, did she discuss with you what she was going to do in London?'

She looked at me. The look and the tone of her voice when she answered told me a lot I needed to know. 'Art school.'

'It wasn't just art school, was it?'

Her fingers stopped their tearing. 'What did she tell you?'

'Nothing.'

'You're lying, aren't you?' The tone wasn't angry, just weary.

'No,' I said, 'Verona didn't tell me anything.'

She looked at me and decided to believe it. Her face went

261

slack with relief. 'They didn't tell me anything either.' The relief was not having to live with the intolerable idea that Verona might have trusted me more than her.

'They?'

'The three of them: her and Ben and Archie.'

'Archie Pritty, her godfather?'

'Yes.'

'You guessed what was happening?'

'I knew there was something. There was . . .' She went quiet, looked out at the expanse of water, then quickly away again. 'There was a kind of excitement about them.'

'Her and Ben?'

'The three of them. Then when this art school business came up I expected Ben to say she couldn't go. He did at first – but that was for my benefit, I could see that. He gave in too quickly. Ben doesn't give in. You know . . .'

There was one of Ben's model ships on her writing table, a delicate little three-master, probably one he'd served on in his cadet days. She picked up a paperknife and used it to pull the model towards her by its rigging. 'You know how it is in the Navy. Sails shot away, sheets dangling, half your crew dead. Never pull down your colours. Sink if you must, but never pull down your colours.'

Her voice was calm and conversational, but all the time she was ripping and stabbing with the paperknife, cutting the intricate threads of the rigging, tearing the miniature sails to shreds. When she'd finished she looked at the wrecked ship with satisfaction and put it back on the table, exactly where it had been.

'So when he said she could go if she wanted to, I knew for certain. It was a secret among the three of them and she wasn't allowed to tell me. Ben thinks I talk too much, you see. He thinks artists talk too much. Well I am, aren't I?'

262

'What did you think she was doing?'

'Secret work at the War Office.'

'What sort of secret work?'

'Secretary, I suppose. After all, they couldn't have just anybody typing letters and filing things. They'd need girls from a background like Verona's.'

'Was she trained as a secretary?'

'They'd have trained her. Those first letters of hers from London, when she was working so hard and didn't come home for Christmas, I thought they were training her.' Her head was down, her hands clasped tightly in her lap. I could see she meant what she was saying, still had no idea of Verona's real work. 'Then, when . . . when it happened and we found out about the things . . . about the . . . about the doping and the baby . . . I thought it was because they'd made her work too hard. A breakdown, I thought. People have breakdowns, don't they? Even young people?'

'Yes. Yes, they do.'

'Was that it, Nell, do you think? They made her work too hard and her mind broke down?'

'Something like that, yes, I think so.'

I was looking at her hands when I said it, wondering what they might do next. I looked up and her eyes were on me, as cold as Burton's in the railway carriage.

'You are *lying*, aren't you? You don't think so at all.'

I had to make the decision there and then, and I still don't know if I made the right one. I didn't think Alex was mad, or no more mad than I might be in the circumstances. Or no more mad than I might be by the end of this. I told her almost everything. There were a few things I left out, like the identity of the lover and how Verona had used me, but I gave her the rest, from Yellow Boater and the other watchers

263

to the railway carriage where Burton had accused me of her murder. She listened, quite still and quiet. All the time the white sails were moving around on the estuary but the tide must have been going out while I told her, because by the end of it the mud banks were shining in the sun.

'She didn't kill herself?'

'No.'

Her head went down in her hands. She started shaking. I knelt down beside her. 'Thank you. Thank you for that.' She was crying. 'It was thinking that she didn't come to me. She was in such trouble, but she didn't come to me.'

She sat there for a long time. After that we walked round the garden, on the landward side away from the view of the boathouse and the estuary. A couple of half-grown Siamese followed us, but she didn't look at them or even talk very much. She seemed calmer but dazed, and when she asked another question it came as a surprise.

'Those men, the watchers you called them, what did they look like?'

'They come in all shapes and sizes. Why?'

'I think they might be watching me.'

'What!'

'One of them came here the other day.'

'When?'

'I think . . . Saturday, probably.'

'What happened?'

'It was Jenny's day off so it must have been Saturday. Mrs Tell let him in. To be honest with you, I wasn't feeling very well. So many people . . . condolences, silences, you know . . . sometimes I couldn't remember who on earth they were. So I told her to show him in. He was quite gentlemanly, not what you'd expect. He had a pleasant voice, I remember, a deep voice. I thought at first he must be a friend of Ben's I'd

264

forgotten meeting, then he said we hadn't met but he was a friend of yours and since he was in the area, he thought . . .'

We'd been walking along the drive. I stopped, and she stopped too, stumbling against me.

'He said he was a friend of *mine?*'

'Yes. I thought it was odd, but . . .'

'Can you remember his name?'

'I don't know. There've been so many names.'

'What did he look like?'

'Quite tall, dark-haired, clean shaven. His face was tanned. That was why I thought he might be one of Ben's golfing friends at first.'

'What did you talk about?'

'What do they all talk about?' Then, after a pause. 'Verona. We talked about her, about her here before she went away. I think . . . I think I quite liked talking to him at the time, but after he'd gone away I thought it was odd he'd called if he was just your friend and now . . . now I wonder if he was . . . one of those.'

She was staring at me. I felt sick and scared.

'Are you sure you can't remember his name? Could it have been Musgrave? Bill Musgrave?'

She shook her head. 'I don't know. Mrs Tell might remember. Was he really a friend of yours?'

'I think so. Yes.'

Alexandra was puzzled, but too dazed by all that had happened to her to be very curious. We went back into the house and found Mrs Tell, the housekeeper. She confirmed that it had been early on Saturday afternoon when the gentleman called and she was quite clear about his name. It was Musgrave.

265

Chapter Twenty-three

I WALKED BACK INTO SHALDON, THE VILLAGE ON the far side of the estuary from Teignmouth. The ferry was in mid-river. I sat down on the shingle to wait for it with the sun hot on my back, and watched an old man in a fisherman's jersey repairing a lobster pot. I asked him if it had been a good season so far.

'Yes, ma'am. Never seen so many visitors so early on. A lot of invalid people for the air and gentlemen for the sailing and sea-fishing.'

There were more yachts and dinghies going out with the tide and half a dozen rowing boats near the opposite bank, some of them being rowed splashily in circles.

'Are those rowing boats for hire?' A memory was nibbling at the edge of my mind.

'Yes, ma'am, just in the estuary. You wouldn't want them going out to sea.'

Back in that railway carriage, Burton had accused me of taking Verona, drugged and helpless, up the estuary in a rowing boat. He or somebody had worked it out very neatly for me. Did they know there were rowing boats for hire, or was that just a lucky guess? The ferry arrived and grounded on the pebbles. With most people at lunch, I was the only passenger back to the Teignmouth side. The ferryman, a lad of sixteen or so, pushed off from the beach with a long oar and started the motor. As we curved out across the estuary I looked back at Shaldon and the red sandstone cliff that local people called the Ness. A small white house, mostly built of white-painted wood, was tucked under the Ness just above the tide-line, with steps running down to the jetty. It looked familiar, then I remembered I'd seen it in the background of one of the photographs of Verona in a dinghy.

'Who lives there?'

'The admiral.' He mumbled the words to his chest, less at ease with people than with boats.

'Admiral Pritty?'

'Yes.'

There were sandbanks at the mouth of the estuary, exposed by the receding tide. An odd-shaped boat, like a little Noah's Ark, seemed to have grounded on the furthest of them. I'd have asked the lad about it, only he was turning the boat again to bring the stern up against the beach on the Teignmouth side, among fish barrels and nets spread out to dry.

'Do you know where I could make a telephone call from?'

He thought about it while he fixed the gangplank. 'The big hotels would have them, the Royal or the Queens.'

The Royal was some way from the fishermen's beach in the fashionable part of the town. It faced the promenade across lawns and flowerbeds planted out in the demented patterns that seaside park-keepers love, clashing pink and red begonias, mauve blobs of ageratum and silver houseleeks crammed together as elaborate as a Persian carpet. Perhaps it's a reaction against all that unruliness of the sea just a pebble's throw away. The foyer of the Royal was sunk in afternoon calm and the man behind the mahogany reception desk shook his head when I asked if they had a telephone I could use.

'Residents only, ma'am.'

*   *   *

267

It took a half-crown tip and an order for tea and crab sandwiches I didn't want to get access to the telephone booth
under the stairs. I leaned against the door that wouldn't shut
properly and asked the operator for the number of the tea
importer under Bill's chambers. The importer's secretary
answered, annoyed, but agreed to go upstairs and get him.
There was a long wait, then footsteps hurrying downstairs
and the sound of the receiver being picked up.

'Bill? It's Nell.'

A silence, and somehow the embarrassment of it came
down the line from Manchester.

'Miss Bray?'

The voice of Bill's clerk. The disappointment told me how
much I'd wanted to talk to Bill.

'Yes.'

'Is Mr Musgrave with you, Miss Bray?'

'What?'

The surprise in my voice made him think he'd offended
me and he started trying to apologise.

'It occurred to us that he might be . . . might be visiting
friends in London. I didn't mean to . . .'

'Isn't he there?'

Another silence then, miserably, 'No, no he isn't. We're
becoming quite worried. In fact . . .'

A tap on the door. A waiter was hovering outside with a
trayful of tea and sandwiches. I signed to him to go away.

'Have you been to his lodgings?'

'Yes, I cycled out there at lunchtime. His landlady said he
left for the weekend on Friday morning and she hasn't seen
him since.'

The telephone booth went dark round me. The phone felt
clammy in my hand.

'He hasn't been in today?'

'No, and he had appointments with clients. It's not like him. Not like him at all. I thought if he'd gone to London, perhaps he'd called on you and . . .'

'I'm not in London, I'm in Devon. He was here on Saturday.'

I think the clerk misunderstood that, because when he spoke again he sounded even more embarrassed.

'Did he tell you where he was going?'

'No, I wasn't here when he was. I just got here today and . . . oh God. Did he say anything to you or the landlady about what he was doing?'

'Only that he wouldn't be into chambers on Friday.'

More silence, apart from crackling on the line. When the clerk spoke again his voice was beginning to distort and go faint.

'Are you still there, Miss Bray?'

'Yes. Look, I'll make some enquiries down here . . . try to find out . . .'

'I'm sorry, I can't hear . . .'

'I'll try to telephone later.'

I was shouting by that time, but the line had gone dead. In the foyer, the waiter had put the tea and sandwiches on a table beside a parlour palm and was standing guard over them. I gulped tea.

'Was there a man named Musgrave staying here on Friday or Saturday night?'

'Reception would know, ma'am.'

Reception was quite sure that nobody of Bill's name or description had stayed at the Royal. They'd been fully booked on both nights and couldn't have taken any new arrivals. In any case, it didn't strike me as Bill's sort of hotel, but then what did I know?

* * *

269

In the next two hours I tramped round about thirty hotels and guesthouses with no result except sore feet and a collection of suspicious looks ranging from mildly curious, through satirical to downright hostile. A woman enquiring after a tall dark-haired man at a holiday resort provokes obvious reactions. The maid at Sea View said she'd been looking for a man like that most of her life and to let her know if I found out where they sold them. The proprietor of a public house that did rooms puffed whisky vapours in my face and said, 'Gone off, has he? Don't worry, he'll be back with his tail between his legs when her husband catches up with them.' A thin woman at the Tamarisks, or it might have been White Horses or Balmoral (they all looked the same), burst into tears and said hers had walked out last Christmas and I'd be better off without him in the long run.

Towards the end of the afternoon, when the musicians on the bandstand were packing up their instruments and families loaded with picnic baskets and buckets and spades were trailing from the beach back to their boarding houses, I stood on the promenade and registered total failure. The tide had turned by then but the sea was still a long way out, the beach patchily inhabited by picnic parties and family groups playing cricket and rounders. A couple of ponies were at work dragging the bathing machines back up the sand out of reach of the night's high tide, the painted huts rocking and lurching on their big metal wheels. Fishermen were digging for worms down at the tide-line. A dog ran up and down barking at the waves.

Then there were the two policemen. I didn't notice them at first but other people on the promenade were staring in their direction and perhaps somebody said something, not sounding alarmed, just curious, amused even. They were to the left of the pier, the part of the beach set aside for women's bathing, so perhaps that had caused the amusement. They walked side by side along the sand, not hurrying. My throat went tight. I started walking fast along the promenade, past the pier, down some steps to the beach. The policemen were still walking quite slowly. They were heading for a man in a navy-blue jersey who was standing waiting for them on the high tide-line of driftwood and dry bladderwrack. There was something odd and skeletal beside him that wasn't driftwood but I couldn't make out what it was. The policemen reached him and stood there, screening it. By then I was running, stumbling over dry uneven sand. People who'd been nearer the scene when the policemen arrived were already gathering, children and dogs with them.

'What is it? What's happened?'

The man in the navy-blue jersey was thin and grey-bearded. He was explaining something to the policemen, making gestures out to sea. Beside him was the skeletal thing, just two big iron wheels joined by an axle. Nothing else.

A woman answered me, 'Someone's taken one of his bathing machines.'

I felt weak with relief, laughed too loudly. 'Is that all? I thought it was somebody hurt.' Or worse. I hadn't admitted it to myself till then.

She was annoyed with me for laughing. 'Sheer devilment, what those boys get up to. Hacked it right off its wheels and now it's stuck out there on the sandbank.' She pointed out to the mouth of the estuary and the shape I'd taken for a stranded boat. 'If it doesn't come in again on the next tide, he'll have to pay somebody to go out and get it off.'

An old man said those boys would be cutting down the pier next and a general debate started on what should be done about them, with a good thrashing being the most popular option. The owner of the missing bathing machine was still describing his loss to the police, showing the wooden struts attached to the wheel axle, where the wooden changing-hut had been hacked free.

I left them to it and walked slowly back to the promenade. My heart had slowed down but it still scared me that I'd been so ready to think of drownings. Back on the other side of the pier people were strolling among flowerbeds or queuing outside the Riviera Cinema for the early evening show. There were a few guesthouses I hadn't tried in a street round the corner from the Royal. At the first two the landladies were busy making dinner and unhelpful. The third came to the door in an apron with a smudge of flour on her nose and at least stood and listened while I described Bill for what felt like the thousandth time.

'Yes, he was here.'

I was so used to 'no' that it didn't strike me at first.

'Here? He stayed here? When?'

'Not stayed. Friday evening, it was. He came here only I didn't have a room because we were all booked up with families. He said did I know anywhere and I told him most places in town were full but he might try down by the back beach. There are a few places there that take in people who've come for the fishing.'

The back beach was the local name for the inside of the sand bar that curved round to make a harbour at the estuary mouth. I'd already been there once when I got off the ferry. It was the artisans' part of the town, where the fishermen and boatbuilders lived and worked, and cargo boats came in and out of the docks at high tide. Narrow streets stopped abruptly at either red sand or lapping water, depending on the state of the tide. There were a few fishing boats tied up, a smell of fish on the warm air and under it a colder earthy

272

whiff from the pale heaps of china clay waiting on the dock-
side to be shipped to the ends of the earth. The houses were
mostly in scrappy terraces of three or four, huddled among
tall net lofts or store sheds. Although they looked hardly
large enough for families, quite a few had 'Room to Let'
signs in the windows. Nobody answered my knock at the
first cottage with a sign. At the second there was a long
silence then the door opened and a brown-haired woman in
her mid-twenties was standing in the doorway.

'Yes. What is it?'

Her voice wasn't local. She was holding a pen and had a
distracted air.

'I'm sorry to bother you, but I see you have a Room to
Let sign and . . .'

She sighed then turned away from me and called up the
narrow flight of stairs, 'John, is the room free or isn't it?'

'What's that?' A man appeared at the top of the stairs,
equally distracted-looking. He wore an old tweed jacket and
glasses, and was carrying a jam-jar full of cloudy water with
a silvery worm inside it.

'She wants the room. Is it free?'

'I don't know. Did he say if he was coming back?'

I said, 'May I come in, please?'

They both stared at me, he from the top of the stairs, she
from the bottom.

'I think the man you're talking about may be a friend of
mine. I'm looking for him. I've been looking for him all day.'

I suppose I must have looked and sounded desperate
because they let me in. The downstairs room where we talked,
looking on to the harbour, was more like an aquarium than
a place where human beings lived. There were shelves all
round the walls with tanks containing a few lethargic fish, a
wooden laboratory bench against the wall with a clerk's

273

writing stool alongside it, a smell of fish and formaldehyde. The woman, who seemed a more forceful character than the man and annoyed at being interrupted, waved a hand at the tanks and explained, 'Marine parasites. John's doing research. He has to be near the harbour for when the fishing boats get in.'

'The man who was staying with you, was that last Friday night?'

They looked at each other blankly. John pushed his spectacles up and rubbed the bridge of his nose.

'Probably, yes.'

'Had he just arrived from Manchester?'

Another pair of blank looks. The woman said, 'I suppose he'd just arrived from somewhere because I think he said all the hotels were full. We don't get many people on the whole because of the smell.'

'And he took a room here?'

'Yes. We explained about not doing breakfast and he said it didn't matter because he'd be out early in the morning anyway.'

'And was he?'

'Yes. He stayed out all day. He got back in the evening and asked if he could take the room for another night.'

'Did he say why?'

'I don't think so. We didn't ask him, did we, John?'

Her manner wasn't as brisk as it had been. She was beginning to sense something wrong.

'So he stayed Saturday night as well?'

'Yes.'

'And left on Sunday morning?' He'd have had to, if he planned to be back in Manchester for work on Monday.

'Yes.'

'Did he say where he was going? Perhaps to the station?'

'I don't know. We didn't speak to him. John had gone out very early because there'd been some boats in the night before and when I got up at about six your friend wasn't here. But he'd left his bag in his room so I assumed he'd come back later and fetch it.'

'And did he come back?'

They looked at each other for a long time and I could feel anxiety stirring in them like some deep undersea creature.

'I'm not sure.'

'I'm not sure, either. You see, the door's always left open . . .'

'. . . because some of the fishermen will leave things on the kitchen floor if they think we might be interested . . .'

'. . . and he insisted on paying in advance.'

'So I suppose we assumed he'd come in and collected his bag and gone.'

'Have you looked in his room since?'

The silences were getting longer. In the end John said reluctantly, 'I might have gone in to get a journal, but I didn't notice if the bag was still there.'

'Come on.'

I followed the woman up the stairs, two at a time. They were steep and uncarpeted, with an old bit of ship's rope rigged at the side instead of a bannister. Three doors opened off a little square of landing. The woman opened the left one and there in the middle of the floor, plumped down on a faded rag rug, was Bill's travelling bag. I recognised the stain he'd told me came from a bottle of retsina that burst at Delphi, when he was hiking round Greece, years before I knew him.

'Is it your friend's?' the woman asked. She sounded scared.

It was a small room, with a window looking towards the wharf and the heaps of china clay. Two of the walls were stacked to waist height with what looked like learned scientific journals. There was a metal-framed bed under the window that might have come out of a barracks with the sheet and blanket folded back and the dent of a head in the pillow, a washstand in the corner with a flower-patterned ewer and basin. I walked over to the washstand, stepping round the bag. There was a little clean water in the basin, just enough to splash your face if you got up early.

'He didn't shave before he went out.'

There was no soap scum or little crusts of dried lather and bristle. A thin white towel was flung over the rail of the washstand as if it had been picked up and used once, but not very crumpled. No trace of razor, brushes or comb. They'd be packed away in the bag.

'What do you think's happened?' the woman said.

'I don't know. Could we go downstairs and talk?'

I liked her, which helped. They were two serious people in a world of their own with their marine parasites, but not uncaring. Her name was Margaret. John must have understood at a look from her as we came downstairs what was happening, because he left his jam-jar on the bench and came through with us to the other room, a combined living-room and kitchen with a cooking range and some sagging armchairs.

I said, 'He called on a relative of mine just up the estuary on Saturday. I don't suppose he mentioned that?'

They shook their heads.

'Can either of you remember anything about what he said or did? Anything at all?'

Margaret said slowly, 'No. He came back early Saturday evening, asked if he could have the room again, then went out to get dinner somewhere, I suppose.'

'After he went out to dinner, what time did he get back?'

'Quite late. It was getting dark.'

'Was there anything you noticed? Did he seem worried, excited?'

'No, nothing like that. Just one thing – I don't know if it's any help. When he went out he had a local map in his pocket. It was still in his pocket when he came back but folded up a different way, as if he'd been looking at it over dinner.'

John was staring at her as if amazed she could be so observant about anything not submarine.

'Did he say anything to you about what he intended to do on the Sunday?'

'No. Unless he did to you, John. They were talking when I went take some warm water upstairs.'

John blinked. 'Were we?'

'Yes, I remember hearing your voices. Was he asking you something?'

He screwed his face up, trying to remember. 'I'm not sure. I was dissecting mackerel.'

'*Think*, John.' From Margaret's voice, she was used to this.

'Oh yes, now you come to mention it he *did* ask me about something but I can't remember what.'

'A person? A place?' I tried to be patient, fighting the impulse to shake it out of him, but he just sat there looking miserable.

'Was it about somewhere he was thinking of going or something he was thinking of doing?'

'Yes.' His face cleared. 'Boats, that was it. He wanted to know who hired out rowing boats.'

'What did you tell him?'

'I said there was a man down at the harbour. I hire from him myself sometimes.'

277

'Can we go and talk to him?'

'What, now?' He looked at me, then longingly towards his workroom, then at Margaret.

'Yes.'

Chapter Twenty-four

&

THE BACK BEACH WAS QUIET NOW WORK WAS mostly over for the day. There were only seagulls shrieking over fish guts and a man and a boy gathering up a net. The hire boats were moored to posts a little way out from the beach, bobbing against each other on the rising tide – but no sign of their owner. Margaret and I waited while John went over to talk to the man with the net.

'He says Matthew's drinking in the New Quay. I'll go over and get him.' And he went, picking his way carefully among lobster pots and fish barrels.

Margaret said, 'If one of the hire boats hadn't been returned I think we'd have heard.'

It seemed a long time before John came back. The man with him was square-built, brown-faced and white-bearded, wearing canvas trousers and a seaman's jersey. He looked as if he'd be the cheerful type normally, but there was a wariness about him, or perhaps it was only that he resented being taken away from his beer.

John said, 'This is Matt Pellew.'

The man looked at me.

'Nell Bray,' I said. 'I think you may have spoken to a friend of mine at the weekend.'

There was a little breeze coming off the water. It ruffled

the edges of his beard and set his flock of hire boats bobbing faster.

'Who would that be, miss?'

I described Bill. Matt took an unlit pipe out of his pocket, sucked on it and slowly nodded his head.

'Yes.'

'When did he talk to you?'

'Saturday evening, just when I was packing up.'

'Did he want to hire a boat?'

'He asked me about them, yes.'

'For Sunday?'

'No particular day.'

'And did he hire one?'

'No.'

'Did you talk about anything else?'

A shake of the head. 'I can't recall, miss. Dare say he wanted to talk about the weather or the fishing. Most of them do.'

Margaret said, sharply: 'Is any of your boats missing, Matt?'

Perhaps he resented the tone because he gave her an annoyed look from under jutting eyebrows.

'No, it's not.'

In a pacifying tone John said, 'This lady's worried, Matt. Her friend was staying with us and now he seems to have gone missing.'

'Well, I'm very sorry, but it weren't in one of my boats.' He looked meaningfully back towards the pub. 'Be that all, then?'

I said yes, I supposed it was, but to let me know at John and Margaret's house if he thought of anything else. He nodded, wished us good evening and went back along the beach.

Margaret waited until he was out of earshot. 'He's lying.'

'Yes, I think so too.'

John looked at the two of us, scandalised.

'Surely not. Matt's as reliable as tide tables. The man's a church warden, for goodness sake.'

Margaret said, 'He could be an archbishop and it wouldn't make any difference. He was lying.'

You could see how unhappy it made John, being at odds with her. I felt guilty about that, but needed Margaret as an ally.

'Perhaps he just doesn't like nosy outsiders. He might talk to you two if I weren't there.'

'Not to me. He might talk to John in the New Quay.'

John looked across at the pub, without enthusiasm. A swallow swished past us, looped out over the water and back.

'But I haven't finished writing up the log.'

'I'll do it from your notes. Go in there, buy him a beer, work round to it gradually. Tell him there won't be any trouble for him, whatever it is.'

Margaret glanced at me. 'We *can* tell him that, can we?'

'Yes.' I hoped so. I wasn't sure of anything.

'There.' Margaret took John by the shoulders and gave him a gentle push towards the public house. He went unhappily.

'Poor John, he hates beer. Still, the fishermen talk to him – all the tall tales they can't get anyone else to listen to. Whatever it is, he'll get it.'

We walked back to their house. She took a black kettle off the range and brewed tea for us, cleared a space on the table and fetched a big cloth-bound book and a sheaf of loose notes from the next room. For a while there was silence apart from the creaking of the chair and the scratch of her fountain pen over the page. The book was ruled in columns for dates, location, variety and size of specimen. An hour later, with the sun throwing a square of gold through the uncurtained window on to the white wall above her head, she sighed and put the cap on the pen.

'John's taking a long time.'

'I'm sorry.'

'Don't be. I liked your friend.' Then she looked annoyed with herself for using the past tense and said, too hurriedly, 'I'm sure he'll be all right.'

'May I stay here tonight? As a paying guest, I mean.'

'You don't have to pay. There's only the one room, the one he had.'

'That's all right.'

'I'll go up and change the sheets.'

'No, don't. They'll be fine as they are.'

'Would you like some cocoa? I was going to wait for John, but . . .'

'Let's wait.'

We sat and talked as the square on the wall spread to wash the whole room in dusty, fish-smelling gold. John's work on parasites was for a thesis that, with luck, might lead to a university post. She had some training as a biologist, but her parents wouldn't let her go to college. Then she had met John.

'At a talk on marine gastropods. We eloped three weeks later.'

Her eyes were shining, her voice full of the wonder of it. The feeling that stabbed through me can't have been envy exactly because I didn't covet a life in a fisherman's cottage surrounded by pickled parasites, but it was something a lot like it. I think what I wanted was their certainty. As it was, I'd already contaminated their lives with my uncertainties because John had spent an unwanted evening in a public house instead of at home.

* * *

282

Soon after we heard steps outside and the door-latch clicked. John came in, his glasses covered in condensation and his hair sticking up as if he'd been running his hands through it.

'You were right, Margaret. I don't know how you knew, but you were right.'

He sat down heavily into an armchair that tilted sideways on uneven feet. It was what I'd expected but my heart plunged.

'You mean Bill did hire a boat from him?'

'No. It's a lot odder than that. Just wait while I get it clear in my mind.' He sat there with his eyes closed. He was perhaps just a little drunk, not being used to it. 'Right. It took a long time. There were a few of them yarning there and he didn't start talking until the others had gone. Then when we were alone he wanted to know what you were doing and where you came from.' He glanced at me. 'I said I didn't know. He said he didn't know what was going on, but he didn't want anything to do with it.'

'What did he mean?'

'I don't know. I stuck to what you wanted to know and asked him if there'd been anything he hadn't told you and yes there had. Apparently your friend went to him as he said on Saturday evening, it must have been just after he left here. They talked a bit about the weather and the fishing and so on, that was true enough, then your friend asked him about the hire boats. But he wasn't interested for himself. He wanted to know about somebody who might have hired a boat a month ago, back at the end of May.'

'Who?'

'A young woman. A young woman of about nineteen with red-brown hair. That was one of the reasons Matt didn't want to tell you about it, you know, your friend and a young woman and so on . . .' His voice trailed away, embarrassed, but Margaret told him to go on.

'Anyway, there had been this young woman. Matt remembered her because he wouldn't usually hire to a woman on her own, but he said you could tell that this one knew what she was doing. So he let her have a boat.'

'Did he know what day that was?'

'No, your friend asked him that and he didn't, only that it was near the end of last month.'

'Did he know where she went with it?'

'No. There were a lot of customers that day. He told her to keep in the estuary and not go out to sea, but he tells everybody that. Anyway, then you get to the bit that really bothers Matt.'

He stopped again and ran his hand through his hair. There were already a few fish scales caught in it, gleaming in the light from the sunset when he moved his head. Margaret told him to get on with the story. He looked at me.

'You have to know what they're like, these people, tough as teak planks but so superstitious they'll . . .'

'John, just tell her what he said.'

My mind made the connection at last.

'Was he by any chance talking about a boat that rowed itself?'

His jaw dropped. 'How in the world did you know?'

'He was?'

'Yes.'

'The boat the girl hired?'

'Yes. The day he let her take it, she didn't bring it back. He wondered at the time whether to alert the police or the coastguard, but then he thought probably she'd rowed over to stay with friends and left the boat tied up somewhere. He wasn't sure whether to be worried or annoyed, so he went off to the New Quay to have a drink and think it over. Well, one drink led to another and he's ashamed of himself for this, but he forgot all about it. He wakes up at first light, remembers and rushes down to the quay and there's the boat come back, tied up with the others, the oars neatly stowed and everything shipshape.'

'But no sign of the young woman?'

'No. That puzzled him, because he'd taken ten shillings deposit off her for the boat. He thought she might come back during the day, but she didn't and he forgot all about it until a few days later.'

'What happened then?'

'I don't suppose you've heard of a man named Commodore Benjamin North?'

Margaret said, 'Of course she won't have. She doesn't live round here.'

I had to trust them, a little at least. 'He's my cousin.'

A silence.

John said, looking more troubled, 'Then you know about . . . ?'

'His daughter? Yes.'

'Well, a small place like this, you can understand that everybody was talking about it. As far as Matt was concerned, he'd never seen her but some of the other fishermen had and they started talking about her, what she looked like and so on, then it gradually dawned on poor Matt. She was the girl who hired his boat. And naturally it struck him that she'd used it to row herself upriver to the boathouse and . . .'

'But the boat came back.'

'That's what I meant about him being a bit other-worldly about it. He thinks a commodore's daughter would see that a boat got back, even if . . .'

'Did he go to the police?'

'That was his other worry. He thought if he did they'd blame him for not raising the alarm. Anyway, he struggled with his conscience a few days, then decided to make a clean breast of it and went off to the police station. He told them his story, they wrote it down and said he'd probably be called to give evidence at the inquest.'

'But he wasn't.'

'No.'

'And he might have been the last person to see Verona alive.' Or the second-to-last, but I didn't want to go into that.

'Anyway, about a week after he'd gone to the police station a policeman came to his house, a man Matt knows. He told Matt he wouldn't be called at the inquest after all but Matt must be careful not to talk to anybody about the girl or the boat.'

'Did he say why?'

'No, and Matt didn't ask. He was just relieved not to have to stand up at the inquest. All above his head, he says. Not his business. But it's still on his mind all the same.' He looked at me. 'But it doesn't help with your friend, does it?'

'I don't know.'

I felt cold. I don't know why, but I hadn't expected the watchers here. They belonged in London, except when I'd decoyed them away from it. But even down here they had influence over the police. Since I'd heard Bill was missing I'd been too concerned about him to worry about being followed. Now I looked at the window and wondered who'd seen us talking to Matt on the quay.

'I'll have to go.'

Margaret said, 'At nine o'clock at night? No, you won't.'

She was worried, I could tell that. I'd have been worried in her place.

'I'm sorry to have got you involved in this.'

'Why? You haven't done anything wrong, have you?'

'No, but some people think I have.'

John said, 'You can stay here tonight and go to the police about your friend in the morning.'

He was a straightforward man. If a person was missing, you went to the police. I imagined standing at the duty officer's desk, reporting Bill like a stray dog. The questions: 'Are you related to the gentleman, ma'am?' Describing Bill as I'd done dozens of times already – just under six foot tall, early forties, dark-haired, clean-shaven. (Perhaps not very clean-shaven now, as his kit was in the bag upstairs.) And I thought of the things you couldn't say in a description to hotel receptionists or police. Like Bill's voice that could make any disturbed thing, animal or human, became calmer. Like his nervy, long-fingered hands and the slow way he smiled.

Margaret said gently, 'You're tired. Why don't you go to bed and I'll bring your cocoa up?'

Bill's well travelled bag on the floor. The pillow with the dent of his head still in it. I wanted to lie my own head there, let what was left of his presence sink through skin and skull into my mind.

'Thanks, but no.'

John said, 'There won't be anybody at the police station now. Better wait till morning.'

'There's somebody else I have to see. Do you know when the tide turns?'

'High tide in just over an hour.' He said it automatically then, 'Why?'

Margaret said, 'Can't we do anything?'

'You've done a lot already. Thank you.'

'Do you know when you'll be back? We'll leave the back door unlocked.'

I thanked them and went out. It was dusk, with the last of the swallows and the first of the bats flying loops round each other over the water. The tide was well up, only a few yards of the back beach above the waterline and the hire boats bobbing beyond wading distance. The windows of the New Quay were lamplit, voices and laughter drifting out, but there was nobody on the back beach to see me going round unlatching boatmen's store sheds, searching until I found a pair of oars. I carried them one at a time to the tide edge, opposite the post where the boats were moored, left my shoes and stockings with them, waded thigh deep, then plunged, grabbed the nearest boat by the stern and scrambled on board, battering my knees and elbows. The noise sounded like sea monsters wallowing and I waited for a shout from the beach, but there was nothing apart from the noise from the New Quay. The knot on the painter was swollen but it came undone at the cost of a few fingernails. I flopped back into the sea, guided the boat to the beach, threw my shoes and stockings into it, shipped the oars, got in and pushed off. It was a long time since I'd rowed a boat on my own and it was a hard pull out from the shelter of the sand bar to mid-channel, but once I'd got there the push of the incoming tide pointed the bows up the estuary. I settled to a rhythm of rowing, looking back towards the dark line of the open sea, the flashing of the lighthouse that marked the sand bar at the harbour entrance and the smaller lights on the sandbanks under the Ness. The layer of salt water between skin and clothes got warm from the rowing until it was almost comfortable to be there, as if nothing existed but the movement of arm and stomach muscles, and the tide carrying the boat along as if this had been the only possible decision.

Chapter Twenty-five

FURTHER UP THE ESTUARY THE TREES CAME DOWN close to the river and lights from scattered houses showed in clearings. The water held the last of the afterglow from the sunset. I tried to keep as close as I could to the south bank, where Ben's house was, and kept glancing over my shoulder for the boathouse. It showed up quite suddenly as a darker rectangle against the dark. I think the tide might have turned by then because rowing had got more difficult and the boat seemed to resist being driven out of the current towards the boathouse. As I came nearer the dark rectangle opened out to show the gleam of water inside, gaping like a whale's jaws. Another few strokes would take me in and now that I'd got there, I didn't want to do it. One stroke, and there was the dinghy's mast. Two more, then the bump of a moored rowing boat against the bows. An oar struck a post. I dropped the oar in the rowlock, reached out and grabbed the post. Inside, there was no glow on the water, only liquid dark and solid dark.

'Anybody there?'

My voice echoed. Something was dripping into the water, the oar probably. Apart from that, nothing. I waited, then fumbled around the post and found a mooring ring. My struggles to tie the painter to the ring set the boat rocking and made the water slap and gulp against the walls. I hoisted the oars and my shoes up on to the wooden walkway then followed them, arms trembling from cold or effort. Let your eyes get used to the dark. Don't try to see yet. Nothing to see. But my eyes had already gone to that patch of the darkness where I'd found Verona and were making shapes in it.

'Bill?'

I stood up, walked a few steps along the wooden platform, reached out into the dark. There was nothing there, nothing hanging, just space and water. For a moment I didn't know which was water and which was space so I must have come near to somersaulting in. I went down on my knees on the planks, gasping and shivering and it felt like a long time before I got back upright. By then my eyes had got used to the dark and there really was nothing there but the boats. I found my shoes and put them on, not bothering with stockings, and went shakily out of the little door at the back on to the walkway over the rushes, through the gate and up the paddock.

From the lawn the house was a blaze of bright, raw light. Naturally, Ben would have electricity. The back downstairs rooms and some upstairs windows were all lit and uncurtained. I scrunched on the gravel to the back door. It was unlocked and opened at a touch into the garden room. I went through the door on the far side, along a corridor to the front hall.

'Alex?'

There was water running somewhere upstairs. I called again, got no answer, and went up the stairs, deep carpet underfoot. The sound of water was coming from a room off the first-floor landing. I rapped it with my knuckles.

'Alex, it's Nell. Are you in there?'

No answer. I pushed open the door, walked in. Through drifts of steam I saw a bathroom almost comfortable enough to be a sitting room. There were piles of white towels on shelves, a rattan chair, an aspidistra on a stand. The bath was mahogany-sided, big enough for two. Gleaming taps were cascading water into it, but there was nobody in sight. Then a hand came down on my shoulder and nails dug in, sharp even through my jacket. I yelled and spun round.

'Alex, for heaven's sake!'

She was wearing a sea-green dressing-gown, belted at the waist. Her hair was down her back and beaded with condensation, her eyes bright and her face white as the soap on the washbasin. She let go of my shoulder.

'Did I scare you, Nell?'

'Yes. You have your bath. I'll wait for you downstairs, then we can talk.'

'Oh, it's not for me.'

She walked over to the bath, moving self-consciously as if in an amateur play, turned the taps off and dabbled her hand in the water.

'It shouldn't be warm, should it? But Ben had the boiler put in and perhaps it would have been – all those slaves and so on.'

'Alex, what are you talking about?'

'Mrs Tell's gone to bed. She sleeps very soundly.' She sat on the edge of the bath, legs crossed, and looked at me.

'Did you know the door's unlocked and all the lights are on?'

'Rows of torches, welcoming him home.' Steam was condensing on the big oval mirror on the wall, making our reflections look like under-sea things. 'Ben's coming back. They put in at Devonport for repairs yesterday and he'll be home tomorrow.'

'Good.'

'Do you think so? You haven't been quite honest with me, Nell, but then nobody has. Scented water, do you think?'

'I don't . . . yes, yes why not.'

It had come to me that she was preparing this bath for her daughter, that she expected Verona to come back out of the sea and the night. Perhaps it had been a ritual every night since she died.

'That bottle there, the pink one. But I expect you think I'm not very clever. Ben does, he's said so. I think probably Verona did as well.'

The bottle was on a shelf in an alcove, pink-tinted milky glass. I gave it to her, she poured, and the steam round us turned rose-scented.

'It makes me angry when I think of it. The two of them, their precious secret and me, the poor stupid wife and mother not allowed to know about it. I guessed, guessed something at least. But if they didn't want me to know, it was . . . it was, well, a kindness not to. Can you understand that?'

'Yes.'

'Only they weren't kind to me, were they? What happened wasn't kind to me?'

'No.'

'When you were here the day before yesterday, you told me she didn't kill herself.' I waited. 'Did you know who did?'

'Not then, no.'

'Not then?' She looked at me, then jumped up, listening. 'What was that?'

'Somebody upstairs.'

'Probably Mrs Tell going to the lavatory.'

Alex took two strides to the door, locked it and dropped the key in her dressing-gown pocket then went back to sit on the side of the bath.

'Why don't you sit down, Nell? Sit down and be comfortable.'

It was a command. I sat in the rattan chair. The rest and the rose-scented warmth should have been welcome, but I wished I were miles away. There was something like a long black stick propped against the side of the bath. In the steam, I couldn't make out what it was.

'Not then, but you know now?'

'Verona came back here of her own free will to put something right. She hired a boat and rowed out into the estuary.'

Verona hadn't been driven back here drugged with Valerie Hergest at the wheel. Her letter had meant what it said. She'd come of her own free will to put something right, she was fit and confident enough to hire a boat and row it on her familiar estuary. And the boat had come back. Bill would have known that from the boat-hire man. He'd always been good at getting people to talk to him. He must have had some idea in his head when he'd come to talk to Alex. I should have pressed her, made her be more specific about the questions he'd asked, but how could I do that to a woman half-mad with grief? Quite easily, now it was too late. Quite easily.

'Alex, when Bill Musgrave came to see you on Saturday . . .'

'Who?' She stared.

'For goodness sake, my friend. He was asking you about Verona, before she went away. There was somebody in particular, wasn't there, somebody he asked about?'

'Yes. I didn't realise at the time but I've been thinking . . . since you told me.'

'Told you what?'

'That she didn't kill herself. I can see what he meant now, what you meant.'

293

She swirled her hand in the water. I looked at the black thing beside the bath. It had a hilt, ornate and silver-plated with a tasselled cord threaded through it. A sword. The kind of sword a naval officer would wear on ceremonial occasions, sheathed in its black scabbard. She stood up, came over and stood behind me, a hand on each shoulder.

'I'm doing it wrong, aren't I? It would be easier in the bath, no struggle. Act as if there's nothing the matter – kind, silly Alex. Water nice and warm, and big soft towels ready. You must be tired from all that travelling. Relax, just relax, my dear.' Her voice was a parody of seduction, curling round me like the scented steam. I kept my eyes on the sword, ready to grab her hands if she made a move towards it. 'You'd drowse in the water probably, wouldn't you, if you'd been travelling all day? Head back against the bath, throat stretched out. Easy. Easy for both of you.'

Her right hand shifted from my shoulder. She was making her move. I twisted in the chair, grabbed both her wrists. She yelled with pain and went down on her knees.

'Alex, I didn't kill Verona. I can guess who told you I did, but it's not true. I didn't kill her.'

She looked up at me, hurt and puzzled. 'I never thought you did, Nell. I never thought you did.'

I let go of her wrists and made her sit down in the chair. She'd started shivering in spite of the warmth of the room so I draped towels over her shoulders and lap.

'But if you didn't think that, why . . . ?'

'What was her name, Nell?'

I really thought then that she'd gone mad and forgotten her own daughter's name.

'Verona?'

'The girl they had to kill before a war could start, the Greek one.'

'Iphigenia?'

The name floated as a whisper in the rose-scented steam. Agamemnon's virgin daughter, sacrificed to the gods to get a fair wind to sail and make war on Troy. But Iphigenia had a mother as well as a father. When Agamemnon came home from the war Clytaemnestra ran a bath for him and . . .

'Ben? You think Ben killed his *own* daughter?'

'She came home, Nell, came back here. You told me that.'

'Yes, but—'

'She'd done things he'd never forgive and she came back to tell him so. She was brave, Nell, always too brave.'

'Yes, but—'

'I wouldn't have done it, Nell, not killed him, at least I don't think I would. Only after you'd gone, after I'd understood, I was so angry I . . . I wanted to know what it would feel like, if I could . . . Do you think I could?'

'No. But Ben didn't kill her! I thought he might have, but he didn't.'

Ben waiting by the boathouse for his daughter to row back, syringe and ropes ready. I'd never liked my cousin, but I'd found it hard to believe. Alex had believed it. In the last few weeks I'd been learning a lot about marriages among other things.

'Are you trying to tell me she killed herself after all?'

'No.' I didn't fancy perching on the edge of the bath, so I sat down on the floor beside her chair. 'We know Verona came back because she wanted to put something right. What she wanted to put right was that they'd made a spy of her. It was a great adventure, until she fell in love with one of the people she was supposed to be spying on and knew she was expecting his baby.'

'That was terrible, Nell. When they told me—'

'She didn't think it was terrible. It was what she wanted.'

295

(Would it have turned out well for them, Verona with her London flat and her career, visiting the Hergests and the baby at weekends? Possibly. Stranger things had turned out well.)

'And, as you say, she was brave. She wanted to start her new life without any lies or secrets. But she was still loyal to the old life in a way – loyal enough to want to hand in her notice as a spy. That was what she'd come back here to do, but not to her father.'

'But if it was here, how did you know it wasn't Ben?'

She wanted to believe me, but there was no great surge of relief. I suppose once you've worked your way to believing your husband killed your daughter, there's no way back to where you were before.

'Because something else has happened that couldn't have anything to do with Ben. My friend Bill's missing. I think he's probably dead too.' There were some gurgles in the pipes, creaking of the rattan chair as Alex moved. She said nothing. 'Bill had guessed. He got there ahead of me. I was meant to follow the ghost boat – come here and walk into a trap. But Bill got there another way and walked into it instead. He was trying to protect me. If only I'd talked to him, hadn't been so sure I was right, it wouldn't have happened.'

I think we stayed there for a long time, Alex in the chair, me kneeling on the mat. The steam settled and the room went cold. Condensation drops ran down the mirror in long wavering lines. Alex started shivering again.

'You should be in bed.'

'What shall we do, Nell?'

'Tomorrow. Go to bed now.'

I saw her to her room, walking and talking quietly so as not to wake Mrs Tell, and sat beside her until she fell asleep.

It was past two in the morning by then. When I went into the bathroom and opened the window everything was so still I could hear the suck of the waves miles away at the mouth of the estuary. Tide on the way out now. Verona's murderer had let the tide be the executioner – as if the rise and fall of the water were an instrument of justice, even justice itself. I let myself quietly out of the back door, over the lawn and down through the paddock to the rock where I'd sat watching the heron or another rock like it – I couldn't be sure in the dark. An hour later the sky was turning from black to blue-black and a shine had come back on the water, a pewter channel between mudflats. I went along the walkway into the boathouse and found that, stupidly, I'd tied the boat to the ring too tightly so that the falling water had left it with bows pulled upward, stern in the mud. While I was struggling with the painter the door at the back of the boathouse opened. Yellow lantern light came in, dazzling so that I couldn't see who was behind it and for a few heartbeats I almost hoped, but it was only Alex.

'I knew you'd try to go without me. Haven't I got a right?'

She had, if only for what it must have cost her to walk into the boathouse. I couldn't have done it in her place. She even managed to unknot the painter as calmly as if for a picnic outing and took her shoes off to help me drag the boat down to the water, wading thigh deep in mud. When we'd got it afloat we washed the mud off our legs in the river then took an oar each and rowed side by side, letting the falling tide take us back towards the mouth of the estuary. Even the salmon fishermen weren't out so early, only herons watching from the banks and a cormorant winging upriver like a black arrow, straight over our heads. Alex rowed calmly, more easily than I did and hardly said a word. All the madness of the night before seemed to have gone from her.

297

It was full light by the time we got among the sandbanks near the mouth of the estuary, with our bow pointing out to sea, between the harbour on one side and the red headland of the Ness on the other. We rounded a sandbank and steered for the Shaldon bank, pulling hard to get out of the grip of the current. The boat came to rest on a beach of red sand under the Ness. It was hard work pulling it up the beach. Alex stumbled in the sand and turned her ankle but still wouldn't leave it to me. Near the cliff red boulders had flung themselves down like a handful of marbles. Between the boulders a landing stage stuck out, left high and dry by the tide, with bladderwrack and limpets clinging to the posts. There was a flagpole on the landing stage. Beyond it a lawn edged with roses and blue hydrangeas sloped steeply up to the little white house. From the landing stage I saw that even at this early hour the French windows were open on to the lawn.

'His bosun keeps sea hours,' Alex said.

We wiped sand off our feet, put our shoes on – Alex gasping from the pain of the ankle but insisting that she was all right – and walked up the lawn towards the smell of coffee.

Chapter Twenty-six

THE BOSUN HAD THE COFFEE-POT IN HIS HAND when Alex and I walked in through the French windows. He'd been going to put it down on the breakfast table neatly laid for one person with a blue plate and a cup the size of a pudding basin on a clean white cloth. There were white rosebuds in a blue pottery bowl, newly picked with the dew still on them. Alex went first and when he saw her the smile on his sun-tanned face was wide and genuine.

'Mrs North. The admiral will be pleased.'

A hint of deference in his voice as well as pleasure. If he'd noticed her wet and muddy skirt and untidy hair he gave no sign of it. No sign either of noticing another person behind her.

Alex said, 'Good morning, Pilcher. Where is he?'

The coffee-pot looked heavy and he was holding it awkwardly in his left hand. There was a bandage round his right hand, padded at the palm.

'Up on the Ness looking out at the traffic, Mrs North. Been there since before daylight. Sit down and I'll pour you a coffee and nip straight up and let him know you're here. Your friend will take coffee?'

He looked over her shoulder at me and nearly dropped the coffee-pot.

299

'Thank you,' I said. 'You didn't offer me coffee on the train.'

He was bare-headed now, grizzled hair neatly combed, but my memory gave him back the ticket collector's cap that had been too small for him and the smell of the raw leather satchel was stronger in my nose than coffee. He stared at me, opened and shut his mouth, put down the coffee-pot and went out. Alex sat down on a dining chair.

'What's going on?'

Somewhere at the back of the house, a door slammed.

'Did the admiral take Pilcher with him on his trips to London?'

'Sometimes. Nell, what . . . what train? The one you told me about . . . ?'

'Yes.'

The unseen man. The head initial.

'Pilcher's gone to warn him. He'll run away.' She stood up, staggered on the hurt ankle and sat down again.

'Why? If you're on the side that always wins and the rules don't apply to you, why run away?'

I poured coffee into the big cup, loaded it with cream and sugar from the blue jug and bowl.

'Go on, drink it.'

She wouldn't take it. 'His. It would poison me.' I put it back on the table. 'Or maybe we could poison *it*, Nell. He keeps morphine in the house somewhere, I know that, for when the pain from his wound gets bad.'

'You might have told me before.'

'How was I to know, Nell? You don't think that way. Until yesterday, I didn't think that way. Do we do it?'

'No. Just wait.'

I left her sitting there and went through the door Pilcher had used. A short corridor ended in a half-open doorway to

300

the kitchen. I opened another door on my left and a wash of blue light hit me from sky and sea. A bay window looked out over the estuary. There was a padded seat in the window, white-painted bookcases all round the room, a light oak desk, all remorselessly tidy. The top of the desk was loaded with framed photographs. Some were of men on ships, but most of them were of Verona, copies of the ones I'd seen in Alex's room. In the very centre, in an ornate frame encrusted with silver scallop shells, was the picture of Verona and her brother in sailor suits, signed across the bottom in schoolgirl hand-writing 'To "Uncle" Archie, with fond regards from your Little Midshipmen'. The brother had his eyes half-closed and his head turned partly away from the camera but Verona beamed out, confident of the world and of her place in it. The desk wasn't even locked. Inside it, among other things, was a red leather case with a syringe inside and little brown packets of powder. I didn't bother to look at the letters and papers but I did notice the book, because it was an old battered thing in such a tidy desk. A pocket edition of *Three Men in a Boat*, edges rounded and furred from frequent handling, with the squashed peach stain from when I'd taken it punting. I left it where it was and closed the desk. Back in the other room, Alex was still sitting at the table.

'Where is he, Nell? He's taking a long time.'

'I'll go and see what's happening.'

'I'll come with you.' She took a step and her ankle gave way.

'Stay there. I'll bring him.'

There was a narrow terrace behind the house then the cliff rose steeply with ferns and brambles clinging to it. A flight of worn steps led from the side of the terrace to a path of packed earth that wound in and out of thickets of dark-leaved holm oaks. Sometimes the path would come close to the edge of the cliff on the left with views down over the estuary and the town on the opposite bank. You could see the pier and the beaches on either side, almost deserted this early in the morning. The sun was well clear of the sea and the tide had turned and was creeping up the sandbanks. About halfway to the top I heard footsteps and there was Pilcher coming down. He looked worried, even more so when he saw me.

'The admiral's compliments and he'll be down below in a minute.'

'Don't worry, I'm going up.'

I stepped past him and went on up the path. There were fishing boats near the sandbanks and, further out, two grey warships. A few more turns of the path and suddenly there was nothing but sea and a platform of trodden earth with an iron rail and a fringe of bushes marking the cliff edge. Either he didn't hear me coming or he pretended well because he was standing there with his telescope, looking down, the bright scar on his face shining in the sun.

I said, 'Watching the warships, Uncle Archie? Like your little midshipman used to?'

It was the only thing I could think of that might begin to hurt him as much as he deserved. At first there was no reaction, then he pivoted to face me, the arm with the telescope coming slowly down to his side as he turned like the movement of a wind-up toy. His face was blank, apart from the pink pulled-down corner of his eye that twitched to a rhythm of its own, faster than heartbeats. It looked like the quivering tendon of a newly killed frog, pinned out in a laboratory.

'You've no right . . .' The three words came out slowly, his lips hardly moving. I thought he was trying to say I had

302

no right to be up there, but after a long pause he added two more words, in the same mechanical voice: '. . . to pry.'

'She used to enjoy coming up here to watch the ships, didn't she? Remember her climbing up the path carrying the basket with the lemonade and ginger biscuits and your telescope? That telescope, was it?'

A nod. His fingers tightened round the telescope as if he expected somebody to take it away from him. The twitch of pink flesh had become a constant fluttering and moisture was gathering there, running down the track of the scar, the wrong side of his eye to be a tear.

'You've no right . . .' The same words, in the same mechanical, squeezed-out voice, the pause, then '. . . to talk about her.'

'But you had a right to kill her?'

He pivoted back, looking down at the sea.

'More than a right. A duty.' His voice was stronger now that he was talking to the sea. 'I was her godfather. I'd watched over her all her life. She was pure, straight, honourable. I gave the dearest thing I owned to my country's service. She made it a tainted sacrifice. She betrayed her country and me.'

'You pushed her into a dirty little schoolboy spying game. Then she grew up and told you what she thought of it. That was the only way she betrayed you – by growing up.'

I hoped he might turn and attack me. As it was, I could have pushed him over while he was standing against the railing looking down. He knew that and knew I wouldn't, or thought he did. His sort didn't just use people's weaknesses against them – they used their decencies too.

'What about the other murder? Was he a traitor as well?'

No response. He had his telescope to his eye, as if it mattered what the fishing boats were doing.

303

'A man came to talk to you on Sunday. Musgrave, his name was. What happened to him?'

Still no response. I moved and grabbed him by the shoulder, ready to shake an answer out of him, but he was so intent on whatever he was looking at, or pretending to be, that I couldn't help looking down too. It wasn't even the fishing boats he was watching. They were further out. From the angle of the telescope it must be something near the base of the cliff, but the only thing there was a sandbank half-uncovered by the tide and perched slantwise on the edge of it, just where the waves were lapping, the lost bathing machine. It looked ridiculous without its wheels, no more than a little wooden shed with a rounded top and steps sticking out from one end. From the crazy angle it was perched on the edge of the sandbank, high tide might have floated it off and landed it back there again. Sooner or later – if nobody caught it in time – the tides would take it away, right out to sea. The bosun had hurt his hand. Why did that matter? A crowd of people round bereaved wheels on the beach – '. . . *what those boys get up to. Hacked it right off its wheels . . .*' That was Monday, so Sunday night was when it went out to sea. A bag unclaimed, a dent in a pillow. I think I intended to push Pritty over. Maybe in the part of his mind that was fatalistic and left the final decision to the sea, he even wanted me to. The only reason I didn't was that if he'd struggled it would have wasted time. As I ran back down the path, sliding on wet earth, cannoning into trees, I didn't even care if he was following me down or not.

At the house, Pilcher tried to stop me getting back into the admiral's study, but I remembered a telephone there and he had to stand watching while I told the operator to ring the police. It wasn't easy to convince them that somebody must, at all costs, get to the bathing machine because – alive or dead, probably dead by now – there was a man inside it.

Chapter Twenty-seven

THE LIFEBOAT GOT HIM OFF, JUST AS THE sea was nudg-
ing the bathing machine away from the sandbank. I
heard later – in the way your mind will keep taking in
irrelevancies when only one thing matters – that a fishing
boat caught the bathing machine on its way out to sea
and towed it back to harbour. I didn't see it. By then I
was sitting on one side of a bed behind screens in the
Victoria ward of the cottage hospital, with Alex on the
other side of the bed and Bill unconscious in between.
His head was wrapped in a turban of bandages, his lips
cracked from dehydration. Every now and then he'd start
shivering so violently that the hand I was holding jerked
itself out of mine. The pyjamas they'd found were too
short in the arm for him and you could see, between wrist
and elbow, a puncture mark with yellow and purple bruising round it. I'd told the doctor when they brought him
in that he'd had a near lethal dose of morphine as well as
everything else. He thought I was raving at first. Nurses
came and went through the screens with fresh hot-water
bottles. They were kind and efficient but wouldn't meet
my eyes. At some point Alex had to go, limping on a
borrowed walking stick, because Ben was coming home.
Goodness knows what she'd say to him.

* * *

The lifeboat must have been busy that morning. Soon after bringing Bill back it had to go out again to recover a body from the rocks under the Ness. The buzz that went round the town when it turned out to be Rear Admiral Archibald Pritty reached the cottage hospital and even penetrated the screens round Bill's bed. I imagined him standing there with his telescope, watching as Bill was carried from the bathing machine to the lifeboat. Perhaps he thought the sea had turned against him at last in not taking Bill away as it was supposed to do, and if the sea wasn't on his side then all the powers of the initials couldn't help him any more. At the time I didn't care. I was only glad that he was dead as I'd never been glad about the death of any creature before.

When the police came to ask me questions, in the matron's office, I told them the whole story. It took two hours because the sergeant wrote it down slowly and carefully, and kept wearing down his pencil and having to sharpen it. I could have told him we were all wasting our time. All I wanted was to get back to Bill. I'd have been right too. I never heard another word about my statement from that day to this. Perhaps it's there somewhere in a file in the War Office stamped 'No Action Recommended'.

There's a superstition that sick people die when the tide's at its lowest. But sometimes they come to life too. I know that because the first low tide on the first day of July was around five in the morning, as the light was beginning to creep round the screens that surrounded Bill's bed. Perhaps I'd been dozing because suddenly Bill was awake and looking at me.

'Nell?' His voice came painfully from a salt-rasped throat.

I don't know what I said.

He said, 'I hate . . .'

306

His fingers clenched round my hand. Hate what? Pritty? The initials? Me?

'I hate to be obvious but . . .'

'Yes?'

'Where the bloody hell am I?'

It still took a week for him to be well enough to travel. I spent a lot of that time by his bed and when he could speak without pain he confirmed most of the things I'd guessed. Pritty had agreed to meet him for a talk but said because of other engagements he couldn't manage it until late on Sunday night. Perhaps Bill would be kind enough to meet him on the beach by the pier, where he was accustomed to walk his dog. Whether there really had been a dog Bill didn't know. He was knocked out by a blow on the head from somebody who came from underneath the pier. The bosun, at a guess, with Pritty waiting behind him with the needle. I still shook with anger when I thought about it, but Bill was more philosophical. He even enjoyed reading Admiral Pritty's obituary in *The Times* about a lifetime of service at sea and, in later years, valuable contributions behind the scenes co-ordinating the work of various committees at the War Office. They buried him at sea, I gathered, with full naval honours. At least Commodore Benjamin North was not among those present.

I stayed with John and Margaret at the fish-smelling house and, between hospital visiting times, did a lot of walking up and down the seafront. The holiday season was in full swing, with bands playing most of the daylight hours, children riding donkeys and eating ice creams, begonias blazing from beds along the promenade, trips round the bay. Only if you looked past the bathers and the tripper boats, further out to sea, there were always the grey warships steaming out on the horizon. There was a terribly purposeful look about them, like huge animals obeying some instinctive call to muster.